Document

Z

Lies, deception and betrayal
—a masterful story of
espionage and intrigue

Document
Z

Andrew Croome

ALLEN&UNWIN

First published in 2009

Allen & Unwin
83 Alexander Street
Crows Nest NSW 2065
Australia
Phone: (61 2) 8425 0100
Fax: (61 2) 9906 2218
Email: info@allenandunwin.com
Web: www.allenandunwin.com

Cataloguing-in-Publication details are available
from the National Library of Australia
www.librariesaustralia.nla.gov.au

ISBN 978 1 74175 743 9

Set in 11/15 pt Fairfield by Midland Typesetters, Australia
Printed in Australia by McPherson's Printing Group

10 9 8 7 6 5 4 3 2 1

For my parents

SOVIET EMBASSY – CANBERRA

FUNCTIONAL ORGANISATION

LIFANOV (Ambassador)
Mrs PETROV (Ambassador's Secretary)

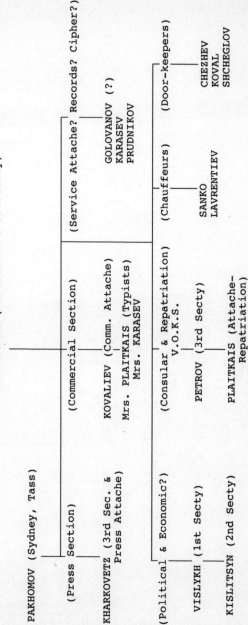

PAKHOMOV (Sydney, Tass)

(Press Section)

KHARKOVETZ (3rd Sec. & Press Attache)

(Political & Economic?)

VISLYKH (1st Secty)

KISLITSYN (2nd Secty)

(Commercial Section)

KOVALIEV (Comm. Attache
Mrs. PLAITKAIS (Typists)
Mrs. KARASEV

(Consular & Repatriation)
V.O.K.S.

PETROV (3rd Secty)

PLAITKAIS (Attache-
Repatriation)

(Service Attache? Records? Cipher?)

GOLOVANOV (?)
KARASEV
PRUDNIKOV

(Chauffeurs)

SANKO
LAVRENTIEV

(Door-keepers)

CHEZHEV
KOVAL
SHCHEGLOV

19 April 1954, Mascot Aerodrome

The car was so long it had the look of a hearse. The crowd watched it arrive via the slip road, an American car of all things, a colossal black Cadillac limousine, hard-tailed and polished. Not quite speeding but not going slow.

The man who stood before it made a lonely figure in a long coat. He raised a hand into the light from its nearing head-lamps and set one foot forward. The crowd waited to see. The Cadillac showed no indication of slowing. For a moment it looked as if man and machine would meet. Then quickly the car veered, tossing up some gravel on the roadside, shooting past the man who turned and shouted something about a sign. Something about an insignia. And before the Cadillac quite reached them, the crowd had flooded its path. They were night breath; forty or fifty people in suits, coats and hats. The car stopped and they surrounded it, peered into its dark windows, a strange feeling overcoming them: acidic and tightening, as if this week's newsprint had entered their bodies and formed there a second blood.

Somebody swore that they could see her. People began trying the handles on the doors.

Staring out the window of the Cadillac, Evdokia knew this crowd was here for her. They were hunting her. They were here to prevent her escaping through the terminal, onto the plane.

The driver, Sanko, high-beamed the lights and revved the limousine hard. The crowd was tapping on the window glass. Evdokia could see angry, desperate expressions on those nearby. Moscow's courier, a man named Karpinsky, turned from the front passenger seat and announced a plan to rush the terminal. Madness, Evdokia thought, though it was madness too not to move. Beside her, Zharkov thrust the door open. She stepped out and was immediately grateful for the man's girth. People everywhere. A silence and then a rising. Just close your eyes, she thought. Keep your feet marching like the Pioneer Youth. In front of her, Karpinsky threw a man to the ground. She heard the click of his skull on concrete, and in the next moment the crowd's voice erupted. The shoving began. She kept an arm on Zharkov and the crowd was targeting him, targeting her, or both.

This might be it, Evdokia realised. A chaos building, a climbing potential. Her escorts had revolvers in their jackets. If it was Moscow's instruction, they'd do away with her here, deliver a misdirected shot amongst these scrambling bodies. Defector's Wife Dies in Airport Riot.

They weren't going to reach the terminal. She and Zharkov were being pushed sideways, heading along the building's edge. She thought maybe there was blood on her gloves, a light red mist. Zharkov locked his arm to hers as they hurried through a gap in a fence and found themselves suddenly on the open tarmac.

An ocean of protesters here. She could not believe it, the number of people, the lights and the shadows. The plane stood distant at a hundred metres. They passed two lone A-frame barriers, overturned, and then three policemen suddenly joined them. They formed a group, a tight, triangular formation: Evdokia between Zharkov and Sanko, Karpinsky with the police in front.

How many people on the apron? One thousand? Two? The protesters roared when they saw the group. The people began to swamp towards them, to push and snarl. Evdokia wanted to stop. She wanted to stop and turn and run. Zharkov at her elbow, insisting otherwise. The crowd's ferocity exponential.

A man with a microphone jogged at their side. 'You can undoubtedly hear the noise going on. Press photographers' bulbs are flashing. People are screaming all around me. Does Mrs Petrov want to go? "Don't let her go," the people are yelling. "She doesn't want to go!"'

She tried to increase her pace and lost a shoe. It came off and her toes scraped against the tarmac. No way to stop. She looked behind to see the shoe held aloft, following like a trophy for the brave.

The plane loomed, an enormous cylinder in the darkness. One of the policemen was swinging his cudgel like a machete in a rainforest, leading them straight for the aircraft's stairs.

'Why don't you stay in Australia? In Moscow, they'll kill you!'

It was a surprise to find her foot on the first step. The staircase rocked as she climbed, and people's hands reached up from beneath the railings, ferociously trying to grab her. There was a terrific shudder when the stairs were pulled free of their moorings, suddenly shifting on their wheels. She heard shouts and screams. Below, the police were beating a man who held the stair's controls in his hands and was refusing to let go. He absorbed the blows like someone being flogged, bending as if shackled to the levers.

Evdokia continued to climb. An official from the plane had come to her side and they were ascending together, a metre from the top, when the stairs finally rolled back into place. Evdokia looked up to see Philip Kislitsyn, the embassy's second secretary, holding the railings with arms outstretched, trying to make the staircase stay flush against the plane.

On the last step, she lurched over a slight air-gap, finding herself inside the plane and its pale, passive light.

When the door was closed, the noise outside fell strangely dead. Zharkov and Karpinsky stood, wiped their foreheads. She could see the shock still on Philip Kislitsyn's face. He brought her a glass of brandy that tasted like fuel.

Karpinksy said the crowd was retreating. Zharkov looked through a window and said they were regrouping to attack the plane.

Evdokia sat and awaited whichever. The minutes passed and she fell into a quiet trance, thinking of her husband, herself, her sister. Everything he had betrayed.

1951

1

Canberra

Lockyer Street was as wide as the streets in a Hollywood dream. The house was a bungalow with bricked pathways and a raised landing, and it sat snugly on its block, hedged by low bushes and a cypress tree. They arrived late in summer. She was expecting palm trees but there was only incandescent heat.

They called it a suburb. Pines and pin oaks. The houses were square bodies with triangular roofs and white window frames, driveways and edged lawns and paths to their front doors. Afternoons, a group of boys would seize the street, gaming with a bat and ball, their shouts punching off the asphalt.

It was a strange town where the roads were curved by design. It was a place for sweeping around in cars.

Their backyard was enormous. A clothes line of strung steel sat alone at the centre like some antennaed monument. Their kitchen was enormous. The oven was new and all its fixtures were bakelite. The bedrooms and the lounge provided enough space for five Moscow families. Evdokia sat on the back porch and imagined she was Mary Pickford in a breakfast robe.

On the way to Manuka was a large white chest called the Capitol Theatre. She walked there, hoping to find a schedule of theatrical performances. The building was a picture house. Nearby, the Forrest Newsagency sold magazines. She bought *Australian Women's Weekly* for the article 'How to be a Woman'. Act dumb, it read. Don't talk about politics, economics, or your theories of relativity.

The weather was knife-blue skies.

Milk was delivered to people's front doors.

She lay awake beside Volodya, wondering if it was possible to be unhappy in a country such as this, where the shopping centres were white-stone temples, where fruit stores sold their produce in the open air, peaches and strawberries in huge boxes.

And the children were so healthy. If there was to be a difficulty living here, it would be their rhapsodic brightness and its propensity to break her heart. They came tumbling from the schools, little girls in high white socks and pleated skirts. It was the kind of pain that couldn't be helped, Mothercraft Centres everywhere you looked.

She imagined Irina with her now. Irina on Lockyer Street in a blue skirt, skipping. Irina leaping into Volodya's arms.

Wear silly shoes, said the magazine. Sensible shoes may be more comfortable, but they are just not feminine.

The Soviet embassy was a double-storeyed lodge. The staff called it Little Moscow, and it sat on a block so large that the gardeners kept an orchard. Nikolai Kovaliev, the commercial attaché, arranged a welcome for the newcomers. Evdokia wore her Stockholm dress with the abstract pattern and her smallest black hat. The other wives were drab. Lifanova, the ambassador's wife, wore a thick tan dress with a hole in it. She had a citation pinned to her chest: the civilians' medal for the defence of Moscow. Almost everyone from the city had received this medal. It made her look like a pantomime scout.

The ambassador, Lifanov, was a man of somewhat crumpled physique with an incredible amount of silver in his teeth. From morning to mid-afternoon, Evdokia was to work as his personal secretary and the embassy accountant. She was assigned a heavy and very formal desk in his antechamber. To make it her own, she cut out a picture of a dog playing a piano and put it under the glass.

Her downstairs duties complete, she was to move each afternoon to the secret section where she carried out her work for the MVD—the Ministry of Internal Affairs. The MVD's traffic was hidden inside the embassy's regular diplomatic cables, identified by a four-digit flag. Evdokia helped her husband decrypt the spy organ's messages using a one-time pad. The matrices were laborious but the job was somehow fulfilling. The results were plain text messages, most littered with secret words. Many of the codes were obvious. 'Fraternal' was the Australian Communist Party. 'The Competitors' were ASIO, Australia's security organisation. 'Voron' was the MVD's agent and so was 'Yakka'. There were other codes that only Volodya understood. Evdokia knew better than to ask.

The third MVD officer at the embassy was Philip Kislitsyr an impossibly tall man who walked with a stoop. He arrived

ter the Petrovs. He had a daughter, Tatiana, and a wife,
.. They all came to dinner, neatly dressed.

You spent the war in London?' Volodya asked.

'That's right,' said Kislitsyn. 'Five years at the embassy there.'

'Were you bombed?'

Kislitsyn shrugged. 'When we arrived it was sporadic.'

'We were in Sweden.'

Volodya produced the photo album of Stockholm: the Grand
Hotel and the Royal Palace, a picture of Evdokia eating strawberries in Gamla Stan. Kislitsyn asked what conditions were
like.

'Terrible,' said Volodya. 'In capitalist countries, goods will
rot on the docks if the people cannot pay.'

'That's right,' said Kislitsyn. 'England was just as bad,
though perhaps they had an excuse with the war. It is difficult
to know.'

Evdokia told the story of their voyage from Archangel,
how their ship had been torpedoed by a pig-shaped German
submarine.

'It surfaced?' asked Anna.

'Right by the lifeboats. We thought we were all about
to die.'

Anna looked impressed. Evdokia told her of the three days
in the lifeboat; how, as the ship was holed and sinking, a child
ipped from the ropes and disappeared. Volodya said they
d their lives to the radio operator who had stayed on board,
lling SOS.

xt time you will be saved by television,' said Kislitsyn.
oing to replace radio. I saw it at the BBC.'

***

The next morning, Kislitsyn came to Evdokia's desk wanting to know if she had any contacts in the Australian business community.

'What do you mean?'

'People who can get people jobs. Captains of industry, they are called.'

He was wearing horn-rimmed glasses, quite an attractive pair. She gave him the embassy rolodex and he flipped through it hungrily, hovering over certain names.

'How can I tell who these people are?'

'I don't know,' she said. 'It's mostly the ambassador's list.'

He groaned.

'Which of us needs a job?' she joked.

He looked at her quietly. She realised now that she'd seen him before, recalling a figure in the Special Cypher Department in Moscow who had usually sat alone in the canteen. Yes, he'd been in the building for a few months, not much more, then he'd disappeared. Purged, she'd thought then, but evidently not so.

'These are our only records?' he asked.

'No, no. There are other lists too. The film nights, for example.'

He looked on eagerly as she began reaching for the files.

She met the Australian prime minister. Ambassador Lifanov came to her desk one afternoon and asked if she wouldn't mind. It was a diplomatic dinner for the Europeans, and he needed staff who spoke English and were suitable. The parliament building was white and, she thought, rather beautiful. Its lights were on, the grasslands around dark black.

‹ Menzies,' said the prime minister.

.sed to meet you.'

. had silver hair and black bushy eyebrows. He was a
.st, or at least had fascist tendencies. He was unfailingly
.lite. He asked them to a cricket match he was organising, a
charity game to raise funds for Legacy. They didn't know what
Legacy was.

There was roast turkey, the huge bird sitting fatly on a plate.
At dinner, Evdokia engaged in small talk with Zizka, the Czech
trade consul, a slight-framed man who she thought worked for
Czech intelligence. Afterwards, there were drinks in a room
with a fireplace. Men stuck to one side, women the other. Prime
Minister Menzies made a toast. Evdokia watched Kovaliev, the
commercial attaché, the way he seemed to hang from Ambassador Lifanov's coat-tails, his equine features making him look
like the man's mule.

Lifanova seemed awkward and out of place. Evdokia
presumed it was her lack of English. She thought the wife
of the Soviet ambassador shouldn't be someone who stood
alone and so she went to her, to help by being there to
translate. The only people who approached them came to
compliment Evdokia on her outfit. The wife of a French
diplomat suggested that she investigate a store named Kosky
Brothers in Melbourne. No one said anything to Lifanova.
.he stood at the edge of the conversations, reduced to
'ding along.

.dokia woke the next day feeling enthused. She smoked a
.te in the backyard and penned a long letter to Tamara,
.teen-year-old sister. This is a koala, she wrote. Here
.we live. This card shows the Harbour Bridge and
. Blue Mountains. She concluded by imploring her

sister to study hard, to take up languages and to read each day *Pravda*'s notes on international affairs. She promised that she would organise Tamara's membership of the Komsomol. She promised that by hard work and struggle Tamara too could go abroad. Capitalism wraps its women in tissue paper, she wrote, but you and I, we are not the beneficiaries but the very benefit of the Great October Revolution.

She had photographs of Irina and Tamara playing with wood-blocks on the floor, her daughter and her mother's daughter, born so close together under the same stars.

She took Tamara's letter to the embassy to post it. She hadn't been there five minutes when Volodya came to her desk with an instruction from Moscow. It had come by telegraph, he said. It was truly the strangest thing. *Please update your records and use the following in correspondence.* The centre had changed her codename. They wanted her to be known as 'Tamara'.

She re-read the telegraph, feeling somewhat confused. It might have been a coincidence, but they knew her whole history, as they knew everyone's, so what were they trying to convey?

She pondered as she worked and by lunchtime couldn't avoid the conclusion that it was some form of threat. Her sister would be their retaliation should anything go awry.

2

'Benson's Games & Goods.' Closed, said a sign on the door. Vladimir Petrov tried it anyway, setting off a small bell on its far side.

'We're shut,' said a voice. 'It's Sunday.' A man's face appeared at the glass. Near to white hair.

'Oh,' said Petrov.

'What is it you want?'

'A rifle.'

The man eyed him. 'What's that accent?'

'Russian.'

'Where're you from?'

'Russia.'

The man looked harder. 'From where I'm standing, you look pretty serious.'

'I need a rifle.'

'I can see you're going to buy one.'

'That's right.'

'It's not a window trip?'

Petrov didn't know what that meant. 'No. This is right.'

'Cash?'

'Oh, yes.'

The store's interior was dim. The man explained that the gun room was in the rear. There was a shade on the skylight, whose string he pulled, dropping a small cloud of dust and bug-mess into the room. The firearms sat like sleek black missions, guns one side, rifles the other.

'Rabbits is it?' asked the storeman, putting a Remington in Petrov's hands. He explained this was their top of the line. Top notch.

Petrov played the bolt. The weapon felt well weighted, solid with a walnut stock. He asked the cost, not truly listening because probably he would take it whatever the price. His first gun had been a hammer-lock, a joke weapon with a replacement stock that he'd bought for two roubles from the village wain-wright. It was a stubborn gun. Ugly. He was fourteen then, and forty-three now, and he would buy this rifle because he wanted to have one nice hunting rifle before he died. He would buy it because this was Australia, land incredible, booming, beautiful, fifteen thousand kilometres from Moscow, and he was intend-ing to enjoy it. Another overseas posting. Not a prize granted to every man, and he would seize it, taking what liberties were possible, knowing the chances against his ever getting a third.

He bought the rifle and two hundred bullets.

'What about a dog?' the man said then.

'A dog?'

'Sure. A hunter buys a rifle, what's the next thing he needs?'

Outside in a yard, Alsatian puppies wriggled in a coop against the fence. Petrov bent down. When the coop was opened, one broke from their number and flopped its way into the Russian's grip. He held it at chest height, a skin of heart and heat.

He thought not of hunting but Evdokia. Of the joy his wife would find in such an improbable thing.

They put the rifle across the back seat of his car, then shook hands. 'Volodya,' Petrov said.

'I'm Jack.'

The Russian laughed. 'Jack,' he repeated, holding the pup. 'Then this will be his name too.'

The embassy's secret section was on the top floor: five cramped rooms at the end of the eastern corridor. Somewhere, the roof leaked. He'd been told that when it rained, the main-wired lighting shorted, which was why each desk in the section had two lamps. Beyond this, the only noticeable difference between these rooms and the rest of the embassy was that each door had two locks and required two keys.

That and the corridor was deadly quiet.

That and it was probably bugged.

This was Petrov's firming opinion. He thought the leak might have been caused by a commando who'd been up there setting microphones at night. He was planning to send Golovanov, the night duty patroller, up to comb the crawl-space.

At the start of the corridor, Prudnikov, the chief cypher clerk and a secret MVD recruit, occupied two rooms. The first was his personal office, where he kept an administrative watch on the section. The second he shared with his wife and baby daughter; it contained a bed and a cot, and in front of these a chest for the family's belongings.

Petrov's office was at the very end of the corridor. It had a small, knee-high fireplace set into the wall, which he liked. Because his MVD role was secret, even from other staff, he had a downstairs office too. The sign there said, 'Third Secretary, Consular Business and Cultural Representation'. His job was to prevent defections. Nina Smirnova, the wife of the embassy's former accountant, had previously attempted to escape. She had arranged herself a job in Sydney working as a nanny to two rich émigrés and, using the Canberra laundrette, had smuggled out two suitcases full of clothes. Her husband had had his suspicions. He had reported nonsense telephone calls, midnight pacings, travel magazines hidden under their mattress. Smirnova was investigated and arrested. The sentence was ten years. Add to this the defectors Gouzenko in Canada and Kravchenko in America, and Moscow was worried, having paranoid visions about any given western outpost. Petrov's Moscow boss, a man known by the codename Sparta, was particularly wary, having promised someone important that nothing would happen again. So he had sent Vladimir Petrov to Canberra, armed with a file on every member of the embassy; Vladimir Petrov who was experienced in containment work; Vladimir Petrov who could be well and truly trusted.

There was a knock at the door. Philip Kislitsyn. The man ducked under the doorframe, sat in the interview chair and tossed Petrov a peach.

'How is your house?' Petrov asked.

'It has a chimney stack, a hedge and a letterbox. Anna is buying appliances. Tatiana wants two kittens, and one of them must be orange.'

Petrov smiled. 'In this country we should take our families on picnics and then we should try golf.'

'You and I?' said Kislitsyn.

'Yes.'

It was a pristine game, Petrov thought. Played in pairs, with dew on the grass and morning sunlight on the fairways, it looked like the kind of thing that made lifelong friendships.

Even with his height, Kislitsyn's jacket was too big. He looked like a second- or third-born child growing into the eldest's suit. Petrov had known him a long time. They had met when Kislitsyn was night liaison at Dzerzhinsky Square and Petrov special cypher clerk. Petrov had handed Kislitsyn late-night decrypts for delivery to Stalin and watched him squirm. That was about the time that Petrov had focused his attentions on Evdokia Kartseva, the beautiful woman two floors below whose husband had recently been purged. Kislitsyn had warned him against it: she was marked, he said, lucky to still be on the streets let alone in the building—a month or two and she'd be gone. But Petrov had persisted, believing he couldn't be tarnished, enjoying the idea that he could be the salvation for this woman and her young child. Yet Evdokia had not been easily persuaded. Before her marriage she'd had many suitors. She was a popular woman, good-looking, and why would she be interested in him, a podgy clerk? She had seemed embarrassed at times by his more public approaches but he did not mind. He began visiting her instead at her apartment, helping Irina—a bright young girl—with her maths, and bringing gifts: coffee and coupons for shoes. In a persistent campaign, he made their Sundays his own. They went to the parks and began to eat together at the MVD restaurant. Carefully, he never mentioned the husband, not once. It was his task to make a new world of Irina, Evdokia and himself. And he knew it was working. He bought Irina a wooden ballet dancer and blue knitted socks and Evdokia squeezed his hand in the doorway. Kislitsyn had thought it incredible: not only had Evdokia Kartseva survived her husband's downfall but she was reciprocating Vladimir Petrov's attentions as well.

Kislitsyn gave his tie a gentle tug. 'This Lifanov is a prick.'

Petrov shrugged. 'He is simply the ambassador.'

'You think his behaviour is natural?'

'We are the MVD and we run a spy ring amongst his staff. We have a separate line to Moscow and who knows what we might say.'

'In Moscow I read his file.'

'Yes, I have a copy.'

'It is very thin. A prick file.'

'His behaviour is only natural.'

Kislitsyn pulled a handkerchief from his pocket, wiped peach juice from his hands. 'I am to tell you things. Firstly, I am the graduate of a course in espionage. Six months intensively freezing my balls in the Urals. Sabotage, explosives, short lessons in coding and in the handling of foreign agents.'

'You are the expert now.'

'Banks, signalling, photography, code work. My instructor says I am a living dictionary of these things.'

'Explosives?'

'Yes. I am to tell you. We are to prepare the ground for an illegal line.'

Petrov looked at him.

'This is an instruction directly from Sparta,' Kislitsyn said.

'How illegal?'

'I have the details.'

'This is in response to Robert Menzies? His war-in-three-years plan?'

'The prime minister has doubled his military budget. Now it is two hundred million pounds.'

'But he can't really believe there'll be war?'

'Korea, Indo-China, Malaya. These are his footnotes for the world situation.'

'Hmm.'

'"A war of aggression is in the highest degree probable."'

'Are they his words or ours?'

'His. Ours.'

'The point is?'

'We are to make preparations.'

'For a network?'

'Yes. We are to prepare the facilities to support a team of independent, dependable, self-resourced spies.'

'Functionals.'

'Men and women to remain incountry in the event that this embassy is withdrawn.'

'In the event?'

'Upon the outbreak of war.'

Kislitsyn put a crumpled yellow envelope on the desk. He wore a very nice watch, Petrov observed; an Omega, not dissimilar to his own.

'Active and aggressive methods,' Kislitsyn continued. 'We are to be bold in our forethought and inventiveness.' He pointed to the envelope. 'I am also ordered to tell you that Sparta apologises that these orders cannot arrive by regular channel. It has been learnt that the FBI have decrypted many communiqués from Washington and other places. The system failure was an accidental double-issuing of one-time pads.'

Petrov groaned.

'To protect us, this envelope contains a new codebook and cypher. I have kept it on my person for three months at all times.' Kislitsyn cut the envelope open and emptied its contents into his hand. 'When you open this channel, further orders will arrive.'

'Further orders?'

'Aggressive methods. In Moscow, men are training. If and when circumstances demand it, they will arrive as experts in subterfuge and long-range wireless.'

'We will place them?'

'We will establish the systems that can bring them into this country and then help them disappear.' Kislitsyn leaned forward and clasped his large hands in front of him. 'And there is something else I am to intimate.'

'All these things you know and I don't.'

'Under your predecessor, a situation existed. It was a set of affairs that hinged on the sympathies of certain well-placed men, internationalists and peace-seekers, acting in the interests of their fellow man. Moscow thought highly of this situation. These were Australian public servants in the Department of External Affairs.'

'Agents?'

'Not ours. They helped the Communist Party, but the Party passed the information on. Documents—US and British papers. Interesting bedtime reading. Moscow found this favourable and would like for steps to be taken to establish such an arrangement again.'

Petrov tossed the peach stone. He picked up the codebook and stood by the fireplace. Having said what was needed, Kislitsyn had seemingly disappeared into the furniture.

The As came first. 'Arkadia', Brisbane. 'Azimut', Perth. Thirteen pages of code. Two hundred and twenty-two of cypher.

'Alright?' said Kislitsyn.

'Golf?' said Petrov.

'Yes, good, sometime.'

3

Michael Howley pulled off Oxley Street and into the car park of the Kingston Hotel. A single light shone over the space. It was past midnight and he sat for a few moments listening to the silence. He'd driven from Sydney non-stop and his back ached.

There was a hole in the Kingston's fence that led to the yard of the funeral home next door. The home was two storeys of white brick, flower boxes on its limit. Howley opened its back door with a key and stood waiting for his eyes to adjust. Coffins in front of him. A chemical odour etched in the air.

He walked slowly up the stairs to the western end of the top floor. The room he came to was small, both windows overlooking a dual carriageway with a wide median strip. Canberra Avenue. Opposite sat the Soviet embassy.

On the windowsill was a pair of binoculars. Howley brought them to bear on the embassy's front gates, on its windows, on the little he could see of its grounds. Darkness and silence. Silence and that impenetrable hedge.

The room was stale. He opened the windows slightly to introduce a breeze. It was more than six months since he'd come here. This room was used sparingly, only for specific operations, not as a general post. It was a question of resources. The organisation's efforts were devoted to the problem of subversives, the Australian Communist Party, various left and far left groups. These were the cancers that needed cutting out. The Russians weren't a sideshow by any means—inside the walls of their embassy was the worst place a secret could end up—but there were simple issues of manpower. The counterespionage division was only four and one half full-time officers, plus the director. Around-the-clock surveillance wasn't on the cards. Instead, this room was used now and again, when it was thought that something useful might be gleaned.

He was here alone for a few days, looking for signs as to which, if any, of the embassy's new arrivals were MVD. It was the kind of work he usually enjoyed. A few days in this room. A few days creeping the streets around. He thought it was a valuable thing, the occasional watch on the Soviet embassy. The building alone handed one a sense of purpose, the dark hedge, the dark walls. It had been built as a guesthouse, something designed to invite, and over this the Soviets had added their layers of menace: the spiked gate, the occasional runs of threatening wire. Howley thought the building played its part terrifically, resisting the observer's attentions as it drew him in.

He made tea in the downstairs kitchen, spooning the minimum dose into the pot. The owner of the funeral home provided use of his premises gratis, and Howley didn't want to indulge.

He returned to the room and sat in the observation chair. A light at the embassy had come on. Top floor, eastern side.

He set his tea down and looked at the light through the binoculars. The window was frosted. He peered, unable to make out anything behind the glass. The window fell again into darkness.

He checked his watch: 1.05 a.m. and well past time to turn in. He pulled a blanket over the observation chair then set his first and second alarm clocks for 5 a.m.

The ambassador's antechamber was near the embassy's main doors. The room had no door and so Evdokia was subject to the noise of everyone's comings and goings, the deliveries and the visitations, the idle chatter of the doormen. There were also the children, who often played at the entrance while their parents worked, chasing each other with fitful squeals.

That morning, it was Lyosha Koukharenko who came into her room. The boy was four or five. He wore a red jumper with his collar sticking up.

'What is it, Lyosha?' she asked.

He was about to speak when something came flying past his head. It hit the near wall with a blunt thud. An orange. The boy turned to see who had thrown it.

Evdokia stood up, enraged. She shouted. She went to Lyosha and smacked him. The sound; the wasted food; Moscow's threats against her sister—she knew it was a tightening vortex of these things. She marched the boy past the dazed doorman, who had been asleep, while the remaining children scattered westward towards the lodges. She yelled after them that this wasn't the place to play.

Lyosha was crying. She took him to his mother, who was an assistant in the consular section.

'Valya, here is your boy. You mothers. Keep your children away from the front gates.'

'What has happened, Evdokia Alexeyevna?'

'They are throwing oranges. They are always so badly behaved.'

She made a ruling, as she was entitled to, that the children must stay away from the embassy during the day. It was a necessary and reasonable act, altogether in keeping with the idea that this was a place of work.

Then she made another ruling. This concerned the furniture in everybody's homes, which was owned by the Ministry of Foreign Affairs and on which rent should be paid. This was a Moscow directive, clearly set out in the embassy regulations.

Ambassador Lifanov came to see her. The staff were unhappy about it, he said. Couldn't she defer her decision? No, she explained. She had to think of the Moscow auditor, who would punish irregularities.

A few days later, Masha Golovanova told her that Lifanova and Koukharenka were spreading stories behind her back. They said she was embezzling money and using it to buy western clothes. This made her laugh. Let them be jealous, she thought. If they had no money and their husbands wouldn't buy them Australian things, what fault was it of hers?

The following week, she attended the regular meeting for Party members. The minutes of these meetings went to the Central Committee of the Party in Moscow. Before the meeting concluded, Kovaliev stood up. 'There is one more matter,' he said with a wooden face.

'Yes,' the ambassador said. 'Comrade Petrova, perhaps you will care to explain it.'

Evdokia looked at him.

'Of course, we are referring to the matter of your desk,' said Kovaliev.

The ambassador nodded. 'Yes, I do not know what to say, it is such a remarkable offence.'

She studied them for a moment. What on earth did they mean? She sensed Volodya stiffen in the chair beside her.

'Come, Comrade Petrova,' said Kovaliev. 'We must sort this out. Under the glass of your desk there is a picture of a dog playing piano, is there not?'

'Yes,' she said carefully.

'You put it there?'

'Yes.'

'What is it for?'

She was quiet. Kovaliev gave her a few moments, then became stern. 'This is a Party meeting, Evdokia Alexeyevna. Come, we are asking you why it is there.'

'It is humorous,' she eventually replied. 'I do not understand your interest. It is a nothing picture.'

The attaché towered over her. 'Then you admit, do you, that this dog is for comic effect?'

'I admit nothing,' she said. 'What is the meaning of this?'

Kovaliev stepped back and pulled on the cuffs of his jacket. 'There is something else, is there not, under the glass?'

'There is,' said the ambassador.

'Yes,' said Kovaliev. 'A portrait of Stalin.'

Her heart sank.

'Tell us, Comrade Petrova, why do you ridicule the Supreme Leader of the Soviet people through comparison to a minstrel dog?'

A toxic taste came to her mouth. 'I meant no insult,' she said warily. 'It is simply that—'

'Then you concede that insult is taken,' Kovaliev interrupted.

She could have kicked herself. It was the silliest of ways to begin.

'She does not concede,' Volodya said suddenly.

His voice was forceful, and as he spoke both Kovaliev and the ambassador shrank a little. Evdokia saw that they were mindful of her husband's authority, and that in hatching this plan they hadn't been sure how he would react.

'That is right,' she began again. 'I must protest. Nikolai Grigorievich, as you must know, this is a very serious charge. Frankly, I do not know why you make it. You know as well as I that these pictures are at the opposite ends of the glass, which itself is a very wide sheet. The idea of offence here is laughable.'

'But, Comrade—'

'Your allegation is baseless,' she continued. 'The two pictures must be half a metre apart. I think it is the allegation that insults the Supreme Leader.' She waited a moment. 'The allegation alone.'

Kovaliev sat. He took out a comb, driving it through his hair, pulling again on the cuffs of his jacket. She knew she'd been underestimated. She was not inexperienced in the means of Party threat.

'I demand that you render my objection in the minutes,' she added quickly.

The ambassador spoke. 'Nevertheless, Evdokia Alexeyevna, you will, of course, remove it.'

'The picture?'

'Yes.'

'As I say, it is nothing.'

'Then you will remove it?'

'Alright,' she said. 'Only to terminate this fuss.'

The meeting ended. She went to her desk and placed the picture in her pocket, then she and Volodya left the embassy by the rear gate. Outdoors, the darkness had newly arrived and a slight, coldish wind had the air on the move.

'You must write a letter,' Volodya said as they walked.

'Yes.'

'Copy each member of the Central Committee.'

'I will.'

'Include a diagram.'

'Yes.'

'Show the charge as a stunt. I will write to Moscow Centre too.'

'I will draw Stalin but not the dog.'

'You have enough black marks already.'

Volodya stopped them at the corner of Lockyer Street, checking the empty stretch. The sound of a radio emanated faintly from an open window at number thirteen.

'You need some insurance,' he said. 'There is a man coming this weekend.'

'An agent?'

'He is a communist, a journalist who wants to help. I have asked him to give us something useful on the political scene, things the newspapers don't print. You handle him. He needs somebody who speaks English. We will put your name on the reports for Moscow.'

The breeze picked up. There was raucous barking from inside their house as they approached. Jack was growling, knowing it was them but putting on a show. When they got to the front door, Volodya tapped the glass, sending the Alsatian into an overblown spin, his whole body leaping like a jack-rabbit. Whenever the dog's hips wobbled, Evdokia thought they were on the verge of giving way.

Volodya went to the kitchen to prepare something to eat. Evdokia sat down at the bureau, reached for some paper, switching on a lamp.

The fish goes to rot, beginning at the head.

Voron. When the agent came to the embassy's front gates Evdokia recognised him straightaway. Rupert Lockwood, journalist and writer of the Australian left. His hair seemed tidier than usual, thin with little grey streaks. He had a high forehead and intent black eyes, and, in a V-necked cardigan and pinstriped jacket, looked decidedly middle-aged.

She led him to the prepared room. There was a round table at its centre holding a water jug, an ashtray, a stack of paper and some pens. She'd hung a picture of Stalin with clenched fist on one wall and in the other was a window. Lockwood stood at the table and set down his briefcase. She told him that the Soviet Union appreciated his presence here today.

'Wait,' he said. 'Is there no typewriter?'

She should, of course, have thought of that. What was a journalist without a typewriter? The only English machine in the embassy was in the commercial section, a battered Royal whose capital A strike rarely worked. She went to fetch it. When she returned, he was staring out the window, watching the children playing in the orchard. He'd placed a chair opposite his at the table. Evidently, she was to watch him work. He began slowly but quickly moved to a pace, smoking and typing with a serious look, like a man at a boxing match with money invested, cigarette stubs piling up, the air in the room becoming increasingly thin. Each page he finished, he gave to her.

She read that before the war the Japanese had established a large espionage network in Australia, including the Japan–Australia Association and the Australia First Movement.

She read that the clique that ran the *Bulletin*—a notorious anti-Soviet and anti-worker magazine—were actually Japanese agents. The managing editor of the *Daily News* was a drunk and a homosexual. He was also a Chinese agent, though completely open to bribes.

She read that all US government agencies in Australia were espionage agencies. The CIA operated extensively. She read that US spies had infiltrated Melbourne's communist circles under the pretence that they were CP of USA, only to appear, after Pearl Harbor, in GI uniform. She read that these spies were now working in the progressive trade unions, doing their best to turn the tide.

She read that the American advertising agency J. Walter Thompson watched the Australian press for the FBI. It was a certain fact that someone from the Thompson offices wrote the right-wing gossip rag *Things I Hear*. W.C. Wentworth, the Australian equivalent of Senator J.R. McCarthy, took direction from this same US agent. Wentworth's organisation, named Political Research, bought Security dossiers from a corrupt officer at four pounds, four shillings a piece; and under his direction Catholic priests met regularly with members of the political police in a café called Mario's, opposite the office of the *Sydney Sun*.

The information had an intensity that surprised her. Hard to reconcile it with the sparse world of Canberra.

Lockwood was looking at her, perhaps seeing something of her thoughts. He announced that he would mark the manuscript with symbols, creating footnotes on his sources for each page. The process took an hour. When it was over, she gave him two bottles of USSR vodka and a tin of caviar. He refused at first, but she insisted.

The next day, he came again, typing twenty or more pages before the Underwood's ribbon depleted and he said perhaps it was time to go. She gave him the same gift, but he would only take the vodka. She also offered him cash.

'Oh, no,' he said.

'Please. It is not a payment.'

'The vodka is sufficient.'

'We understand you are not interested in money. This is simply to refund your expenses, the hotel room and the train pass. The embassy cannot have you out of pocket.'

Lockwood paused a moment, checking his watch and then some papers in his jacket. Eventually he said, 'Fair enough,' and took a portion of the money, perhaps only a third of the total sum. Then he and Evdokia shook hands, and he left in darkness, this time via the embassy's rear door.

Upstairs, she, Volodya and Kislitsyn sat down and read Lockwood's document twice. She forwarded it to Moscow and, two weeks later, the Centre replied by cable. *Congratulations. Keep a close watch on Voron with a view to acquainting him more fully with our work.*

Volodya was happy. Such praise was hard to find. They drank two beers on the back porch, rugged up in a blanket, rain rocketing through the yard.

4

B2 kept an office on the top floor, at the opposite end of the building to Colonel Spry's. On the door was an embossed plate: DIRECTOR COUNTERESPIONAGE. He was seated there now, in his reading chair, a comfortable and heavily stained lounge that he'd had since university. Around him, the chaos of the room sprawled in all directions: memoranda, scribbled notes, cuttings from the *Sydney Morning Herald* and the Melbourne *Truth*, layers of reports written by his section officers, telephone messages typed by the secretarial pool, carbon-copied sets of the working Russian files, ten-year-old issues of the *Government Gazette*. The office felt like you didn't want to smoke in it, which was how B2 wanted it to seem. He was a literary man, after all, the author of two books of poetry and he had an order going here, a product of history and connective patterns only he could decode. The cleaning staff had long learned to stop coming.

On the walls were maps: Sydney, Melbourne, London, and a particularly large one of the USSR, placenames in Cyrillic, repeated underneath in English, pins showing the known birthplaces and life trajectories of the men, and some of the women, today residing at the Soviet embassy in Canberra. It was in front of this map that B2 sat examining Michael Howley's latest report. He thought it was a fair bet that one of these new Russians was Sadovnikov's MVD replacement and he was trying to think up some way to tell. Petrov, Kharkovetz, Kislitsyn, Koukharenko? An MI5 memorandum he had on the subject of identifying intelligence workers was, he thought, particularly unimaginative, its only interesting analysis a statistical measure of the number of confirmed MVD and GRU men per embassy vocation. VOKS—the Soviet cultural organisation—seemed the most popular cover for the MVD, at least in the United States and Britain. Other suggestions were less helpful: look for men with excellent English, for example, or men with the ability to drive motor cars. Spry was in America this week, meeting today or tomorrow with J. Edgar Hoover. B2 wondered whether the FBI would lend them their analysis instead.

He looked at the photographs of Philip Kislitsyn that MI5 had sent. He read and re-read the background histories and service records of the newcomers where recorded. He got out pins and stuck them to the map. Then he stood back from the map and looked.

Nothing jumping out.

He thought perhaps they needed some better sources. Perhaps someone they could place a little closer to these men.

On his desk was a small stack of incidental reports from the subversives section, occasions where their agents had come into contact with proper Soviet personnel. What was the name of that chap of theirs—the New Australian doctor, who seemed to know Pakhomov quite well?

Michael Bialoguski. Top-secret source Crane.

Crane said he treated Anna Pakhomova, wife of Tass correspondent, for a urinary tract infection at her home. Flat reportedly filthy, infested. Personally sighted adult bedbug, recently satisfied, moving along a blanket's edge.

B2 thought for a moment. He picked up the internal rig and made a call one floor below, to the office of the director of subversives. When the man came on, B2 got to the point quickly, asking what he knew about Crane.

'Oh,' the director said, 'I know he comes with certain difficulties.'

'Do you think he's reliable?'

'I'm not aware.'

'You think he's a mercenary?'

'He doesn't work for king and country.'

'Because he's a Pole?'

'Because he's a mercenary.' The voice on the line slowed. 'Actually, I believe we may drop him.'

'Any reason?'

'He's often very insistent that his salary is disproportionate.'

'Is it?'

'His information is second-rate.'

'He's not Party?'

'He attends meetings of the satellite groups. Peace Council. Various charities and committees.'

'The Russian Social Club, I see?'

'That's right.'

'Perhaps we'll take him.'

'If you like,' said the director. 'My advice would be to get him off balance and see how cheaply he'll come along.'

'Secrets in his blood, do you think?'

'The world grows strange. I guarantee Crane sees people following him and habitually stops in front of shop windows.'

'You think he lies in bed mouthing his codename, pondering its meaning in a thousand different contexts?'

'Why we gave it to him. Why we author the codes and the agents don't. Is this a new approach for you?'

'I'm seeking someone closer,' said B2. 'A source we can talk to firsthand.'

'Find someone good to manage him, my suggestion.'

'I'm going to give him to Michael Howley. Would you mind loaning me his file?'

They disconnected. B2 leaned back into the depths of his chair. He worried at times about how he was perceived by the other directors. They had military and police backgrounds. He was a poet. He worried they didn't understand his utility in the field of counterespionage; why Spry had recruited him, an interpreter of words. He wasn't one of them, but he hoped they understood him and didn't somehow think him weak.

They drove through Queanbeyan just as the sun was coming up, Petrov and Kislitsyn in the embassy's black BMW with Petrov's rifle, a few spare fishing rods, a set of crayons and an easel. Crisp air shot through the car. They slowed coming into town, and Kislitsyn thought to maybe make a phone call, so they stopped at the post office and he stood in the booth with the receiver to his ear and watched the road. Nothing came.

They left the highway for a dirt track four kilometres out. Farmland of some type, a frosty carpet catching some heat and glistening. The road crested and Petrov stopped. Kislitsyn popped the bonnet and feigned an examination of the engine. Both watched the road and nothing came.

In the next gully the road forked, and they followed left and saw a rail line in the distance. They came to it and found that the road dipped under the line, which ran above them on a bridge. They nosed off and got out. The bridge was made of greying sleepers and ironwork and there was the red globe of an ants' nest on the northern embankment.

'Here,' said Petrov.

'Where are we, the Sydney line?'

Petrov struggled up the southern embankment to inspect the bridge. Some of the overhead sleepers had dry cracks, fissures that ran deep into the wood. One had cracked remarkably, and after a splintered opening was a hollow cavity. He brushed out some cobwebs, thinking them a good sign. Kislitsyn threw him a matchbox and a cigarette packet. Both could be stuck straight in.

'What do you think? Alright?'

'Yes, alright.'

They drove on, Kislitsyn taking note of the odometer. The road became more worn, centred by a stretch of wild grass, and eucalypts appeared. Petrov pumped his window down to catch the strange smell. The car reached a river and they followed the bank. They stopped at a willow tree, got out the rod and rifle and began to walk. Eventually they came to a grey gum that was peeling; in its base was a blackened hollow. Petrov examined the hole.

'Alright?'

'Yes, alright.'

They drove back towards the highway. To be sure, Petrov parked the car again on the hill crest and Kislitsyn popped the bonnet and watched the road. Nothing came. He put the bonnet down and Petrov started the car again, only now the engine seemed unwilling to kick over.

'Is it flooded?'

'What's flooded? No, it's okay.'

Petrov twisted the key. The engine whirred but didn't catch. Kislitsyn opened the bonnet and this time the look was real.

'Try again,' he said.

'Do you see anything?'

'Where's your foot? Put your foot on the gas.'

'It's on. It's down.'

'I can't see anything. Take it off.'

'Anything now?'

'No. Try again.'

Petrov twisted the key. Nothing. They swapped roles.

'It's not happening.'

'Hit the alternator with a wrench.'

'The alternator or the carburettor?'

'With a wrench.'

'It's no good.'

'I'm on the gas. Do you see?'

'Nothing.'

Kislitsyn sighed. He pulled his tall frame out of the driver's seat. 'This is Vasili Sanko's fault. What system of maintenance does he have for these cars?'

Looking downhill, Petrov suggested a push start. He got into the driver's seat and Kislitsyn re-tied his shoelaces and put his jacket in the back. Then he put two long arms on the car's rear end and kicked into the dirt. The car took the hill quickly, Kislitsyn sprinting behind, Petrov twisting the key and pumping his foot. The engine kicked once but didn't catch. The car coasted ghostly to the sound of road noise until it hit the flat and all momentum tapered off. They were thirty metres from the highway. Now Petrov pushed and Kislitsyn drove but the car registered no response. They pushed the car to the highway and the hard shoulder. That at least might cover their tracks.

Kislitsyn opened the bonnet and tugged at the hoses. With a towel, he opened the radiator cap and a thriving hiss came boiling out. He put his hand wherever it would reach, searching for little mechanical mysteries. Nothing helped.

After a few minutes a utility appeared. Both men watched as it came over the lip of the horizon, slowed, and then went somewhat past them before stopping. It reversed and came off the road. A man and a boy got out, the man quite fat, the boy in shorts.

'Fellas got trouble,' said the man.

'Yes,' said Kislitsyn. 'This car won't start.'

'Working the Snowy?'

Kislitsyn didn't understand.

'New blokes?'

'Yes,' said Petrov.

'Right,' said the man. He bent into the engine. Umms and ahhs. Petrov turned and took note of the utility's plate number, and saw that the boy was picking pebbles from the road and throwing them with cocked arm towards the paddock, trying to hit a fencepost.

'Beats me. I've got a tow rope. Queanbeyan alright?'

Kislitsyn looked to Petrov. Petrov said, 'Yes, alright.'

The car lurched onto the road, pulled by the axle. Petrov sat steering. Kislitsyn asked how much they should pay this farmer. Petrov wasn't sure. They would let him suggest the figure.

In Queanbeyan, there was activity on the streets: morning traffic, small trucks and sedans, a school bus. A handyman's utility went past, strung with ladders, paint tins and tools, the handyman smoking and staring at the car on tow. The farmer brought them to a halt by the service station and Petrov got out. He shook the farmer's hand and thanked him and shook his hand again. They undid the tow rope together and then Petrov sent Kislitsyn into the station to get an ice-cream for the boy. The boy said a polite thankyou, the farmer gave them a nod and the utility drove off.

'He didn't ask for money?' said Kislitsyn.

'No, nothing at all.'

The response came a fortnight later: *Concerning Secret Hiding Places For Documents.* Petrov sat decrypting, substituting codewords, revealing piecemeal the message and its sting. Moscow was not impressed. The hiding places were defective, they wrote. It was their opinion that a crack between the boards of a railway bridge was substandard because railway bridges were probably inspected by appropriate persons and, upon the outbreak of 'exceptional circumstances', would likely have military guard. They complained that he hadn't sent sketches of the areas nor an explanation of the signalling system to be employed. They thought the selections much too close to one another, facilitating easy detection by counterintelligence. To right their errant station leader, they included fifteen paragraphs of secret hiding place advice, including a small treatise on the destructive habits of rodents.

Petrov read and re-read. It was their masterly tone that irked him most, as if he wasn't a colonel in the MVD but a

Komsomol scout who couldn't pitch his tent. He got a small bottle of whisky from the bottom drawer and drank. He raged a little. It was clear the writer wrongly believed the railway bridge to be over a river and not a road. He wondered who it was, this petty bureaucrat without the clout to sign his name, content with his missive and sitting at lunch in the canteen. It wouldn't be Sparta, but it might be someone with his ear.

Shadows down there that were blunt, suffering from a lack of contrast, losing their conspiratorial edge. ASIO had just left. From the window of his third-floor surgery at 195 Macquarie Street, Michael Bialoguski, a tall figure with a goatee beard, was looking down at parked cars, memorising numberplates for practice. It was a few minutes after 10 p.m. and the new handler had just visited. Michael Howley, Attorney-General's Department, D Branch. They shared the coincidence of a first name and the doctor liked the fact. Howley seemed less regimented than his former handlers, younger, with an edge to his voice that the doctor hoped concealed a desire for action over surveillance—but with these ASIO types, who knew. Bialoguski was considering the change to counterespionage a promotion, and once there was a rapport, he'd find a way to secure a raise. Not that that was his motivation. Just that, for the time and resources invested, he was terrifically underpaid.

Did he have money problems? The answer wasn't always clear. His medical practice in these rooms was busy enough but it was all contract and lodge, a shilling a week for un-limited treatment, and he was making little headway on his loans. It was a problem of his background. His was one of the more popular surgeries on Macquarie Street, but his

41

clients were New Australians, Balts and Poles like himself, hardly a well-financed segment of the social order and a difficult base from which to make a fortune. So he had other incomes and projects. His violin and his orchestral work, for example. He was playing for the famous conductor Eugene Goossens as a member of the Sydney Symphony Orchestra, a much-loved but again underpaid commitment, part of his own plan to one day conduct. Then there were other services he provided: women's procedures that weren't particularly good for his practising licence, but whose execution he considered to be an enlightened—and sometimes well-paying—responsibility.

His practice had two rooms: this small consulting office, and a second he used to keep supplies. At the end of the corridor was a reception area he shared with Halley Beckett, an ophthalmologist. The 195 building was medical men top to bottom, most of whom were part-time or retiring. Bialoguski had moved in two years ago, having transferred his practice from Thirroul.

He collected his keys, locked up and made his way down to the car park at the building's rear. Buick Sedan, BN 422 (white). Velox Tourer, EK 732 (white). Nineteen forty-nine Pontiac, DL 902. Howley had wanted to know about his political persuasions. He'd told the ASIO man he didn't have any, unless you counted believing in the rights of the individual and being against fascism of any kind. This was the only part of their conversation that had annoyed him. How was it relevant, his politics? He didn't have a view, not in the way they meant it in this country, whose political scene was, in comparison to where he'd come from, essentially simplistic. Which wasn't a bad thing. A two-party system, where the close balance between Labor and Liberal meant that elections were decided by voters of no fixed allegiance. This, he thought, coupled with the fair observation that, when voting, most Australians put instinct above processes of rational thought, was a recipe for a good democracy, where ideology—of any kind—found it difficult to get ahead. Not that this excused the country—through his paid agency—from keeping at least some kind of eye on the revolutionary beast.

He drove home through the city towards Point Piper. The Cliveden was a luxurious apartment building, in the deeper fold of Blackburn Cove. The flats had a palm garden and an outdoor pool and a view into the harbour over Double Bay. He was living in number nine, the property of the Poynters, patrons of the orchestra who were on sabbatical in London. The best feature at Cliveden was in its garages: each had a revolving floor. He parked in garage number nine, hit the switch and watched his Holden arc.

The flat was on the fourth storey. All conveniences, three bedrooms, including one for a maid. He kept things tidy because, where this place was concerned, there were appearances to maintain.

He poured a nightcap and sat in darkness looking at the view: Sydney nearing midnight and at half-light. Howley's talk had been full of promise. He'd be targeting the embassy now. Forget the petty communist émigrés and romantic left-wing dupes he usually hung around. Cultivate Pakhomov, the Soviet Tass journalist, in particular. See what shadowy contacts of his could be unearthed. The mission impressed Bialoguski greatly. He'd arrived in Australia almost ten years ago, landing with only a violin and thirteen pounds. He'd paid his passage using diamonds from a toothpaste tube. And look at him now: a qualified doctor and a state-sanctioned spy, living rent free in a luxury flat. Still, it wasn't quite enough. He'd given a lot here. This country owed him.

5

An interesting letter arrived at the Soviet embassy. It was on purple paper and written carefully in Russian. The sender, a man named Arkady Wassilieff, wrote that he was 'the holder of progressive views'. He said he ran an aviation factory in Melbourne. Government contracts. He said he had an industrial secret that he wished to share.

Petrov showed the letter to Kislitsyn, who suggested it might be a Security trap. Petrov wasn't so sure. He checked the embassy's consular record to find that Arkady Wassilieff had been denied a Soviet visa at the close of 1949.

He was in Melbourne two weeks later. He spoke to Zizka at the Czech embassy beforehand to get some idea about the city, asking what the man knew of good places to stay. Kislitsyn had tried to accompany him, but Petrov persuaded him to stay on the grounds that the Moscow couriers were soon to arrive. Really, it was just that he wanted the freedom in Melbourne to do as he pleased. He wanted to go anonymous and unrecorded. He wanted to act like a man not watched.

He arrived at Spencer Street by sleeper train, and had a haircut at Solomon's Barber Shop in Collins Street, at the hands of Isaac Tyger, a Pole who distributed Soviet literature to his clients. The haircut was a good one. Isaac spent the entire time talking world affairs and refused to let Petrov pay. Afterwards, he walked to Flinders Street Station and dropped into the pub on the corner of Swanston Street. He felt good, clean and good; 9.30 a.m. with a beer and a cigarette, watching the steps of the station where men in suits broke from the turnstiles onto the street, checking hats and watches, feeding the Monday busyness. After a time, he waved to the barman for a second glass and the second glass came and he savoured it even more than the first. A boy arrived with a stack of newspapers, and he sat reading and drinking and watching the sunlit activity. Just past midday he checked into the hotel on Bourke Street that Zizka had recommended. He sat in the room there for a moment looking through his pockets, making sure he had the Czech's other suggestions: a Collins Street watchmaker and an address in Fitzroy.

He took the tram to Clarendon Street, the ride much smoother than any of Moscow's trolleys. As the tram crossed the river, he produced a map and pretended to consult it while trying to get a view of the three men he thought were following him. The one with the moustache, staring carefully now at a timetable—he'd been smoking on the footpath outside the hotel. Definitely. That thin black tie. About the other two he wasn't certain, but they had the feel of a unit and certainly looked the part. Petrov winced. He didn't want these kinds of problems in his day.

The conductor stood in the tram's centre by the doors. Petrov approached him and loudly asked directions to a fake address. Then, at the next stop, he jumped from the tram just as the doors closed, striking out east at pace, checking over his shoulder. None of the men got off.

The factory was a white-bricked building, sparking flecks of iron and a deal of deafening noise. Arkady Wassilieff shook his hand at the entrance and led him to an upstairs office with glass windows overlooking the factory floor. They stood there watching, and Wassilieff opened them each a beer.

'Aircraft,' the man said, pointing to a particularly large machine. 'This one coils wire for the Stratocruisers. The wire is used for all purposes and each plane requires two thousand feet.'

The industrialist in Petrov was impressed. Wassilieff pointed again. 'Those vats you see are new. I am trying to refine the glue used to seal internal fittings for low pressures. The chemistry is fascinating, I assure you.'

They sat down at a small desk. Covering the walls of the office were rosters and diagrams and photographs of race-horses.

'I have made some modest scientific discoveries here,' said Wassilieff. 'Currently, the Australian government has the total benefit, but I think all of humanity should have it too.'

The man had a mousy face, Petrov thought. 'Two years ago you asked for a visa,' he said.

'Yes, I have relatives in Russia. In Voroshilovgrad.'

'Voroshilovgrad? A visa there would be difficult. Moscow is better. Get a visa for the capital.'

'No, no,' said Wassilieff. 'I want only to visit Voroshilovgrad. You know how it is. Men do well and they want to visit their past.'

Petrov said nothing.

'Listen,' Wassilieff pleaded, 'you don't need to worry about me. When we were boys, Marshal Voroshilov and I were in the same union. He may even remember. I could perhaps write to him, but I want to use the regular channels, which is why I aim to prove my loyalty to you.'

'Tell me about this loyalty.'

Wassilieff had Petrov stand once more at the window. He pointed to a third machine on the floor. It was spherical, two alternately rotating discs that were pressed tightly together, moving fast. 'Hard-wearing aviation ball bearings,' Wassilieff said. He showed Petrov a glass jar brimming with pellets. 'Their life span is twenty times that of regular stock.'

Petrov picked one up. It was hard. He held it to the light.

'I have developed a secret process to produce them in large numbers,' said Wassilieff. 'Each bearing is a small enigma, exactly the same. There are no defects at any stage. Consider that. It is a perfect process. Place one in each hand and I can almost swear you are holding the same number of atoms.'

Petrov took a fistful. They felt like futuristic gunshot, each its own galactic sphere.

'Take them,' said Wassilieff.

Petrov held the jar. 'I don't know,' he said. 'It is likely we have this technology already.'

The factory owner put his fingers on his chin. 'Yes, of course. But take it anyway, for *comparison*. And if the Soviet engineers would like to compare their processes to mine, you let me know. I will send them everything I have.'

'Just to compare.'

'Yes, yes. For that purpose. And then maybe we will see about my visa?'

Petrov smiled. They shook hands again and he left.

At the tram stop, one of the men was waiting. Petrov stopped on the street corner, lit a cigarette, and began to feel sick. They had probably followed him to the factory. They probably planned on following him all day. He felt a weakness in his knees, in his stomach—a disgusting base liquid rolling in its hollows. He could have vomited. He took a moment to compose himself, then stood at the stop only a few metres from the follower.

They both boarded the next city-bound ride. At the following stop, the man with the thin black tie got on, and then at the next the last man was waiting. This actually made Petrov feel better. Positioned like that, they must have lost him; and there wasn't much chance they could have been at the factory and reached these stops in time. They'd just been hoping he'd go back to the city the same way. Which meant he was stupid. He should have stayed on the south side of the river and crossed somewhere else.

The men were careful not to watch him directly. He was careful not to watch them directly. He retied his shoelaces and waited for the tram to reach the city. If he'd lost them once, he could do it again.

He got off on Bourke Street at the corner of Elizabeth Street. Black Tie and Brown Hat joined him on the footpath. He walked east along Bourke Street and turned into the first arcade he came to, moving quickly past a luggage shop and a shoe store. He gathered speed, examining his watch as cover: just a man with an appointment who is late. Pursuing footsteps sounded on the arcade floor. He passed into the light of Little Collins Street, then into another arcade, and he didn't look back. He went quickly into a café and asked for the toilet, and went past it, through the kitchen and out a back door. In the alley he reversed his heading, doubling back to Little Collins

Street. He turned there for Swanston Street and hopped on a northbound tram. It pulled away and he watched from the windows until satisfied he was untracked.

An hour later he was at the bar of a pub in Fitzroy. He'd walked the entire distance, using his map, arriving sweaty in his long coat. It was half past three. He checked the address Zizka had provided: 71 King William Street. It was a while since Petrov had done this, not since his and Evdokia's last weeks in Stockholm, in fact. Of course there were such places in Moscow, but those he knew were under MVD surveillance and half the girls were co-opted workers; a visit there was a dangerous, foolish act for someone who knew any kind of state secret. Trapped by his position, he'd never attempted it. Things weren't the same here though, just as they hadn't been in Stockholm. Here, he was no one. He was just another body on the street and the street didn't know anybody's name. It was the only thing he had savoured about his years in the navy: the feeling of being the outsider, the man in port, in transit, free of consequence. He and his shipmates had visited the houses and he'd liked the girls then, enjoyed his ability to chat with them, to be accepting of their vulgarity. In Stockholm, his pleasure had been more in the physical act itself, the grip of his hand on the skin of a side or stomach. He'd been much less interested in the girl and far more, he guessed, in himself. It was addictive, and he'd arranged his activities to free himself as much as possible from the embassy's watch. Not so difficult in Stockholm; even easier in Melbourne when the one block of official Soviet soil in the country was five hundred kilometres away.

He finished his beer, feeling a little glum. Seventy-one King William Street was the main reason he'd come to Melbourne, but the encounter with the bastard followers had ruined his mood.

The building was a thin terrace, thick curtains in the windows. He knocked loudly, wanting to be off the front doorstep as quickly as possible, yet, paradoxically, feeling both powerful and uncaring to the same degree. Nobody answered. He looked up and down the street and knocked once more. Eventually, he was greeted by a man in a dressing gown who had the look of recent sleep.

'Yes?'

'Hello,' said Petrov.

They looked at each other.

'A friend gives me this address,' said Petrov.

'Does he?'

'That's right.'

'It's very early.'

'It's a good time.'

The man looked past him to the street, then pulled back the door. The Russian walked in. They stood in the front room, dark and abundantly furnished with armchairs, drink tables and ashtrays.

'Ford,' said the man.

'Karpitch,' said Petrov.

It seemed that whichever girl was available had to be roused and was unhappy about it, for a minute or two after Ford left him he heard the sounds of a suppressed argument. But after a time she emerged. A big-hipped woman with brown hair. She smiled at him, took his hand and walked him up the stairs. In the large bedroom at the front, they stopped at the foot of the bed. He put his hand on her breast and then undressed her.

***

ANDREW CROOME

Julius and Ethel Rosenberg were going to die on the electric chair at Sing Sing. Evdokia sat at her desk with the newspapers and a pair of scissors and made clippings for Moscow. US atom spy couple, parents of Michael and Robert, their crime 'worse than murder'. The secret the Rosenbergs had shared was a new type of bomb, a beryllium sphere, enclosed in plutonium, hugged by barium; thirty-six high-explosive lenses, each with two detonators, seventy-two condensers to fire them. Evdokia thought that detonators were detonators, but in the atom world there was always a further caveat on any basic fact. The judge said the Rosenbergs were part of a diabolical conspiracy to destroy a God-fearing nation and that the Russian international spy ring was a well-organised beast, with tentacles that reached into the most vital of places. The jury made no recommendation for mercy. Only the Lord could offer forgiveness for what the Rosenbergs had done.

If Moscow wanted these articles, Evdokia thought, something about the case must be true. The defence was claiming Political Hysteria. Evdokia clipped a photograph of Mrs Ethel Rosenberg: thirty-five years old, stern but delicate in black and white.

Ambassador Lifanov came into the room. The knot of his tie was minuscule, perfectly positioned on his throat, and the chain of a fob watch hung below his breast. He stood beside her and watched. She put the clippings in a folder and faced him. His glasses were low on his nose.

'Petrova . . . these figures.'

'Ambassador?'

He put some papers on her desk—the embassy's monthly payroll. She had prepared and submitted it that morning.

'Is it correct, this figure?'

She looked. Everyone's salary was twofold: an allowance in Australian pounds, furthering a direct deposit in roubles into a Moscow account. The ambassador was pointing to Volodya's name and his one hundred and one Australian units.

'Oh, yes,' she said.

The ambassador looked taken aback. He pointed out her own name.

'Seventy-five Australian units,' she said. 'Is something wrong?'

He frowned, gauging her. 'Well,' he said, 'it seems *unbalanced*. Wouldn't you agree?'

'Oh?'

'Yes. The Pipniakovs, for instance. They have six mouths to feed. And here, look: twenty-six units. I think it is unfair. That is all. Alexandra agrees.'

'Your wife, Comrade . . .' She was not sure what to say. 'Nicolai Nikhailovich, these figures are set in Moscow . . . You are comparing a *dvornik*'s wage to a diplomatic post.'

'Still, it is unreasonable. Do you not think?'

'The figures are what the Foreign Ministry have decided.' She did not add that the payroll showed only her and Volodya's ostensible income—that the MVD served them additional salary as well. 'Perhaps the Pipniakovs should receive more,' she said. 'But my responsibility is only to ensure that the correct monies are paid.'

The ambassador shrugged. 'I am simply saying that, without children, you and your husband are very well off.'

Hatred welled. She stood and left the room without looking at his face. The corridor was airless. Volodya was out of his downstairs office. She shut the door. She took a teacup from his desk and gripped it, applying tremendous pressure against the cup and its handle until the pain felt like it might damage her bones.

The national sheepdog trials. The weather was warm and the embassy accepted an invitation en masse and embarked on a Sunday morning, the cars sardined with children. The trials were at an oval in Yarralumla. The Soviets parked on the boundary and set down rugs and served themselves cordial, wine and bread. The next day would be Constitution Day, a holiday.

The dogs competed one at a time, herding three sheep through a series of obstacles. Evdokia and Volodya stood at the rail with Philip Kislitsyn and his wife. Anna wore a suit that was neutral in colour but modern in its look. She and Evdokia looked at poor Zaryezova. The girl's husband was in the commercial section and tense about his money. Her suit was ill-fitting, its shoulders uneven like some parallax mistake.

The dogs dashed and stalked and came around. The men, in crumpled suits and crumpled hats, whistled, waved sticks, split sheep and penned them, sometimes shouting 'Hup'. There was a crowd of a few hundred, annexing the land around their cars, picnicking, a six-metre tally board and a loudspeaker broadcasting.

The secretary of the Trial Association walked past exhibiting the trophy and welcomed the Soviets to the event. The ambassador told him they had sheepdogs everywhere across Russia, but all of them with shaggy hair.

They drank from coloured metallic cups. Evdokia watched as Alexandra Lifanova poured all the women champagne except her. Anna stood for the toast but did so looking sympathetic and distressed. Volodya poured his wife a little brandy instead, and Kislitsyn asked for a share. The children chased one another through the shining maze of cars.

It turned out that the Czechs had come too. She walked with Volodya to their encampment under the shade of a tree. On the oval, a dog crossed between the sheep and his master and was disqualified. The company were despondent for it. Volodya, in a happy mood, shouted that it should be allowed to start again, and the Czechs chimed in, but with no result. Volodya and the Czech consul, Zizka, began drinking vodka. Evdokia watched the way he did it, gulping the drink down. Her husband and the consul stood clasping each other by the shoulder, smiling in the grassy sunshine. They drank and smoked and ate sausage and cured meats and they applauded the dogs and laughed together as they drank some more.

Evdokia sat on a rug with the consul's wife. The woman wore tinted glasses and had trouble watching the events on the oval, so Evdokia tried to describe what was happening, but it was such a poor sport to commentate on that they gave up, laughing. Lunch was chicken sandwiches.

Vasili Sanko came to say that Ambassador Lifanov felt ill and wanted driving home. Volodya looked at him, chewing. 'That's your job.'

'He says I am too drunk.'

Volodya examined him and grinned. 'You are an ox. You are not too drunk.'

Zizka gave Sanko a glass. The driver paused briefly, then tipped it down his throat. He clapped once and said, 'Volodya, the ambassador wants you to take him. He declares that you have the most practised hands.'

Volodya laughed. 'He is wrong, I can't drive. I'll crash like a cartoon.'

Evdokia spoke up. 'Tell the ambassador that my husband is too drunk. He is bleary-eyed.'

Sanko waited for his cup to fill again. He watched a dog finish its round. 'Alright. We are all too drunk.'

Zizka cheered and laughed.

'Tell Lifanov we're happy here,' said Volodya. 'And say that while the Czechs' vodka might be inferior, at least they serve more of it.'

Sanko smiled and turned. He walked along the boundary, white pegs of timber, back to the Russian camp. Evdokia watched him go. A while later, they saw the Zim departing for Mueller Street. She wondered who was at the helm and turned to give Volodya a goading stare. He wasn't watching her. She saw him give the car a small wave and continue his cheering of the dogs.

The next day was Monday. In the Lockyer Street house, she stood at the door of the spare room. They'd planned to create a garden box that morning in the space below the porch, but Volodya was in here, snoring.

On the street, sprinklers flared in a few front yards. She walked to the Manuka shops. For the first time there she felt utterly lonely, somehow purposeless, a schism between herself and the physical world.

The house was empty when she came back. The car gone, Jack too. The afternoon arrived and went. She swept the house and used a duster. She put furniture oil on the chairs. The radio played serials that she didn't have the concentration to follow. It was enough for her to listen to the drama, the sound of family empires, humming.

She wrote to her mother. She wanted to write the things she couldn't: this growing isolation, the hollowness. The letter was so far removed. She sat the pen on the bureau and stopped.

Volodya came home before dinner, not saying where he'd been. Jack was muddy and she washed his feet in a bucket. The sun gone, they ate sausages from the freezer. She watched Volodya chew and told him that this was a wasted day, that miserable failure had come visiting their plans.

He looked at her and gave a nod. 'The sausage is good. The potatoes.'

'Are they?'

'Tomorrow,' he said, 'I need to go to Sydney.'

'I thought maybe you'd gone there now.'

'No. I'd tell you!'

He put pepper on the meat.

'You went to the spare room last night?' she asked.

He nodded. 'I woke myself from snoring. I was uncomfortable. I slept there for your benefit.'

'Where did you go today?'

He paused. 'Oh, errands.'

'Errands where? In the country?'

'Hmm?'

'Jack's paws. Mud all over.'

Volodya shrugged. 'We crossed a creek.'

'You were hunting?'

'Doing errands.'

'Errands, but crossing creeks?'

'Yes.'

'With dogs and rifles?'

'Just cover. Hunting as cover.'

She knew that was a lie. 'You decided to go hunting and forget the garden box,' she said.

'No.'

'Tell the truth.'

'You don't know, Doosia. I needed to do some things, country things, I needed Jack for a story.'

'You took Kislitsyn too? Did you take Zizka?'

'Of course not.'

'Perhaps I will ask them. Whether, this holiday, they were at home with their wives?'

He stood up from the table and changed the tuning of the radio, giving the dial a violent jerk.

'What will you do in Sydney?' she asked.

He collected his plate to leave the room. 'That is official,' he told her. 'Not yet any business of yours.'

The ambassador laughed into the phone. Evdokia was taking notes while he spoke with his Swiss counterpart. The Swiss man was now making jokes. Lifanov's laugh started and ended in his gut, lifting him from his seat. On telephone calls, his habit was to jam his finger under the cradle, as if the spring in the mechanism might fail at any moment and the cradle give way under its own weight, disconnecting him.

At the conversation's end, he had Evdokia read him back the notes. On her way out, she said to him, 'Nicolai Nikhailovich, I hope you are not angry about the dog trials. The men were very drunk. It would have been dangerous for them to drive.'

He laughed happily and looked at her. He said that Vasili Sanko had driven safely. The chauffeur's wife had promised the ambassador the chance to cut off her husband's head should the pair arrive anything less than sound. They'd sung a song and negotiated the corners slowly.

'You arrived safely then?'

'Sanko has a head.' The ambassador smiled.

That afternoon she went upstairs. The silence of the secret section was the same silence you heard in the corridors of Dzerzhinsky Square. She worked quietly at the administrative desk, tabulating the results of a stocktake of MVD equipment, cataloguing anything of security interest that couldn't be burnt.

2 × Nagant M1895 revolvers
1 × radio receiver (dismantled)
4 × official MVD seal
1 × photographic enlarger . . .

Suddenly, Prudnikov was whispering from the door. The chief cypher clerk had one foot in the hall and was holding a square of paper. They were the only two in the section. 'Nina and I are sorry,' he said. 'About what is happening. We must follow the ambassador's lead.' He looked down the corridor, towards the stairs. 'But we are friends, we hope you know. Volodya is in Sydney?'

'Yes.'

'Then I will show you this so that you may know.'

The page he held was a private cable from Lifanov to Moscow. It said that Third Secretary Petrov was drunk on duty and disobeying direct orders.

'I am cyphering this,' said Prudnikov. 'It will go tomorrow.'

She thanked him. He put the cable into a folder and disappeared.

***

Volodya rang from the Oriental Hotel. Sydney had seen sun showers, which was the impossible situation of rain on your face and the sun on your skin. It was seven o'clock now. He was going to have dinner. He sounded crisp and a little contrite.

'Mirabel,' he said.

'Mirabel?'

'That child. The daughter at 16 Lefroy Street.'

Evdokia knew the girl. Six or seven years old, brown hair, little red sandals. She walked by the house every morning on her way to the Telopea Park school. She played sometimes with the boys in the street, and she'd come to their door once, without escort, selling tickets for a raffle.

'I think we should ask her parents whether we can adopt her,' said Volodya.

Evdokia was silent.

'I think it is a good idea,' her husband continued. 'We can promise she will be well looked after. We can tell her parents that she will be given a good home and a good education in Russia.'

She had been going to tell him about Lifanov. Instead, she stood there somewhat stunned.

'When I am back,' Volodya said before disconnecting. 'We will talk more about it then.'

She walked through the house, switching on all the lights. It was a crazy idea, Mirabel in their apartment in Moscow, a novelty Australian daughter. Was Volodya serious, or was he simply up there in Sydney halfway drunk? Thinking it over, it eventually occurred to her that his suggestion was probably an attempt at making amends for his hunting. An apology of sorts. The idea was actually quite galling—Volodya presenting the possibility of a child to her as if the suggestion of a

60

daughter was a peace offering equivalent to bunched flowers, a piece of jewellery or some coffee. It stung. It was infuriating. She began thinking about Irina—the slight that her husband had just delivered on herself and her daughter both. Then she pictured Volodya's face again from that day's end; his arrival at her apartment, her struggle to relay the news and his developing of that crippled look that she'd never forget, her daughter's lifeless body in its bed. The forty strange hours of flu and fever; the nausea, the cold limbs and the flights through delirium; the lucid hours that were perfect resurrections until each time the fever hit again and with increased vigour. Until the last.

It was difficult to reconcile Volodya's kindness at that time with now. Still, she thought their marriage was strong. In the beginning, after their wedding in Moscow, he'd directed upon them a focus that was at times overbearing, their lives overlapping to the degree that she often complained she needed release. But it was an intensity that had had its uses, allowing her to cope. Perhaps it was just the natural way of things that, since then, his attentions had been slowly travelling beyond them. She thought he was increasingly self-focused, progressively more foreclosed. On their excursions or at the gatherings they attended as a couple, there was a developing sense of his acting alone, of needs that excluded her, a selfishness in his behaviour that wasn't malicious but that was there all the same. The secrecy did not help. In Sweden, and here in Australia, he seemed to know full well that he could cloak whatever he wished by evoking the MVD's name. Still, none of this concerned her too much. She thought that these were ordinary pressures—the same as those on any union. What husband wasn't selfish and unthinking at times?

She had arrived at the window of the spare bedroom. About to draw the curtains, she saw through the window two human shapes: two pin-prick glints of cigarette, two men sitting outside in a car—the car where you'd park if you were trying to surveil or intimidate the house.

She was being paranoid, she knew. She closed the curtains and went and reheated some stew; dropped bits of potato into Jack's mouth while listening to a news broadcast on the radio. Returning to the bedroom, she looked through the gap between the curtains, with the light off. The car was still there.

Modes of fear. She wasn't afraid to begin with, but as time wore on a nervousness set in, a tightening sensation in the blood. She rang the operator and asked the girl to pass a message to the police: a suspicious car on Lockyer Street. Prowlers?

The police came in a gleaming white utility with a loud-speaker on its roof. One officer, turning into the street from Canberra Avenue, parking right behind the car with his head-lamps ionising the back bumper. He spent a few moments at the wheel of the utility, as if pondering the object in front and gathering his thoughts. Then he got out and walked up the gutter and leaned into the car. The conversation lasted a few minutes. The policeman wrote something on a pad and went back. He sat in the utility—Evdokia thought maybe talking on his radio—then he cut half the power to his headlamps and drove away.

The car remained. One figure looked directly at the house now, the other behind and around.

There was a heavy spanner in the bathroom where Volodya had been changing washers. She stood with this weapon in one hand and Jack's collar in the other. Jack knew that something was happening but not quite what. He pulled against her grip, low vibrations in his throat. The people in the car wound down their windows. She decided to switch on the outdoor light. Its glow fell weakly on the road, hardly more than a gravesman's lamp.

Even as the engine started, the car's occupants seemed coolly unperturbed. They moved slowly to Lefroy Street, turning right, headlamps off. She was taking a long breath at the window when she had the feeling that there was someone in the room. Jack barked. The sound rang out like a shot in an enclosed space and she dropped the spanner and swung around.

There was no one. She cursed the dog quietly as her heart came to rest. She cursed and patted him at the same time.

At the back door she checked the bolts. She went to their bedroom and set down a towel. The flex cord on the telephone extended a few inches under the door. She moved it into the room, put the reading chair against the door, the dog on the towel and the spanner by the bedside lamp. These were practical precautions. She was no longer afraid. Life had just seen enough trouble caused by men breaking through doors in the middle of the night not to act in cases of fair warning.

They met at the Canberra railway, a station like a weatherboard homestead, black tar on the platform and a cracking concrete area for travellers' cars, turning circles marked by white stone. It was only a few hundred metres from the house. Volodya carried his suitcase, Evdokia his satchel.

Crossing the avenue, she informed him of the ambassador's report.

'He's sent it already?' Volodya said.

'Yes.'

'It will be alright.'

'No, it won't.'

'Well.'

'You gave him things to cite. Drunkenness, refusing his command. You were foolish.'

Volodya unlocked their front door. 'Who is Lifanov to command?' he spat. 'Which of us is the fearsome MVD?'

'He is winning.'

'We need something on him. If necessary, we'll make it up.'

'I don't want this again.'

'It's alright. I'm not your last husband, a weak target. I am different. You will see.'

They went to bed.

She didn't like Volodya talking about Irina's father that way but she said nothing. It was cruel to suggest that the arrest was Alexei's fault: the random nature of the terror; you couldn't assign blame, and you couldn't truly think that weakness made a difference. But then again, perhaps it did. Take herself as the example. Her husband arrested in their flat after midnight, never to be heard of again: it should have been a fate shared by association, but in the weeks following she'd put up a terrific fight for herself, for Irina, had proved them strong enough to survive.

She'd done the necessary things, visited the right people with the right powers, committed acts that needed strength. She'd been so focused that there had been no time to fret over Alexei's vanishing. He was gone; no point in asking questions, in dwelling on him as if he might somewhere still exist. In fact, to do so could have been dangerous. Not so strange then, that her memories of him now were split from her memories of

Irina; two entities, unrelated, existing in the same lifetime, the same places, the same flat, but in wholly different lives, no bridge between; Alexei hanging so far from everything that most times, when encountered in some accidental thought, the man was a complete surprise.

She wasn't sure what to make of it, the fact he could be so easily erased. She'd been young when she'd moved in with him. She had felt that she loved him fiercely. He was bright: only twenty-two and already researching and teaching in a university, a respected radio engineer, part of a specialist team developing a new and more reliable form of valve. It was a project that the military had an interest in, and secrecy prevented him telling her much about it, but he would bring drawings home to amend and she would watch his careful diagramming from the other side of the room, eventually seeking to distract him by standing behind him, placing an arm along his, or leaning her weight against him. He was an intense and quiet person, which was what Volodya meant by weak. They had been living together for two years before the arrest. She had come to suspect that the event had something to do with the project—a jealous member of the team, perhaps, putting Alexei in: a target who as a result of his introverted nature appeared isolated, more disconnected than others, a man who could disappear with little consequent fuss. But who really knew? Years later, she saw a former colleague of his who told her that he was in a prison not far from Moscow. By this time she was married to Volodya and, within this new existence, the idea of Alexei had become abstract. Perhaps, at the time, Volodya's voluble, borderless personality had swallowed quiet Alexei up.

6

Saturday night and Doctor Bialoguski was at the Russian Social Club, wearing a grey suit and a red bow tie, sitting against the wall, drinking beer and smoking cigarettes, listening to the jump and swell of the band; a poor lot of musicians to his mind, completely uninventive and not particularly well rehearsed.

The club was in the basement of a building on George Street. It was one cavernous space and a few smaller rooms, thick velvet curtains—draped with Soviet flags—over the walls, which gave the music a muggy tone and swallowed the noise of conversation.

Tonight, he had a good spot for observing. The crowd was a large one, even by weekend standards. The club had recently been banned by the Labor Party, who were now considering it a communist front. The news had made the papers. It seemed the publicity was serving it well.

Across the room, he saw Bela Weiner. The girl was entertaining a table of young men, sailors probably, all seemingly transfixed by her diminutive and quite intoxicating Jewish features—good wrapping for the eloquent communism that was her inner light. He had to admire Bela. She would have recruited these boys off the ship this morning, entranced them, handed them a card for the club. She was a prolific promoter, spoke several languages, and he respected her commitment— even if she was deluded—to the communist cause.

He counted the men at the table. Felt certain they were speaking Hungarian.

The band started another song, people dancing at the foot of the stage. He saw Mrs Klodnitsky, the club's president, approaching him. She was too thin, he thought, and had a nose like a bird.

'Good evening, Doctor,' she said, holding a champagne flute, smiling. He was the toast of the club at the moment, a Macquarie Street practitioner whom they all thought respect-able and politically sound. Mrs Klodnitsky had taken to suggesting he run for the club's committee.

He stood and gave what he hoped was a charming bow.

'Are you interested in drama?' she asked.

'Drama. Oh.'

'I am trying to organise a circle for the study of the new Russian writers. I think it will attract some intellectuals to the club. Are you persuaded?'

'The new Russians?'

'That's right. Bela Weiner has agreed, and Lydia Mokras also. I would like some men to be involved. A drama circle.'

He looked into the crowd. 'Lydia Mokras?' he asked.

'Have you not met?' Mrs Klodnitsky said. 'Lydia is new to Sydney, a member for a few months now. It's rumoured that her father is an important colonel for the MVD in Moscow.'

He attempted to look impressed.

'Let me introduce you,' she said.

They walked through the smoky drift that engulfed the tables. She led him to a table at the edge of the dancers where a woman, who couldn't have been more than twenty, was sitting with two men. The first of these men was Ivan Pakhomov, the Soviet Tass journalist based in Sydney, and Bialoguski admonished himself for not realising the Russian was at the club. The second man was round, almost barrel-shaped, a little floppy at the edges, neatly dressed, smoking a cigarette and staring at the room through black-rimmed spectacles.

'Lydia, this is Doctor Bialoguski,' said the chairwoman.

'Please,' he announced, leaning down to take the girl's hand, 'my name is Michael.'

Lydia smiled. Pakhomov invited the doctor to sit. Mrs Klodnitsky declared she would fetch the table some champagne.

'How is your boy, Ivan?' Bialoguski asked Pakhomov.

'He recovers well.'

'That's good news.'

'Are you a medical doctor?' Lydia asked. She wore a small hat, and underneath it he saw blonde hair. A broad face, but attractive.

'That's right,' he said.

'Do you have rooms?'

'Yes.'

'I must visit you. I have a complaint with my ear.'

'It will be this band.'

'The doctor does house calls too!' said Pakhomov. 'Very good.' The Russian gestured to his friend. 'Doctor, this is Vladimir Petrov. He is VOKS, the embassy's new cultural representative.'

They shook hands. Bialoguski went to say something, but Lydia interrupted.

'Will you be joining our drama circle, Doctor? Mrs Klodnitsky has told me about you. She says we need some good members. You don't look like the kind of man who's regularly here.'

He asked what she meant.

'Oh, I mean that you appear sure of yourself. Radically. Many of the men this place attracts seem raggedy to me.'

'Raggedy?'

'Yes. They are communists but of the type who wear scrappy jackets and seem to carry chips on their shoulder about some fact or other. They're easy to set off. They want to argue about politics, but once you do they get angry and close up. My experience anyway.'

'You speak excellent Russian. Are you Russian?'

'Maybe.'

'I hear you have relatives in Moscow.'

'Yes, I have an uncle there.'

'And are you a communist?'

She looked at him as if he were strange. 'Of course,' she said. 'I believe the revolution in Australia is, at maximum, five years away.'

Mrs Klodnitsky returned with the champagne. Bialoguski opened the bottle and poured. 'Why don't you make the toast, Lydia?' he asked.

'To Soviet planes on our runways!' She raised her glass.

They drank. The man named Petrov grinned and seemed to be enjoying himself. Bialoguski leaned towards him. 'Mr Petrov, how are you finding Australia?'

'Oh, very warm.'

They laughed.

'You are the VOKS man,' said Bialoguski. 'Has someone shown you the club's library?'

'Yes. I am going to arrange for more journals. Science and literature. Full colour. Perhaps even some medical texts.'

'I would be interested.'

'Alright.'

Bela Weiner went past, drawing two boys with her to the dance floor. Lydia Mokras looked at them all watching her, then leaned forward suddenly. 'Doctor,' she said, 'it must be a discreet profession you are in.'

'Discreet?'

'Yes. People must trust you. You must keep secret what ails them.'

'I suppose.' He smiled.

'Do you have a car, Doctor?' She was looking at Petrov as she said this.

'I do,' Bialoguski replied.

'That's interesting. I will keep that in mind. Are you much of a photographer?'

He looked at them both. 'Well,' he said, 'I have an old Pentax I used to use.'

She smiled and nodded, and he was sure she was smiling and nodding at Petrov. Slowly, the night wore on. He purchased the table a second bottle of champagne and, at Pakhomov's urging, made blunt criticisms of the band. Lydia kept asking him questions, raking his personal history in a way he thought was too interrogatory to be without purpose, Petrov listening the whole time. Near the end of the evening, the girl departed the table for the bathroom, and Bialoguski was left alone with the two Russians.

'My knees,' said Petrov.

'Your knees.'

'There is an ache they have. Here, in the joint.'

'An ache.'

'Yes. Some kind of pain.'

'I will look at it.'

'Not now. I think perhaps I should visit you professionally. Sometime soon.'

'I have a card.'

The Soviet accepted it, placed it carefully in his breast pocket. Then he stood and looked at Pakhomov, who announced they would leave. Bialoguski followed them to the bar, where he ordered a beer, said his goodbyes, and waited for Lydia Mokras.

She never returned. He waited until closing time, wondering how she'd escaped the club, chatting here and there with a few people who knew him, making mental note of the things they said, writing everything down a short time later, regardless of its Security interest, onto a leather-bound pad he kept for the purpose in the glove box of his car.

'Kings Cross,' the driver announced.

Buildings lit up at night, a huge sign, 'Capstan', cheering from a rooftop. Petrov had heard from Zizka there was a witch out here. There was a sex witch who had a cult of worshippers, hedonistic black magicians, sex acts performed in ritual circles by occultists or sex barbarians posing as occultists. It was a flat somewhere in the Cross, sorcery and spiritism, corrupt as Berlin. People in masks, arranging their bodies in dark and elementary geometries, lowly chanting rites with their sex organs exposed.

Petrov asked insistently, but the taxi driver knew nothing about this. Gave him instead the address of some kind of club. He would go there later tonight. He wanted a drink in his hotel room first. He'd had a few beers at the Russian Social Club, but that was work. He'd needed to watch his behaviour under Pakhomov's nose.

His room at the Oriental looked onto the fire escape of the building next door. He found the bottle of brandy he'd bought at the terminal at Mascot and drank straight from it.

His mission was to report to Sparta on the state of the club. That doctor, Bialoguski, looked like an interesting prospect. A man in his position would be a good source of information, even a good agent perhaps. Petrov supposed he should sketch the night's events on a piece of paper—the personalities, the conversations—but he couldn't be bothered. Instead, lamplight and this brandy. The sounds of traffic and the skip of city voices through the open window.

The girl, Lydia, seemed a player. Pakhomov had introduced them, whispered that she had some kind of intelligence connection, maybe the Czechs; or was she even, he'd suggested, a *novator*—an agent on their own illegal line? Petrov had laughed. He'd said that as far as he knew there were no illegals incountry. But the girl did seem mysterious: she knew her politics, appeared overly connected for someone who claimed to have been in Sydney only six months. Someone to keep an eye on. He would ask Moscow Centre what they knew.

Down on the street, the air seemed warmer and people were walking unsteadily or in loud groups. At the address the taxi driver had offered there was no signage, simply a staircase leading down to basement rooms. He could hear the dull and muffled sound of music. He stood near the doorway, his thumb clipped into his belt, finishing his cigarette, watching people go by, hunting for any shadowy figures that weren't passing as much as staying, noticing nobody before going down.

A Sunday afternoon at home; Bialoguski trying to write his violin concerto. It was music about two lovers. He had a beginning and a middle, now he was looking for things to go wrong. It had to be a case of fate conspiring, only he was stuck, couldn't think. His ideas were somewhere else, possibly ahead or behind him, which was why he had coffee brewing and why he was wearing a fez.

The doorbell rang. Lydia Mokras in a raincoat: Ta da! 'Hello, Doctor,' she said.

Bialoguski wondered how she'd found where he lived, but guessed it wasn't an A-1 secret. His first reaction to women alone on his doorstep was to get his doctor's case. Instead, they sat together on the couch. Lydia had a smile that wouldn't disappear.

'You have a beautiful flat,' she said, studying a page of score.

'Is it raining outside?'

'Hmmm?'

'Your coat.'

'I wanted something dark.'

She was more blonde than he remembered. Small hands and smaller shoes. Under her coat was a blouse so drab it was definitely Russian. He pictured them lovemaking, her wearing nothing but the blouse, on the Poynters' U-shaped lounge.

'I am here to invite you to dinner,' she said. 'Myself and Vladimir Petrov at the Adria Café.'

First she was Lydia Mokras with connections in Russian intelligence; now she was Lydia Mokras, Soviet embassy go-between. She removed her coat. On the blouse, just over her left breast, was a large white flower, crepe paper and plastic.

Turn the dinner down, he told himself. As if I can take it or leave it. As if eating with spies is a bore.

'That would be delightful.'

She was pleased. He decided her head was fishbowl-round, and got up to put a record on the gramophone. When he came back, she was pointing a camera at him.

'Happy birthday,' she said.

'Oh?'

'It's a gift.'

'What is it?'

'A 35mm Russian Leica.'

He took it from her to inspect. She was not lying. The camera's top plate was crystal clear: 'Manufactured Kharkov, NKVD.'

'It's not my birthday.'

'Who says?'

The coffee pot was howling. He stood with the Leica to his eye, peering down the finder.

She wanted to photograph military installations. Okay. They drove to Beacon Hill. Bialoguski felt somewhat invincible, thinking about a surprise arrest and an overnight stay in a holding cell. To their captors he'd bark on about his rights.

Away from Lydia, he'd dress down some shithead military policeman for disrupting a Security operation.

She loaded the camera on her lap with her knees showing. He thought it no accident; that was the kind of effect he had on women, at least those who were slightly unhooked. The landscape was prickly. Hard rocks sprouting grass. Some construction was happening: fibro cottages or their empty shells, earth-moving machines with their dirt-pulling teeth. The radar station was on the hilltop. Bialoguski thought it looked like the conning tower of a battleship. There'd be men inside, scopers, short-sighted operators with caffeine addictions and polished hair. He wondered at what point he should stop the car; or did spies just drive right up?

LOOK OUT. NEXT LEFT.

They pulled into a flat picnic area right below the target. He slammed the door hard, like a fearless tourist admiring the ten-mile view. Lydia wasted no time pointing the Leica. Snap. She had him stand with the station in the background. Snap, snap. He took the camera from her and they did the reverse. Snap. Nothing happened, but then what did they expect? They walked obliquely from the lookout, circumnavigating the hilltop. They tried to project the idea that they were an ordinary Sunday couple. Lydia took him by the arm.

'Let's drive to Mascot,' she said. They did. Snap.

'There's a US warship in the harbour,' she said. There was. Snap.

They needed fuel. She insisted on giving him money, reimbursement for his costs. The afternoon was ending. She suggested they see a film and lie low. She bought them tickets to *The Day the Earth Stood Still* and they sat at the rear of the cinema and watched an alien named Klaatu warn America about atomic power. The message was find peace or be destroyed. Afterwards, they returned to his flat and had a glass of wine and went to bed much faster than even he thought warranted. As it happened, this release occurred in the maid's room, not the lounge. When the act was over, Lydia lay smiling. 'There's something about you,' she said.

Night had arrived. He went to the lounge room and drew the Poynters' curtains and then went to the bathroom, and then came back and got into bed and asked what their photography was for.

'I won't lie,' she said.

He asked whether she was engaged in espionage. Whether she was an agent for the Soviets.

'I won't lie,' was all she said.

'I'm married,' he told her. 'Separated, however.'

She looked at him. She broke open the back plate of the camera and removed the film.

'Good,' she said. 'As am I.'

7

Philip Kislitsyn was eating bread in the kitchen of the Dominion Circuit house, examining the day's newspaper with interest. Tatiana sat opposite, dipping a slice of toast into an egg yolk. She turned seven a week from today. He told her that seven year olds did not toy with their food. She looked at him, her hair knotted and bed-messed, and grinned.

The *Canberra Times* was reporting that all meat was being declared 'black' because an abattoir in Cowra had used non-union labour. Meat workers were downing tools and no butchers would open tomorrow. It was also reporting that Britain was soon to detonate its first atomic bomb, possibly at Monte Bello Island in Western Australia. Kislitsyn read this second story carefully and twice. To simulate the physical effects of watching the explosion, it said, stand in a dark room two inches from a hundred-watt bulb and hit the switch.

He reached for the *Sydney Morning Herald* only to find that Tatiana was scribbling over the faces on its front page. He told her he needed this paper now. She put down the pencil and swung herself from her chair.

The same news; the same advertisements for Kodak, for 'Free Chest X-rays' to test for TB. But on page six was a different story: VANISHED DIPLOMAT'S WIFE NOW MISSING. This stopped Kislitsyn completely. The diplomat was Donald Duart Maclean. The article explained that Mrs Maclean and her three children had vanished from Switzerland two years after the disappearance of her husband and his fellow British diplomat Guy Burgess. Kislitsyn smiled. He wondered whether to risk sending his congratulations in the diplomatic bag. Maclean had been important to him: a friend, but also the cornerstone of his career. It had begun in London, 1944, when Kislitsyn was a cadre worker for the GRU. The war was being won, and they had a man, codename Homer, in Foreign Affairs. Every second week, sometimes more often, Kislitsyn's senior, Gorsky, would disappear for a rendezvous, returning to the embassy in a muddy state, always carrying a briefcase. While Gorsky changed his coat, Kislitsyn would open the case and photograph the things inside: British documents, peace policies, diplomatic agendas and so forth. This system went on for years without Kislitsyn ever knowing who Homer was. Eventually, cases were arriving every other day. The volume was too much, and someone somewhere in Moscow was chided for their slowness in processing the material and failing to provide it to the departments where it could be used. Kislitsyn was recalled and took over the job. He created a special section, his own one-man operation in a crisp room on the top floor of Dzerzhinsky Square. It was there that he learned of the others: Stanley, Hicks and Johnson, Cambridge men in high places, Stanley in the top echelon of MI6.

It was an impressive operation, and so too the size of Kislit-syn's archive. As much as he could figure, he used the indexing systems of the British departments where the original documents had been held. The other workers on the top floor called his room the British Public Service; shelves housing file after file on photographic paper, military, political and economic questions, reports on the colonies, attitudes on America, China, Russia and what to do about the coming of the atomic age. The operation's masters were the more ruthless thinkers of the First Directorate. One day they received an urgent cable from Stanley. The word in MI6 was that the FBI had Maclean and Burgess fingered. An emergency evacuation plan swung into action. The men disap-peared on a Friday evening; arrived in Moscow via Paris and Prague, their plane landing in a slight and floodlit snowfall at 2 a.m. They stepped wide-eyed from the aircraft, like moon men on the surface of a distant world, and Kislitsyn drove them to their new home in the Moscow suburbs, their faces with this questioning look, what-have-we-called-home. He became their dogsbody, these two men in the service of an empire they'd never seen, and whatever they wanted, he found. That week was a welcome of the first order. Together, they toured the regime's monuments: the Kremlin, Red Square, the tomb of Vladimir Lenin. They went to the theatre and they drank and smoked. There were medals and honorary titles, parties and dinners with officials so high ranking that Kislitsyn was afraid to attend. They met Beria and Stalin. The Generalissimo shook Burgess's hand with a certain effete limpness, like some kind of inside joke. Maclean got so drunk he broke a lamp and broke down crying. Kislitsyn thought they should have jobs, and the Anglo-Amer-ican section of Foreign Affairs recruited their most qualified theorists yet.

Guy Burgess asked for cigars, vodka, warmer clothing and an automatic pistol.

Donald Maclean asked for his wife and three kids.

More meetings. It was decided that the direct approach was best. A London worker tried to contact Maclean's wife for three months. Not much came of it. The watch on her was too tight: men in long coats, women talking together while pushing what were surely plastic dolls in prams. They managed to get her one word: holiday. The agent stood beside her at a crowded bus stop and said the word with his Russian accent several times so it had to have been understood. It was about this time that Kislitsyn was sent to Australia. He had one last dinner with Donald Maclean, who wanted to know whether this plan would work. Kislitsyn had assured him that it would. And now, by the look of things, it had. It was a glad feeling. Good to create a little happiness through espionage for a change.

He cut the article from the page, intending to send it to Moscow. The hole it left stared back at him and he realised that holes in the wrong hands were clues, and so he took the newspaper to the incinerator and burned it.

Petrov sat upstairs in the MVD section, jotting notes on a report and chomping on an apple. It was two o'clock and Evdokia might soon arrive, so he was considering exactly what she could do. There were some personality reports on some students at Sydney University from their agent there, Yakka. Moscow was always wanting these and so perhaps she could encode them.

His door was ajar. From downstairs came a noise. He heard children arguing and tramping down the halls. But that wasn't quite it. There was adult shouting. He got up and stood at the door and heard his name.

He met Kovaliev coming up the stairs.

'It's your bastard dog, Volodya. He is making a disturbance.'

They went down. In the hallway, a chair had been knocked over. They heard a growl. Koslova was staring from her office. They went past her and turned and saw Jack's glossy coat flash from the antechamber and into the first secretary's room. They found him running circles, jumping and snarling and refusing to be caught.

'Sit,' Petrov said.

The dog bounced towards him. Petrov took him by the collar and held him. The dog gave a snorting bark and flung himself to the floor.

The ambassador appeared.

'Vladimir Mikhailovich,' he thundered. 'What is this animal doing running amok? This is an official Soviet outpost. The Swiss ambassador visits us in moments. Is he coming to a nation or to a farm!'

Petrov said the dog must have escaped the yard. Kovaliev said that Petrov's ground-floor window was open and accused Jack of jumping through.

'This is not fitting,' said the ambassador. 'It will be reported.'

Petrov went to protest, but then said nothing. He took Jack home and shut him whimpering in the laundry.

The next day Moscow wrote. They had two messages. Firstly, they said that Mokras, Lydia, was unknown to them. She seemed far too erratic to be a Czech worker or a Czech illegal. They advised that he remain cautious in his relations with her. Secondly, they complained that his intelligence work was at a standstill. He was not producing discernable results. His reports concerning his agents were deficient in their formulation. He often sent them materials that they knew were gleaned from public sources, newspapers and the like. They urged him to be more daring. He should adopt a harder line.

He burned the letter. The words seeped from his mind to his gut and hung there, and he felt indignant, then apologetic, and then doomed and afraid.

That afternoon the Tass man, Pakhomov, rang from Sydney, breathing heavily, static gusts heaving down the phone.

'What is it, Comrade?'

'Trouble, Vladimir. Myself and Charlie—we've been given the Hollywood treatment.'

'You've been photographed?'

'Yes, together and brazenly.'

Petrov groaned. 'The competitors?'

'I don't know by whom.'

'You're certain though? We should be certain before alerting Moscow.'

'I am certain. I apologise.'

Petrov stared intently at a fingernail. Pakhomov was silent while he thought. In the background, he could hear Pakhomova washing dishes, cutlery and porcelain clashing in the sink.

'Do not see him again. Not for a long time,' he said.

'No, Comrade. It was Hyde Park. Much too open.'

'Alright.'

'But listen, Charlie has a message for you.'

'Is it important?'

'You should contact him, I think.'

'You won't tell me?'

'Best you hear it from him. I don't want to say it on the phone.'

When the call had disconnected, it took Petrov only a moment to pour himself a drink. He went downstairs then, to his consular office, looking for work that was easy and rhythmic, that couldn't end in mild disaster. He found his list of Russian émigrés and copied out in hand the form letter urging repatriation. *The USSR misses her children*, he wrote. *Punitive measures against non-returnees have ceased, and now is the time to hear the homeland's call, when there are jobs and production is booming. Perhaps you have relatives waiting?* He enclosed an illustrated pamphlet, 'We Returned to Our Own Land', which showed a gelatin silver photograph of smiling repatriates in the gardens of the Neskuchny Palace, pictures of ferocious corn and sunflower fields, of peasants at festival, of crowds rallying in Moscow, and of the busy floor in a radio factory. All of it real. All of it the Russia of your dreams.

The plane came with a drift from the north, sounding the bay with its chop and roar and keeling into the water. It fell from the sky midway across the alighting zone, a perfect landing, the span flight-taut before bouncing with its floats against the water. It snorted and came towards the base, the propellers on their wing-mounts. The sunset caught it from the west. There was an obvious weight in the hull and the plane sat low, as if it were a submarine travelling the surface to exhaust.

Petrov stood on the balcony of the Rose Bay Flying Boat Base. The building was white with a jetty that extended into the bay, a maintenance apron hugging the shore beyond the slipway to his right. He watched as a small launch departed for the plane, carrying two men in sailing uniforms. Below, people were milling on the jetty.

'The skyways are today's highways,' said a voice from behind.

Petrov turned to see 'Charlie', Rex Chiplin, wearing a scarf but no coat. He was peeling the wrapper from a boiled sweet that he must have bought from the waiting lounge. He grinned and shook Petrov's hand.

'Hello, Rex.'

'Vladimir.'

Chiplin looked over the bay. The air was cold. A windsock rattled above them on a mast. Chiplin threw the sweet around his mouth. 'Ask me if I was followed,' he joked. 'You should have seen Pakhomov after we were photographed. Scared witless.'

'He has no diplomatic immunity.'

'Bastard snuck up with the camera down his shorts. Two snaps. He's no one I know.' Chiplin was a writer for the Communist Party's Sydney newspaper, *Tribune*. He turned and leaned back against the rail. 'Might have been Security. Might have been a nose for Willy Wentworth or some prick on behalf of the Pope.'

Petrov said that the embassy and the Party shouldn't meet again. Instead, they'd find an intermediary who could move between them. Chiplin said that was a terrible shame.

'Pakhomov tells me something is urgent,' Petrov said.

Chiplin removed his scarf and re-tied it. 'It's Walter Clayton.' He lowered his voice. 'I was a sceptic at first—this whole notion of our own Special Branch. I thought, we're so loaded with moles that whatever we find will leak. But Clayton's running everything and doing it very quietly. He's got a committee off the books, our very own MVD. Dossiers, indoctrinations, the works. There's an office somewhere that's wall-to-wall safes and cabinets. Unless he's personally vetted you, you're not even allowed to know.'

The seaplane finally cut its engines, an iron cormorant in the swell.

Chiplin said, 'One of his sources is a man in the Post Office, a telephone technician. When an order comes through from the police or Security, he tells us whose phone's on the tap. We can look into the embassy if you like?'

Petrov shook his head.

'Anyway,' said Chiplin, 'Walter's finally got an informer in Security.'

'In counterintelligence?'

The man was nodding. 'She's a young girl. In the dark. She's a member of the secretarial pool, which probably means she wanders the corridors making the gnomes their tea. But she is in a position to see documents, and to bring them out. Which she hasn't just yet.'

'How in the dark?'

'Poor girl's in love with a communist, one of Walter's new best friends. Said communist asks her what she sees, which is how we've come to know . . .' He hesitated for a moment. 'Well, the newsflash is she's seen some kind of chart. In the section engaged with your embassy's surveillance. The name Petrova in big red letters.'

Petrov winced a little. 'My wife?'

'That's right.'

'This is what you told Pakhomov?'

'Yes.'

'You think they suspect her?'

'I think her name was in big red letters.'

'And you told this to Pakhomov?'

'Just before the photographer struck. Should I not have said?'

'No. It's alright.'

'We don't know with you blokes. We're not sure who's in charge.'

'I am in charge. Do you think you can recruit this girl?'

Chiplin shrugged. 'Not now. She's off to London for a holiday.' He stood upright to go, then pointed to the plane and said, 'You can play golf in that. They'll set you up with a practice net if you can swing the club alright.'

He left Petrov standing on the balcony, wondering how Evdokia's name had ended up in red, wondering whether there was a way to stop Pakhomov sending Moscow the news.

He arrived at the Adria Café to find Lydia already seated with Doctor Bialoguski. They spoke Russian, mostly about the weather until Lydia mentioned Korea and there was a discussion of the latest movements; the 38th parallel; defence lines in towering mountains; a new make of Chinese tank. About Australian involvement, Bialoguski seemed noncommittal. They ordered a bottle of wine and the conversation somehow drifted onto British strategy in Hong Kong.

Eventually, Lydia sat a film canister on the table. 'Michael and I have been taking photographs of navy destroyers in the harbour,' she said.

Petrov looked at the canister and then at Bialoguski. The man looked back warily, perhaps trying to gauge whether the film's production had been an order of Petrov's.

'In the harbour?' repeated the Russian.

'Yes,' said Lydia. 'Including American ships.'

He left the film sitting by the salt. Silence fell until Bialoguski said he was thinking of quitting the Russian Social Club.

'It's becoming dull,' the doctor explained. 'The cabaret is uncultured.'

Petrov made no comment.

'What do you think, Vladimir?' asked Lydia. 'I say quitting is a good idea. The club is full of people who talk but take no action. Bela, for example. She yaps and yaps, but do her recruits stay longer than it takes them to realise she has no real interest in bedding them?' She looked for agreement. 'No. Before the revolution, action will be required. That is why the social club wastes us. It is all boards and committees and no one willing to make a stand.'

Petrov picked up the menu. He wondered whether Bialoguski would now hammer home the charge, and was pleased when the man did not.

The following day, he rang the doctor and went to visit him at his clinic. The signs in the cramped waiting room were in Polish, Latvian and Russian. The walls needed painting. Bialoguski's name was on his door on an attractive gold plate. There was a bill for the Sydney Symphony Orchestra pinned to the wall. The doctor shared a secretary with an eye specialist down the hall, a woman with a cleft palate and what appeared to be bad eczema. She ushered Petrov in.

'Ah, Vladimir,' said Bialoguski. He stood up from his desk. In his hands was a copy of the *Polish Bulletin*.

'No. Call me Volodya,' Petrov encouraged.

He was put in the examination chair.

'Now, let's see about this knee.' Bialoguski leaned down.

'I think it is my circulation.'

The doctor prodded. 'Does that hurt?'

'No, it is less painful today. Do you have appointments now? We should drink.'

They went to a nearby hotel. Compared to his mood at the Adria, Bialoguski seemed more relaxed. They discussed his practice at first. How many patients? What nationalities? Bialoguski said that the Australian medical system was obviously inferior to that of Russia.

'That is true,' said Petrov. 'Moscow has the best hospitals.'

Bialoguski asked about the world's most expensive painting, Raphael's *Alba Madonna*, which both America and the USSR claimed to have. Petrov joked that either the Americans' was a fraud or the master had painted two. They had whisky, embassy shout. It felt good to buy and better to drink. Bialoguski talked about horses, a system he was developing to make money from the races. Petrov said he'd loved horses since he was born.

'What do you know about Lydia Mokras?' asked Petrov.

'I don't know.'

'Her history . . . I don't know.'

'This uncle in the Cheka.'

Laughter.

'She says her family is rich. In Prague they have an electrical shop, a house and two motor cars.'

'She says she is Czech and she says she is Russian. She can't decide.'

'I know she is trying to cancel the certification of her marriage.'

'I've heard it said she is an agent of Security. Have you noticed her head is fishbowl-round?'

They drank on. At about half past five came the rush. It was a long bar and they sat at its end, the room dense with smoke, the ceiling fan churning a slow current, voices carpeting one side of the room to the other, men in suits, and a gang of them playing crib, and boys not sixteen offering a small commission on trips to the bar. The diplomat and the doctor ate sandwiches standing up.

'What do you think of Australian women?'

'Yes, they are alright.'

'I want to see Bondi Beach.'

'The coast is better. What shall we do now?'

Petrov said he knew a place. He took them both to the club he'd found. There was a girl on stage. The stage was small and the girl danced in a bathing suit. They stood there watching. They bought Swans from the bar and sat on two stools either side of a high table. He saw that Bialoguski was staring at the drinks waitress's enormous breasts. She lit cigarettes for them. They smoked and watched the girl on stage and she watched them back as she moved. Enlivened, Petrov decided to see what kind of source this man might turn out to be.

'Doctor,' he said, 'do you know a man, a Russian, named Efim?'

It was someone Moscow was searching for; a possible escapee to Australia sometime before the war.

'Efim?' Bialoguski asked.

'Through your practice perhaps?'

The girl produced a parasol. She sat its stem in one hand and spun it with the other, her hips cocked to one side.

'I don't think so,' said the doctor.

'We are looking for a man by this name, should you meet him.'

There was a screen of frosted glass by the girl. She disappeared behind it then stuck her leg out. Petrov clapped and cheered. He asked Bialoguski what he knew about passports. He asked what papers were necessary for migrants to enter the country.

The doctor looked from Petrov to the girl and then to Petrov again. He was drinking rum now. 'I can get the papers for you,' he said. 'I can get them from the department.'

'What about passport blanks?' Petrov asked. Procuring these would win him a reprieve from Moscow's scoldings.

Bialoguski seemed to take the question in his stride. 'I think that would be very difficult. There are likely security measures that prevent the distribution of such things.'

The girl held the bathing suit at arm's length, twirling it. She was hard to see through the glass. The music on the gramophone was melancholy but had punch. The girl put her breasts on the glass and moved her hips round and round, and the men in the room clapped for the two white and lonely circles and for the hips below them that moved.

They went to the Metropole Hotel for gin. Bialoguski was becoming certain that this man was MVD; all this probing about passports and names. They listened to 2UW on the bar's radio while Petrov chained three cigarettes. The place was empty except for themselves. Sinatra came on and Petrov said, 'Who is this?' and Bialoguski said Sinatra.

The Russian began tapping his pockets.

'What's the matter?' asked Bialoguski.

'Keys. I've dropped the Oriental's keys somewhere.'

'The keys to your hotel room?'

'I'll have to leave early,' said Petrov. 'While the doorman is still on.'

Bialoguski thought. 'Forget the Oriental,' he said slowly. 'Why not stay at my flat? It has a magnitude of space.'

He was mostly being polite. He presumed that Russian diplomats had strict rules against staying with locals. Petrov looked across and said, 'Okay.'

Inspired, Bialoguski decided it was time for a small stunt. 'Pakhomov asks about you,' he said. 'At the club. He wants to know, have I seen you? Have you been in town? I get the impression he's keeping tabs.'

Petrov peered up at the wireless. 'What do you say?'

'Nothing.' The doctor shrugged. 'I say that I haven't seen you. I make jokes about how he's your countryman and how on earth would I know where you are.'

Silence. Petrov began to toy with the flame of his lighter.

'Leave the club,' he said.

'Oh?'

'Yes. It attracts too much interest from Security.'

The doctor didn't reply. He reached over the bar for the ice spade. Petrov looked pensive now and Bialoguski wondered what he'd done.

That night, Bialoguski lay awake, the flat quiet except for the dull hum of rain. He was tossing an idea slowly in his mind. It was to do with listening. He thought that sounds had surfaces, and he wanted to penetrate that plane and listen deeply to whatever lay underneath. He thought that there, in noise just as in music, maybe he would hear the truth.

He sat up breathlessly and listened, using all the training he could muster. Between the master bedroom and the guest room was a bathroom, and between the bathroom and the guest room was a line of creaking boards. He listened like somebody superhuman, like a comic-book hero using a secret force. He was certain that Petrov was sleeping.

He got up and began to move. At the bathroom, he opened the door slightly and switched on a light and stood listening to the Soviet's breath. He didn't think it possible to step over the creaking boards and into Petrov's room without making a noise. He put one foot where he knew the boards would creak, and they did creak and he listened. No change to the Soviet. He raised his foot and set it down again, one hand on the bathroom doorframe, preparing to yank him towards an excuse.

He went carefully into the room. Petrov was turned towards him, his glasses on the night table. If he woke, they'd be staring at each other. His coat was on the door knob. Bialoguski put his fingers in the inner right-hand pocket. Nothing. He checked the outer right-hand pocket. Nothing. In the inner left he felt a booklet. He memorised its position with his hand: spirals facing out, the thread pointed down. The master spy at work. He took the booklet to his bedroom and turned on a lamp. The book was names and numbers, a mixture of scribble and Cyrillic. Bialoguski copied each page. He copied not only the numerals but also the layout, just in case the layout was a secret in itself. There were twelve pages and forty-two names. It took him the best part of an hour.

He replaced the book. Petrov looked whale-ish rugged up in

his blankets. In the next pocket was the Russian's wallet, and in its cash fold the beginnings of a letter, unaddressed. It was a request for a meeting. Petrov's cursive was horrific and hard to read. At points Bialoguski was reduced to copying simply the shape and clash of the scrawl.

The remainder of the wallet was identification, business cards and scrap. Bialoguski copied each item with an artist's precision. He thought that the true facts of the wallet would ionise around the smaller, literal details—the slant of a phone number or the fade in the circumference of an official stamp. He drew a diagram mapping the wallet and the position of each item. By the time he'd finished, the sun was coming up. A wide white yawn beyond the hill that broke the light.

Petrov's flight back to Canberra rattled in the morning sun. Golden light belting the crests and valleys below, working on the palette of paddocks.

He was trying to read the newspaper when he realised there were blurry spots in his vision. He rubbed his eyes and looked west. The spots didn't move. They were unlike anything he'd known. He read on, hoping they would disappear.

That night, he and Evdokia lay together in the dark.

'My eyes,' he said.

'Your eyes?'

'I have spots.'

'Spots. Do you mean flecks?'

'I mean spots are clouding my vision, like small warpings in glass.'

'Is it dust?'

'I don't think so.'

'It hurts?'

'Painless.'

'Did you do something?'

'Why are they there? I don't know.'

'Tell your doctor friend.'

'Oh, yes.'

'You sound worried.'

'Are you worried?'

'About your eyes?'

'No . . .'

Evdokia rolled towards him and the mattress sank a little.

He said, 'I think the ambassador will relax. He will decide we are no threat.'

Silence.

'You don't?' he asked.

'I think we will be recalled.'

'If we are recalled . . .'

'Ten years.'

'No, not prison.'

'Death then.'

'Not death.'

'Poverty and nothingness.'

'Perhaps expulsion.'

'Perhaps.'

They lay awake for a time. It was so dark he thought maybe someone had broken the streetlight. He put his hand on her belly. They lay listening and not moving. He didn't tell her about the Security service's interest in her and the fact that Pakhomov would report it. He wondered instead whether he were going blind. In so much darkness his eyes were okay. He wondered if the blind man saw the world in darkness or in light, or in some nothing state beyond both that only blind men knew. He took his hand back and rolled over. He reached for his Omega on the bedside table and wound it five or six times and put it back. He lay there listening to its tick. It was the only noise in the quiet room and quiet house and darkened street.

8

A sign said, 'Cake Needs'. Bialoguski sat in his car in the parking area of a food and liquor store in Willoughby. It was midnight; the store was closed and nobody was there. He watched the way the light fell from the street across the car park as he sat in the Holden and smoked through the driver's window.

A few moments past the hour, Michael Howley appeared. He came from nowhere, from the darkness beyond the yard like some spirit of the moor, and he stood beside the car with his hat pulled tightly on his head. Bialoguski leaned across to unlock the door. The man got in, Bialoguski pointed the Holden onto the road, and they drove for ten or so minutes, the car breathing heat into the winter air, the men silent beyond Howley's occasional low instruction to turn.

The wind on the coast was biting. They pulled up on a gravel circle on a cliff. Bialoguski left the engine on to run the heater.

'He's left you?' asked the ASIO man.

As Bialoguski went to reply, he was wondering how he could make some money from the things he was about to say. 'That's right. He stayed at Cliveden. The extra room. He said he'd lost his hotel keys but I think that was a lie.'

Howley had a minifon. The doctor could see it strapped over his shirt. He thought: I'm important enough that they're recording my every word.

'Yesterday he went to Redfern,' he said. 'He told me where and I found the address for him on a map. He's recruiting me, I'm sure.'

'You think he'll stay with you again?'

'He finds Cliveden useful. He knows I'll be there to support him. I think he's decided to use it as a base.'

The ASIO man was watching him talk, sitting turned slightly towards him, spectating from close range.

'It's a shame,' Bialoguski said.

'Oh?'

'Yes. I'm struggling to keep up with the Cliveden payments. The rent is very high. I may have to move and it will likely be somewhere less convenient.'

Howley didn't respond.

Bialoguski reached into the back for a satchel. He dragged it forward and tossed the flap open. 'It would be better for everyone if I managed to keep my flat,' he said. 'Here, for example, are the contents of Petrov's pockets.'

He revelled in his description of the previous evening's hunt. He narrated the position and precise content of the items copied and handed the copies over. He was the masterful secret agent, the Queen's trusted spy. Howley examined everything but showed him emotionally next to nothing. Bialoguski knew that this was very much part of the game.

'Did he spot you doing this?' Howley asked.

'No. He was snoring like a pig.' The doctor pointed to the address list. 'This is very good for you. Here. These names, they are Australian names.'

'Yes, I see them.'

'You know these men?'

'Some.'

'You can turn these men. Doublecross. You can feed them false information, false documents. You can control what the Soviets know. Petrov is MVD. Positive. He is recruiting me non-stop.'

The ASIO man had a small electric lamp, which he ran over Bialoguski's schematics.

Bialoguski said, 'These are his agents. No doubt.'

'No doubt?'

'Positive. This is treasure for you. This is as good as it gets.'

Howley produced an envelope—cash for the doctor's retainer. Seeing this, Bialoguski reached into his satchel for an envelope of his own. Inside:

EXPENSES INCURRED IN THE FORTNIGHT: CRANE

(Report) Car	15	0
(Report) Transport	12	0
(Report) Incidentals	8	0
Transport	3	0
(Lunch) Car	10	0
(With Petrov) Chocolates, cigs	1 5	0
(Report) Car	15	0
(Peace Council Donation Meeting) 'to Stalin's		
Memorial Fund'	1 0	0

(Petrov) Dinner at Adria	2	10	0
Entertainment at home		10	0
Camera film		10	6
Food		15	0
Wine	1	10	1
Car		15	0
(Report) Car		15	0

TOTAL: £13 13s 6d

'All legitimate,' said Bialoguski.

Howley read the list by the lamplight. There was a noise outside in the wind, a sudden scrape. The lamp was turned off and both men looked. The wind whipped around the Holden. They peered. There was nothing but darkness and nothing, the cliff edge and the black, crashing sea.

Howley flicked the lamp back on. 'You want us to fund Stalin?'

'I am at the coalface. That is what sympathy costs.'

The man was quiet for a moment. Then he gave Bialoguski the list and put his hands to the heater. 'You'd best add the date. I think you can't be too careful where money's concerned and it doesn't belong to you.'

Bialoguski got out a pencil. 'Agreed,' he said. 'And the rent on my flat? You will talk to someone? You will talk to Colonel Spry?'

Howley told him that they'd see. 'Don't use your codename for the finances,' he said. 'Use a natural-looking pseudonym. Jack Baker.'

Ocean spray was misting on the windshield. An extended silence meant the meeting was over. Bialoguski put the car into gear and returned them to the car park. Howley said goodnight and disappeared the way he'd come.

The doctor had a cigarette and felt ecstatic. He wondered whether Howley knew that he was sitting the flat for free. Even if he did, that might be better. They would understand each other that way. And he wouldn't call his bluff when Bialoguski was adding so much information to the pot.

He put the car on the road. He decided to go and find Lydia.

B2 looked again at the monochrome photographs, grainy samples shot at odd angles, only the moderate suggestion of depth. Petrov with briefcase and double-breasted suit. Petrov in crowd in grey-tone hat, shorter than those around, staring, waiting. There was a business card in elegant cursive: *Vladimir Petrov, Third Secretary of the Embassy of the USSR, Canberra.* B2 looked at these things, searching for some form of meaning. All he could find was sadness.

He got up to make tea. What did Petrov think he was doing? B2 was almost certain now that they had enough material to burn him. A well-delivered threat about his drunkenness and weakness for prostitutes; spy for us, or go home in Russian handcuffs. Probably they'd never do it. They couldn't be too reckless while their organisation was still on trial. But the point was that Petrov was leaving himself open. He knew they were following him and still he visited houses of poor repute. This was the mystery that B2 couldn't reconcile. Was Petrov baiting them? Was the whole thing a Soviet dare? He thought hard. If it was possible, it was only possible because everything was possible.

Petrov bears a striking physical resemblance to Mr Harold Holt, Minister for Immigration; could be described as slightly shorter, thicker-set, slightly fatter edition of Holt. He has longish hair, turning prematurely grey, like Holt's, brushed straight back, also like Holt.

B2 shovelled the tea leaves quickly, digging deep into the box. He set the pot and waited, rereading the account of Crane's latest report. B2 never met personally with agents. His job was to provide the vision, to be the omniscient paragon who rearranged the puzzle pieces of counterespionage so that they joined and found coherence. He thought Crane was a compulsive liar and completely out of control. But concerning Petrov's strained relations with the other Russians, perhaps the doctor had a point.

He went to a filing cabinet and pulled on a drawer. There was a program in here somewhere: Operation Cabin 12, detailing the preparations to protect a hunted defector. B2 liked the name, one of his own concoctions, a certain ring to it, the suggestion of shelter and branding. He opened the file on his desk. It was a plan and nothing more. Wired safe houses in Sydney and Melbourne, body swaps and speedy rendezvous on the Wombeyan Caves Road. The Riley was to be used, its dashboard fitted with sound recorders. There were shopping lists for the safe houses, whisky at the top. Two officers were to be resident at all times, and then two men from Special Branch with guns. B2 saw that someone had selected opportune suburbs, even possible streets.

He wrote a memorandum headed 'Possible Cabin Candidates'. Vladimir Mikhailovich Petrov topped the list. Almost everything that western intelligence knew about Soviet espionage had come from the mouth of a defector—Gouzenko,

Kravchenko, Tokaev. The history wasn't so good. Gouzenko had spent days pressing his case to every agency in Canada before the mounted police caught on. Then there was Oksana Kasenkina. She'd leapt from the third-floor window of the Soviet consulate in New York, having been locked up by the Russians when the US State Department refused her initial attempt. Given the man's limitless travel and constant meetings with communists, B2 was certain now that if the embassy had an MVD resident it was Petrov. He wrote an opinion outlining the best possible circumstances for having him defect. The core need was documents, Cyrillic proof. The wisdom was trust the record. Defectors had strange ideas about loyalty and betrayal and you could never be sure of the truth.

Bialoguski was a problem. If it came down to him managing a potential defection then they might as well not bother. He wrote a heading, 'Third Vector', and jotted some thoughts. Naturally, they couldn't induce a defection—External Affairs would have a fit. The offering would need to be modest, perhaps lifetime protection and cash for a house. The director of counterespionage drafted an induction sheet in triplicate and put Spry's name first. He sealed it and the memorandum in an outgoing envelope. The unstated message was that if the organisation could do this, any question marks about its existence would disappear. If elected, Labor wouldn't fold an apparatus that was turning Soviet spies. And if Petrov was MVD, then his public testimony might land the man's bastard agents in gaol.

B2 returned to his chair. The light in the room was dissipating. He picked a magazine from the shelf and turned to a poem by A.D. Hope. He'd shared an office with Alec over one desolate Melbourne winter, and had never known for a moment that he wrote.

The Kingston Mothercraft Centre stood in an eerie, sunset light. Evdokia walked that side of the street, going by the building, its stretches of lawn, the young elm trees pegged to the slope.

She went into the Kingston newsagency. There had been a letter that week from Tamara. Things weren't going well in Moscow. Their father was ill. It was difficult to decode the inferences in her sister's words—like those of any fifteen year old, a poor conduit for bad news—but it seemed to be cancer. In any case, the doctors were using radium.

At least it wasn't her mother. Was that an awful thought? She couldn't bear the idea of her mother falling ill. If it had been her mother, she would have requested the next plane home.

She scanned the shelves for something her father might like. They had a souvenir range here: Canberra mementos in Shelley china. She looked but couldn't choose. The news-agency closed.

Outside, the dusk had reddened. She walked south past the Kingston Oval and over the avenue as the street lamps came on. Coming to Lockyer Street, she could see something large protruding from their letterbox. It was a package of string and paper, a note taped to the outside: *Communism is a movement of scientific intellects originating in Godlessness and material-ism and exploiting poverty and it must be met in the battlefield.* No signature. No stamps. Inside the package was a hard-cover book. The King James Bible.

Evdokia stood with it in her hand, hate rising at the back of her neck. She looked up and down the street but saw no one. She opened the book, grabbed a wad of pages and bent them in her hand. She held the front and back covers and applied a shearing force. The book didn't break. She threw it into the outside bin, wondering when whoever had delivered it had followed her, whether they had crept alongside or behind her, wondering on what expedition she had been marked out and tracked.

His eyes were getting worse. The specks were gone, but now a spasmodic grey smudge clouded his sight, dropping a muddy curtain between himself and the world. Reading the newspapers was becoming difficult. He knew his depth perception was shot. He was going blind. That was his conclusion, and when it happened it would probably spell the end of him.

Michael Bialoguski told him to stop worrying. They were sitting together in Bialoguski's waiting room, which was also Doctor Beckett's. When the ophthalmologist finally appeared, Petrov judged him to be about fifty. He wore a brown jacket with a red tie and over these a white coat. He said Petrov's name and they shook hands.

In the doctor's room, Petrov complained about slowly going blind. Beckett turned off the light in the room, got a pen-light, and shone it in his eye.

'How long has this been happening?'

'I don't know. A few weeks ago there appeared these specks.'

The man stood with his waist bent, two hands on the instrument, leaning into Petrov as if he were some form of intricate machine. The idea pleased Petrov. Whenever his health broke down he wanted to be treated as a man of nuts and bolts, a thing of mechanical logic, of processes designed and knowable and capable of being returned to working order. Anything other than the sublime terror he suspected the body really was.

'We're looking at the beginnings of a macular star,' said Beckett. He stood and found the light, pulled a book from a shelf. They looked together as he flipped the pages. 'Here,' he said. It was a black and white shot of the optic nerve, produced by special camera. Near the centre was a dazzling firework, an explosion of white dots, thick in the middle then petering out. It looked like an astral event or some form of bursting flare.

'Yours isn't as acute.'

'Acute?' asked Petrov.

'Sharp. Severe. Intense.'

'Oh.' He looked at the page again.

Beckett said, 'Have you had any contact with cats?'

'Cats. The animal?' asked Petrov.

'Yes. This condition is often caused by cats. Usually the scratches of young kittens.'

Petrov waited a moment to check that the doctor wasn't joking. 'No cats,' he eventually said. The surgeon wrote a script. Petrov was to take pills for two weeks, and if nothing got better he was to come back. In the meantime, he shouldn't drive.

The MVD at the embassy ran a system of checks on incoming mail. This was part of the MVD's SK work: maintaining an eye on the staff, watching for traitors or discontents. In many cases the letters were abuse: *Go fuck yourselves*, etc; random thoughts that arrived like stinging dust from the winds of public sentiment, unsigned and barely addressed. Other times they were from lunatics requesting money, or from men and women who thought the Australian government was persecuting them and wrote seeking the Soviet Union's intervention in their personal affairs.

In a cramped room on the ground floor, Evdokia examined the day's mail under a reading lamp, the bulb's heat across her knuckles. Lifanov thought himself in charge of this monitoring, which in turn he delegated to her. Yet while she passed him the mundane things—the anti-Soviet pamphlets, the true maniacs of mind-splatter—the more interesting material she kept for intelligence work. The monitoring was no secret: the staff expected to receive their mail opened. Except Lifanov, of course, who made a point of inspecting his post alone.

In the mail was a letter addressed to the ambassador 'Nicolai Lifanov'—no honorific, which piqued her attention. She held the envelope to the lamp and saw inside the veins of a hand-written message.

The MVD knew various ways to open envelopes, but the best method was to read the message without opening its packaging at all. For this task, she used a strand of wire, inserting it into the fold through the top corner, twisting monotonously until the letter coiled itself around the implement and she was able to delicately remove both.

The note was from a friend, an Australian using the initials M.T. *Nicolai Nikhailovich, you are popular here. Think of the better future for your wife and son.* It was an encouragement to defect, personal, deliberate, reckless. She could hardly believe her luck. She tore open the envelope, looking to see that there was nothing else inside.

Upstairs, Volodya was reading a story on the Rosenbergs, the newspaper sprawled across his desk.

She gave him the letter. She expected at least a smile, but when he looked at her she saw no joy in his eyes. They read the letter again. Volodya got up and locked the door. He would write and she would cypher. They would send the report right now; two hours until the post office closed. He put the letter itself in the upstairs safe.

The following morning, Prudnikov gave them three priority cables. Moscow's response was perfect. The first cable informed them to wait; the report was going to the special committee. The second and third were from this committee's secretary— palpable panic. He wanted to know what kind of paper was used, how the letter was delivered. Had Lifanov seen it? Had he made any remarks?

Volodya took his time with their reply.

Lifanov's mood changes dramatically, he wrote.

'He is unpredictable,' Evdokia added.

He seems under great strain, as if an important decision weighs on his mind.

He spends long hours in his office.

There are rumours of impropriety in some of his relations.

We suggest his previous secretarial assistant, in Moscow, be interviewed.

He and Kovaliev are increasingly inseparable. They drink with the commercial section at the ambassador's home, and it is reported that the telling of anecdotes is encouraged.

Lifanov is known to engage in lies.

We have prevented him from sighting this letter.

We remain vigilant. Above his every action, a question mark.

Please forward your instructions and advice.

9

They drew lots in the early morning freeze, each man's breath crisp and fierce, white moisture barking into the air. Trimmed grass and dew. The green blade of the first fairway twisted slightly to the right. In Kislitsyn's hands the club resembled a toy. Petrov and Prudnikov watched to see how this experiment would go. Kislitsyn put the face against the ball, judged the weight of the weapon, drew himself slightly to one side and practised a swing. He stood at the ball, deciding with a beginner's unease the best place to hold the stick.

'Is the tee too high?'

'Aim with your feet.'

'Yes, alright, quiet.'

He threw the club backwards and swung. The sound was a snap and then a fizz and the ball flew high, gathering a slow fade, falling to earth in the right-side rough.

They were impressed.

Prudnikov stepped forward and jammed his tee into the

grass. He stood behind the ball and peered, his stroke soon skipping down the fairway, losing pace with each dense bounce.

Petrov shot last, making a chip of it really, high and aloft and with no great measure of forward motion.

They walked towards the white dots on the landscape.

'Loosen the limbs.'

'How. Gymnastics?'

The trees each side had a yellow tinge. Petrov struck another chip, dull and weightless. They smiled at one another in their efforts to reach the green.

Putting was worse, the ball unpredictable and too light.

The next hole was a long one.

'Don't swing so hard.'

'Watch as you hit.'

'How do you watch?'

'Swing less.'

'No. Alright.'

Thwack. An upward curve, spinning out flatly on the grass.

They walked, buggies trailing. In the rough, three birds pecked and flapped. The watery smell of drowned and breaking leaves.

'I have news that will interest you,' said Prudnikov.

'What is that?' asked Kislitsyn.

'A cable that came late afternoon yesterday. For Lifanov.'

'Yes?'

'He's been recalled. I decrypted it.'

Petrov stopped. 'He's going?'

'That's right. Moscow says his posting is at an end.'

'How soon?' said Kislitsyn.

'He's to book on the first flight via London.'

The men smiled.

'This is very good,' Kislitsyn said, moving into position to strike his ball. 'Goodbye to the prick.'

Petrov watched Kislitsyn's shot sing down the fairway. He felt steely.

'Do you think he'll be alright?' asked Prudnikov.

'I don't think the ambassador is worried,' said Kislitsyn. 'He probably has assurances.'

'If he has assurances, he'll end up shot,' said Petrov.

Prudnikov grinned, enjoying himself. This wasn't actually them talking; it was the game, the arrangement of things, their ulterior selves in a rare and peculiar set-up—Kislitsyn's and Petrov's trust, Prudnikov's agency with the MVD—a licence given for the next few hours: here we can speak the truth.

'The bastard must have told Kovaliev,' said Prudnikov. 'I saw our unflappable commercial attaché moping in the corridor like an orphan with no supper.'

They crossed a long white bridge over the Molonglo, blue flags on the river's margin. At the next tee, Kislitsyn readied his shot, the low roof-points of the Hotel Canberra visible in the distance. Petrov watched, trying to understand the method behind Kislitsyn's swing, distracted by the Lifanov news, imagining Evdokia's relief at it.

On the next hole, they met a machine on the fairway, a tractor pulling a contraption of lawnmowers, an improvised-looking thing, a Frankenstein. Petrov stared at it and realised his eyes were almost clear. Whatever was in those tablets was a miracle. There was a blurriness now and again, but nothing that felt like it wouldn't eventually depart, and nothing that seemed to be affecting his aim.

***

It was true—Lifanov was departing. She wouldn't denigrate him. Best to be saddened; not as if Moscow had made the wrong decision (they never did), but as if they had made this one, at least, that was cheerless.

She walked into the antechamber to find the ambassador at her desk. She caught his posture before he straightened: an indignant slump, shoulders beaten and forward, forehead frowning. When he turned to her, she saw his eyes were alert, his mind ticking.

'Evdokia Alexeyevna,' he said. 'There will be a meeting of the staff in one hour. You will organise this, please.'

'All staff, Ambassador?'

'Yes, everyone.'

He took his jacket and went out into the hall.

She went from room to room, her voice flat and unhurried.

From the back step of the embassy, the staff gathered on the grass, Lifanov made his speech. He had been given another posting, Europe, probably Madrid. He had enjoyed his years here, and was thankful for the trust of the department and the camaraderie amongst his staff. He would be leaving posthaste, but there would be time for a celebration tomorrow afternoon and he could properly say goodbye. It was very much friends, colleagues, fellow comrades-in-arms; a speech so amiable she gave up her intuition that his conspirators would be denounced.

Sad applause bounced from the red-brick walls.

A week later, the day of his departure passed with little fuss. Evdokia was at her desk by 7.30 a.m., sorting the last of the cards that had come from Canberra's various ambassadors and consuls, some of the messages warm and handwritten, others just simple notes in type. Lifanov came into the antechamber, examined the messages she was filing, and pleasantly said, 'Good morning'.

'Your tickets, Ambassador.' She gave him a folder from the BOAC office.

He thanked her and said that he'd left some instructions on her desk, small things to be attended to for which he didn't have the time.

'Of course, Ambassador,' she said.

He went through to his office and drew a handkerchief from his breast pocket. He ran the cloth over the planar surfaces, the desk and the sideboard, the various cabinets, the windowsills and the shelving. He wiped each surface then examined it closely. It seemed he was erasing the dust.

He came out and locked the door, then asked Evdokia to seal the key in an envelope.

As she stamped the sealing wax, Lifanov said, 'Comrade, we have had our disagreements, certain things, certain ways you have behaved. But I think we understand each other; we know the pressures we have been under. When we see each other in Moscow, I hope we will stop and say hello and recall our time here favourably. Please tell Vladimir that I wish him good luck. I will not have time to visit him this morning.'

He took the envelope lightly from her grasp. She looked at him and saw in his face a rare expression, fresh and energised, the strain that usually worked a stress of wrinkled tension across his forehead gone.

'Yes. Thank you, Ambassador,' she said. 'Enjoy your journey.'

In the hallway, Moscow's two couriers sat opposite one another: Shcherbakov and Kopeikin. They were grim-looking men wearing coarse suits of Russian manufacture, both with zip-up woollen vests underneath. Each had a diplomatic satchel, but all presumed their real escort was Lifanov himself. Kopeikin's revolver bulged at his chest.

The party left at five minutes to midday, the car easing through the gates onto Canberra Avenue, Vasili Sanko at the helm, the Lifanovs and the couriers in the back. The entire staff gathered to watch it go. Afterwards, they returned silently to the building, performed their duties for ten or so minutes and then took lunch.

The doorbell rang at Lockyer Street. It was Masha Golovanova with Anna Kislitsyna and Tatiana, the child's hands around her mother's neck. It was an invitation to walk. Minutes later, they were all proceeding through the stripped emptiness of York Park, crossing the Circuit to the equally bare nothingness of Capital Hill, their shoes sinking slightly in the earth.

Reaching the hilltop, they saw the tops of the trees on the western side and, between them, the corrugated-iron sheds of the Capital Hill hostel. Faraway, a tube of white cloud hung over the Brindabella Hills.

They were facing east. Free of her mother, Tatiana ran down the slope with an unsteady gait.

'You look tired again, Masha,' Anna said suddenly.

Masha laughed. Looking into her wide, round face, Evdokia saw nothing of Anna's observation. She thought Masha looked awake enough, lively even.

'That's Ivan's fault,' Masha said. 'He has been sick of late, a horrible cough. I have been doing his round in the mornings.'

Her husband was the night duty officer, charged with patrolling the embassy's grounds and buildings.

'Is he very ill?' asked Evdokia.

'He'll be alright. He needs to eat more beets.'

Tatiana fell. They expected tears and small chaos, but she picked herself up and continued unperturbed, her spirits too high for breaking.

Evdokia suddenly had an awful thought. She knew that, as the embassy's most menial workers, the Golovanovs didn't receive much, if any, allowance in Australian pounds. What if they had no means to shop in stores for food? What if the food they received at the embassy was not enough?

'Masha,' she said, 'you know, Volodya and I have a garden at Lockyer Street that goes to waste. He talks always of a vegetable patch but nothing happens. If Ivan wants a plot, we have the room.'

The pariah offering her help. Evdokia expected Masha to at least find a way to give the idea some thought, but the woman's response was instantaneous.

'Evdokia Alexeyevna!' she said, delighted. 'Ivan has asked for some earth at the embassy, but the gardeners won't allow it. I will tell him—he will be pleased.' She paused. 'But what will we give you in return?'

'Nothing, Masha. The garden will do well being used.'

'Well, we will help you somehow. We will make it collective! You, me, our husbands.'

Tatiana had reached the bottom of the hill and was staring across the Circuit. She wore a brown gaberdine coat that now had dirty marks on one sleeve. Anna called her back. The girl waited a moment longer, then turned and came, plonking one foot before the other, elephantine.

***

The walk to Capital Hill was the first in a number of friendly excursions. A small Russian party set out for the Capitol Theatre's picture show, watching newsreels from the Olympics in Helsinki where the Soviet gymnastics team were collecting medals unprecedented, hungry in their first appearance for a half-century. The medal-winning vaulter stood on the podium as the Soviet banner dropped—a flash of the Union's flag against grey skies—and in the Capitol Theatre, hard, round sweets were sent skittling down the aisles.

Expeditions were mounted to Civic, to the J.B. Young department store with its manchester, fashion and home furnishings. They marvelled at a shoe display—shoes that weren't for wearing but simply for trying on. There were children's books and Bibles, vacuum cleaners and brooms. There were seven grades of sheet and four pillow stuffings with gradients in between. In kitchenware, they found labour-saving implements for stuffing chickens and cutting eggs. There were bakelite containers with the English letter for the foodstuff marked on the side. It wasn't always easy to know what was for buying and what was simply for display. The woman in ladieswear was a New Australian who spoke to them quietly, furtively, pointing things out in Russian when her supervisor wasn't near. They made mental checklists of their needs, which grew as they circumnavigated the floor. Salt and pepper shakers, automatic cigarette dispensers. They went from department to department, led by a tiled walkway with straights and oblong turns that together formed an embracing geometric shape.

Nobody purchased anything without checking Evdokia's opinion of it first. She thought certain colours were better. The others thought so too. She thought certain designs more fashionable; a red peplum jacket, for example. She said that Nina Prudnikova's black floral skirt was dashing but slightly under-sized. Nina thought so too.

They walked a wary lap of the Civic centre, an oversized monument of rounded archways and balcony, Spanish white, banking institutions facing the empty intersections at its corners—twin buildings, mirror copies, fifty metres apart with a garden in between, low-cut lawns and towering trees where the Russians sat for a moment on two benches, a midwinter scene, the sun out, the children chasing one another from trunk to trunk and a man with a bucket and brush scrubbing an oil stain from otherwise unspoilt concrete. McGlade's Gift Store. Ansett ANA. The City Butchery and the Canberra City Post Office. The Christian Supply Depot and the National Mutual Life. Evdokia thought the people walking here were dream-like, verging on the edge of impossible, their suits with a sun-bitten sheen, skirts and dresses incredible. She looked for signs of the downtrodden, the oppressed, the capitalist enslaved. If this town had them, she couldn't see them. Not amongst these hopeful buildings, this place where everything seemed squared away. The perfect city, she thought. A paradise of conifers.

Weighted by their packages, they caught the bus home. There were only two routes, One and Two, and they caught One, crossing the Molonglo, disembarking at Manuka. From there they went in various directions, most to the embassy, some to the houses they had in the different streets around. Evdokia and Masha went together to Lockyer Street and saw what Ivan had done with the vegetable plot, black earth upturned in preparation.

'Let's take Jack for a walk,' said Evdokia. 'The day's not over, Masha. We'll go to Red Hill and the reservoir.'

Red Hill was southwest across Griffith Park and Bass Gardens. The women walked with the Alsatian leading in front. Beyond the last roadway was a fenced paddock, poplars at its edge. The hill itself was patterned by eucalypts and tall grasses, its gradient a measure of work, their footfalls drumming harder as they climbed. The walk took them to the lookout: a gravel turning circle with a single concrete bench. The view was Capital Hill and then over the river to Duntroon. Down the gravel track was the reservoir, where, after a time, they went and stood, two communists and a dog on the edge of a town supply. The water was a dark and bloody brown, a slight breeze rippling its surface.

'I can't read or write,' said Masha.

Evdokia turned to look at her companion.

'I'm not asking you to teach me,' Masha went on.

'I will if you would like.'

The woman shook her head, explaining that she just wanted Evdokia to know. That it was important a woman of Evdokia's cleverness knew how uneducated she was. Evdokia frowned.

They sat at the water's edge, talking. Masha had two brothers and one sister; one brother had been killed in a riding accident, the other by flu. Evdokia had four brothers and two sisters; one brother killed by dysentery, one by typhus, one by a fall. One sister killed by dysentery, the other a fifteen year old in Moscow.

Masha had three children, all grown adults: a boy in Moscow, two girls in Siberia, all Ivan's. Evdokia had one girl, killed by meningitis.

Masha was afraid of Moscow, afraid of the people, the noise. Evdokia loved the city, the old buildings and the parks.

117

It was her familiar place, home, that snoring, body-strewn room where she'd grown up.

Masha knew they were lucky to live with the privileges of departmental work. Evdokia thought it was no real crime to bring out bread in a handbag for family and friends. To use tickets to get things for others, even if it wasn't necessarily approved.

Masha was too old to join the Party. Anyway, she didn't remember half the revolutions that had occurred. When Evdokia had applied to join the Party, a Colonel Kharkevich had asked what was she doing before the revolution. She said that before the revolution she was three years old.

Masha knew nothing of the English language although she had lived in Australia for almost four years. Evdokia spoke English, Swedish and, for whatever undeclared reason, a few touches of Japanese.

Masha thought the landscape in Australia was a drier, less earthly Siberia without snow. She thought the hills were smaller, the dirt harder, and she wondered whether the gravity situation was doing her body any harm. Evdokia had expected more animals. She had yet to sight a koala, and wondered why, with all these animals at hand, the town didn't have some kind of zoo.

Masha thought the embassy's children had the perfect childhood—sunshine, long summers, sacred days. They wanted for nothing and the idea of it made her glad. Evdokia remembered the famine year in which she had turned five. While no one watched them, her grandfather had taken a cup of milk from her and poured its contents on the floor. Because if hunger is a burden, then so too are the hungry.

Masha worried about the atomic bomb. Ivan was talking about the new American designs, hydrogen. The simpler the element, the greater the devastation.

They both wanted to get out of Canberra. Masha had a poster in her bedroom of Tasmania, billed as the Switzerland of the south. Evdokia wanted to see Sydney again, one of the most modern cities in the world.

On night patrol, Masha said, Ivan's main problem was the possums. From about ten o'clock they began leaping from the heights of the eastern roof onto the tin eaves below, making a thumping din. There was also a group of boys who thought it was a game to penetrate the Soviet embassy hedge and lurk noisily in the orchard. Volodya was away days at a time. Evdokia knew only the city he was in: Melbourne, Sydney, Newcastle. He called her now from phone boxes, from the phones in cafés or restaurants. Never from his hotel.

Before she went home, Masha planned to save some money and buy a lifetime's supply of shoes. She never wanted to beg or plead for a footwear coupon ever again. Evdokia had promised her mother a fur coat. She was cutting pictures from catalogues—removing the prices—so her mother would be able to choose.

Masha wondered why they hadn't come to sit here before. She thought some of the women in the embassy were green-eyed and resentful, angry at how this country held a mirror to their peasantry. Evdokia thought there were certain ringleaders. Others at the embassy had simply decided which way to jump.

The two women eventually walked the track from the water back to the lookout. They went slowly downhill, towards the lines of poplars and elms along the crescents and avenues, the roofs of the houses catching the afternoon sun, glinting on their left-hand sides and shadowed to the right. Some of the roads were freshly made, sitting more atop the landscape than in it, expanses of grassland like bits of puzzle in between, impossible to say whether they were future sites for housing or parklands unmade.

Masha explained that she and Ivan were at first to be posted to Vienna, then Rome, then Ottawa. She said she'd always been told that cities created their nations. Only here it was the other way around.

'I have an idea,' said Petrov.

Bialoguski was flipping through the Poynters' record collection, looking for something that wasn't so plain as to be pointless. The two men were drinking whisky with ice and brandy at the same time.

'The embassy has a liquor merchant, Crawford & Co,' Petrov was saying. 'On embassy liquor, we don't pay Australian taxes. We buy duty free.'

The doctor gave up and played Dick Jurgens. They'd be heading to the Adria soon anyway.

'We buy in bulk too,' Petrov went on. 'Bottles by the crate. I haven't tested it, but I'm sure Crawford would supply any quantity we like.'

'How cheap?' said Bialoguski.

Petrov leaned forward. 'It's boom times, isn't it?' he said. 'Fortunes are being made.'

'Only by some,' replied the doctor, waving his hand at the apartment. 'Only by those who already have the cash.'

'It's a criminal system.'

'If you like.'

'We could team up, you and I.'

'You're a diplomat, Vladimir.'

Petrov grinned. 'But you're not. I can't do business, but I

have an idea and I can't do it alone. There will be good profits in it. We'll split them down the middle.'

Bialoguski had a notion of what was about to be said. He took a packet of cigarettes from the coffee table and handed the Russian one. 'What do you get below the sticker price?' he asked.

'In bulk and without taxes, the discount is almost half. On Bell's Special Whisky, even more. I can issue purchases on the embassy account. We pay with our own money, the embassy never knows. You sell them discreetly to pubs or whoever else. We beat the legal price by a fair amount and we pocket whatever is the difference.'

Bialoguski saw Petrov was watching him carefully, attempting to see what he thought. What was he doing? Was this a real scam, or was the MVD just trying to get him involved in something black?

'What do you say?' asked Petrov.

Bialoguski picked up the bottle of Bell's that Petrov had brought, added a splash to both their glasses. 'How's your vision, Vladimir?'

'Beautiful. One hundred per cent. He is a good man, your friend Beckett.'

'I treated Anna Pakhomova this week.'

'Oh?'

'She says the ambassadorship is changing hands.'

Petrov looked pleased. 'Yes, we are ridding ourselves of the incumbent. It's a great relief for many of us; you have no idea, Doctor, the bastardry that goes on, always the encouragement to put each other in. You take the tiniest of inconsequential things and make deadly errors out of them. Who knows what might happen in the case of an actual crime.'

Like exploiting the embassy's liquor privileges, Bialoguski thought.

'Let's do one case,' he said.

'Test the water?'

'Start slowly with a dozen and see what happens from there. Come, I'll buy you dinner.'

At the Adria, they ordered beer and bread to begin. The café was lit by milk-coloured lights that hung like alien ornaments. Their waitress turned out to be a patient of Bialoguski's, Eliska Kysilka, a stern woman in her forties who got tremendous ear infections to the extent she suffered vertigo. Their entrées were complimentary.

'Before I forget,' said the doctor, 'the Rosenbergs. I have been asked to join a delegation petitioning the American ambassador in Canberra. Lily Williams is behind it. She is the secretary of the Jewish Council to Combat Fascism. And Anti-Semitism. I think it is the council that combats both.'

'Who are the delegates?'

'Tom Wright from the Sheet Metal Workers' Union. Some left-leaning City Council members. They say I am needed to add an effect of realism, a balance against the high number of registered communists.'

'That's good.' Petrov seemed in a buoyant mood. 'But don't stick out too far. Don't attract too much attention.'

'From Security, you mean?'

Petrov shrugged.

'I've been wanting to ask you.' Bialoguski lowered his voice. 'What is your embassy's opinion of the Security here? What do you think of their capabilities?'

The Russian spoke without pause. 'Getting better. They trace our movements now. Noticeable pressure at times. I think they have hired more or smarter men. Of course, it's all of no consequence. They are wasting their time.'

Bialoguski nodded. Petrov fell silent when their two steaks arrived. Afterwards they drank coffee, and only when Bialoguski had asked for their bill and was walking to the register to settle did he remember that he'd spent the last of his cash that afternoon on petrol.

'Eliska,' he said, embarrassed, 'I've made a mistake. I haven't brought my chequebook.' This was Security's bloody fault. If they paid him a retainer in advance, like they should do, he'd have money in his wallet right now. 'I thought I had cash, but I don't,' he went on. 'Can I be inconvenient and pay tomorrow?'

The woman looked at him. 'I don't see why not, Doctor,' she said. 'But I'll need to ask.'

'Thank you,' he said, and waited uncomfortably while she sought the Adria's manager, whom he knew, which made the situation more humiliating, even though the man didn't hesitate to give him credit.

As they got into Bialoguski's car, Petrov said, 'Let's find some company tonight.'

'What do you mean?'

'There are some girls I met the other day.'

'Whores?'

Petrov laughed. 'What's put you in a mood? No, they're just some girls. Drive me over to collect them. I've been telling them about your flat.'

Bialoguski started the car. Perhaps the flat was a good idea; going anywhere else would require money.

The address was a crumbling terrace off the far end of Darlinghurst Road. It looked on the verge of collapse, a dozen or more living there, the smell of cooking baked into the walls. Bialoguski stood on the doorstep while the Russian went inside. Two girls came downstairs, looking only half as bad as the doctor thought they might. Neither were New, which relaxed him. They'd been drinking, he saw. One asked his name and smiled, and he knew then they weren't professional girls at all.

At Cliveden, he played host and fixed drinks. Petrov seemed most interested in Dorothy, a largish woman who said she was a clerk for the Chamber of Manufactures. Bialoguski sat with Lucinda on the sofa. She told him he must be in a lucrative business if he could afford a place like this.

'I'm in metals,' he said.

She asked what he thought about flying saucers. She thought they were Soviet aircraft, cycloid planes flying at high altitudes. Experimental, atomic probably, the reason for the disc shape. He told her he wasn't sure Soviet science had reached such heights. They watched in silence as Dorothy and Petrov left the room.

'Outside sources, then,' said Lucinda.

'Hmm?'

'The alternative saucer theory. Sources outside this planet.'

'This is the choice we face? The Soviets or outer space.'

'Weather balloons also, but you'd be mad to believe that. I think the outer space theory is an understandable reaction. Mysterious third parties. We're looking for someone to save us.'

They opened a champagne bottle. He invited Lucinda to stand on the small balcony with all the lights off so there was no dampener on the view. Dark ocean mass and a carpet of lights. Lucinda said she'd come from Adelaide three months ago. This was her first view of the city from any height. He felt like volunteering something, some pristine fact. He told her about his marriage, a failed holiday in New Guinea he'd had

with his wife, and the coming divorce. He felt himself performing, which was disappointing, because this wasn't an act but
the truth. She seemed to be sympathetic. They watched boats
moving as lights on the harbour.

'Your friend's a strange man,' Lucinda said.

'Oh?'

'He tells Dorothy he's Polish. Later he's Bulgarian. He
says he's a bonds trader, then an importer and exporter of
antiques.'

'He said he was Polish? He may have been drunk.'

They heard giggling from the guest room.

A few hours later he drove both women home. The front
door to the terrace was wide open and unattended, light
spilling onto the street. He suggested checking the house for
intruders, but Lucinda said the door often willed itself ajar,
some broken impulse in the lock.

'Goodnight,' she said.

Outside Lydia's flat, he was shocked to find an Essex tourer
against the kerb. He stood in the dark, watching. He knew
the car's plate. It was driven by Claude Watts, a young man
from the club. There was no light on in the flat. Why Lydia
was doing this he didn't know. He considered breaking his way
through her front door, confronting them; the lover, jilted. But
that would be Claude's win. Best to challenge the bitch alone.

Gleaming wounds. He found a rock and gashed the paint-
work on the tourer, a coarse squeaking and a long mark, pale in
the lamplight, on the driver's side. He kept the rock in his hand
and lowered his Holden's window and drove past the car and
released the rock. Loud crack on the windshield.

10

Vasili Sanko gave the horn a half-toot, bringing the staff running. They stood on the lawn at the front to watch the ambassador arrive. Nikolai Ivanovich Generalov wanted his door opened. He got out of the car and looked into the waiting faces. He was larger than Lifanov, with a definite military build, silver hair over his ears and a receding scalp-line. Generalova was more solid, taller than her husband and broader. Not too awful a dress, Evdokia thought, for someone straight from Russia.

The new ambassador took a tour. The grounds first, the tennis court and orchard. Evdokia went to her desk to work and so she was there when he came in.

'Ah. My office?' he said.

'That's right,' answered Kovaliev, behind him.

The men waited, without a word of greeting, while Evdokia retrieved the official envelope in which the key had been sealed. Generalov broke it open, and the two men went inside. She stayed in the antechamber listening to Kovaliev point things out—the telephone, the lighting board, the combination cabinet with the embassy's top-secret files.

'Evdokia Alexeyevna,' said Generalov's voice. She went into the room to find his hand pointing at a vase. 'These flowers have died,' he said. She awaited further instruction until she realised he simply wanted them removed. Kovaliev was staring at her. She collected the vase and was on her way out when the ambassador spoke again.

'Comrade, various reports of your behaviour have found their way to Moscow. I will warn you once. I am not a man as gracious and lenient as Lifanov. You will not be permitted to be a disruptive influence on my staff.'

She glanced at the commercial attaché. 'Ambassador,' she said, 'I can assure you that any reports you have read have been slander. A campaign has been made against my husband and me, the result of petty jealousies.'

'Yes, you remind me,' he said. 'Please tell your husband that the Central Committee of the Communist Party of the Soviet Union has ordered that he no longer bring his dog into the precincts of our embassy.'

She poured the flower water down a drain, feeling angry and a little panicked. As it happened, there was little time to marvel at the ambassador's words. When she came back to the antechamber, the unimaginable had occurred. Kovaliev was standing with the embassy's external phone in his hand. 'Evdokia,' he said. 'Talk to this man.'

She picked up. It was a journalist from the *Argus* wanting to confirm that Stalin had died.

***

Generalov became sickly pale. After the *Argus* came the *Sydney Morning Herald*, the *Courier*, and the ABC. They didn't know what to tell them.

The senior staff huddled around Sanko who was trying to repair the broken radio set that received news broadcasts from Moscow.

2CA were knocking at the embassy's front door. 'We're not sure,' Evdokia told them. 'Please go away.'

The rest of the embassy got word of the happenings, the children, in quiet awe, creeping along the corridors of the ground floor, looking for out-of-the-way vantage points where the cross-legged might disappear.

'We can call Auckland,' she suggested to the ambassador. 'We can ask the legation in New Zealand.'

The operator booked the trunk call for quarter past the hour. Each time the ringer went it was a journalist not an operator. Eventually, it was Sanko's radio that brought the Soviet outpost their news.

The Supreme Leader had passed at 11.32 p.m. Moscow time. Stroke.

Generalov agreed to speak first with the ABC. He gave a heartfelt eulogy, saying that he spoke for a shocked nation, a nation that had lost a great revolutionary equal to Lenin and Kirov.

The ABC journalist wanted to know who would lead the USSR now. The Party would decide, said the ambassador, but the people, as ever, would continue to be well served.

What had been Stalin's legacy? The Generalissimo's bringing about of the Soviet Union as a world power. His showing of the way forward after Marx and Lenin.

Would the ruler's death encourage dissidents in the USSR

to find a greater voice? No one was opposed to the regime. Why would they be when it took care of their every need?

Was Stalin the greatest dictator the world would ever see? The Generalissimo opposed dictatorial rule. He was a man for the people, even if the west could not bring itself to understand this fact.

Were they sure he died of natural causes?

Generalov permitted no further questions. He created a statement, which Evdokia read aloud to the newspapers, and made no further comment. On Pakhomov's advice, the only other journalist given audience with the ambassador was Rupert Lockwood for the *Tribune*, whose enquiries were bound to be less embarrassing.

Late that night, Evdokia left for home. On her way out, Generalov gave her an unexpected appreciative nod. She called in at the embassy kitchen and collected two servings from a hot soup that was sitting on the stove.

At Lockyer Street, Volodya was on the back porch, smoking. 'Well,' he said.

'Stalin dies.'

'Seventy-four years old.'

'Is this a good thing? I don't know.'

'Chaos, you think?'

'Possibly.'

'Here we have a power vacuum with yet-to-be-felt destabilising effects.'

'If they say he is dead tonight, probably he has been dead for weeks.'

'There will be a succession plan in place.'

'Several plans, I would think.'

'Now moves the mercury of terror.'

'Hmm.'

'Did you know that Karasev has a portrait of Molotov in his living room?'

'Yes, but it is not his. The house rents it from the embassy.'

She transferred the soup into bowls. They sat in the lounge room by the wireless, listening to 2CA report the news.

Bialoguski lost his job with the orchestra. He should have seen it coming. It was the fault of the ABC, who, with the Musicians' Union, had decided that nine in ten members of the symphony be Australian-born and not New. It didn't matter that he was a naturalised subject, only that once he'd been a Pole. The unfairness grated. He suspected that Goossens was behind the move. They'd booted six foreign players but kept nine, which meant they'd conspired to put him out. Had he got wind of it earlier, he could have mounted some kind of defence.

He wrote Goossens a death threat that he knew he wouldn't send, typing it out on the Poynters' Hanimex, wearing gloves and redrafting twice.

On the telephone, Lydia refused his dinner invitation. 'This was a busy week, Michael. Perhaps another time.'

'Are you sure?' he demanded. 'Are you certain that busyness is your best excuse?'

'What are you talking about?'

'You're not a very good liar, Lydia. It's not an appealing quality, being easy to see straight through.'

He jammed the phone into its cradle, and then rang Howley in a mood. The man's voice was distant, disappearing into static. Noises and scratches meant only one thing.

'This handset is bugged,' Bialoguski said.

'Come again,' said the Security man.

'This line or this handset. Your voice is vanishing in the feedback.'

A pause. 'Well, it's not us,' said Howley. 'You're our agent. If we'd bugged you, we'd say.'

Bialoguski thought hard. 'What if there are two files?' he said. 'In one file I'm Crane, but in the other I'm a regular communist, Michael Bialoguski. My cover but a real file.'

'We don't double-keep.'

'Are you sure? Perhaps a colleague hears about me, starts a file on me, a communist falling under notice. What stops him tapping my phone and ordering surveillance?'

'Are you under surveillance?'

'Men follow me all the time.'

'Is that a joke?'

'What's it called? Banter.'

The voice was strained. 'Followed or not?'

'Once or twice.'

'Where?'

'From my practice, certainly. Last month perhaps. There's a feeling you have, an awareness. You think, what do I look like? Where do I think I'm going? What does my left arm usually do as I walk—in fact, how do I walk at all?'

'Did you see who it was?'

'I didn't want to look in case he disappeared.'

The voice slowed. 'Well, it wasn't us. The Russians, maybe. Might have been the communists too.'

'They follow people, the communists?'

'The ones who are serious about things, yes.'

The doctor tried to picture the room where Howley was.

There was nothing to hear in the background. Perhaps it was the background that was the foreground, noise falling apart, vanishing. He thought the man would be sitting on a chair.

'I see you've written me a letter,' Howley said.

'That's right. Just some grievances I have.'

'Money.'

'It's a ridiculous system, this keeping of receipts. What kind of spy keeps an ice-cream container of papers and tabulates his expenses? Petrov is here all the time. What do I say if he finds them?'

'You want a flat twenty-five pounds a week.'

'That's right. It's an average expense. I've learnt that the well-equipped agent needs cash on hand to satisfy contingencies when they occur.'

'It can't be done.'

'Why not?'

'Other people's money.'

They were silent for a moment.

The doctor said, 'Should I buy a gun, do you think?'

'A gun?'

'If it's the communists following me. Aren't they men of intent? Aren't they capable of violence?'

'No gun.'

The *Argus* form guide was on the floor beside him, race listings covered in scribble. On an intellectual level he knew his own writing but that didn't stop a sudden, instinctive sense that someone else had circled the bets. Certain marks were definitely his, the small crosses and the slant lines under the jockeys. But the diving verticals? He'd never noticed himself making those before.

'I think I might resign,' he said.

'What do you mean?'

'I don't know. Is it worth it? I should be doctoring, concentrating on building my practice. Presumably you haven't read the *Polish News*? Here it is, the front-page story: "Doctor Bialoguski Petitions for the Rosenbergs!" How do you think that will run with my patients, the majority being New Australians well known for their conservative views?'

'Petrov is important to us.'

'Yes, and a flat retainer is all I ask.'

'Michael, it's been denied by those above. I can register disappointment, not much more.'

'Fine tactics. You're like the branch manager at my bank. Whenever he's tugging at my overdraft he pretends it's head office on the strings.'

'Where's Petrov right now?'

'I don't know. But listen. A flat retainer. I'm demanding it or I quit.'

He thought there would be a note about the Generalissimo on the MVD channel, not a mourning necessarily but at least a resolute statement. Stalin is dead. Long live the Union. But there was nothing, not a breath of stasis. The work went on and the regular messages came out.

The processes described by Arkady Wassilieff for the production of hard-wearing aviation bearings are already known to Soviet industry. Permission for a visit to Russia cannot be granted at this time.

Kislitsyn thought Beria destined to take control. They'd each met the man, Petrov twice. 'An administrator of the highest order,' said Kislitsyn. 'Watch him unite the Ministries of State Security and Internal Affairs.'

Stalin, dead. Still it wasn't quite believable. The mourning at the embassy was becoming high farce. Koukharenko had a room set up with the Georgian's picture, and staff were going in there, coming out with wet faces. It was show, completely. No one in their right mind was sad to see the author of the Yezhovshchina pass.

Four days went by before Generalov called him into his office to hand him the rebuke. A single line from the Central Committee of the Communist Party of the Soviet Union commanding Vladimir Petrov not to bring his dog to work. Generalov added nothing to the missive. Petrov had known it was coming but the forewarning didn't prevent him feeling ill.

The following evening, he was carrying a crate of Bell's Special from the car to the garage in darkness when he saw a figure standing at the end of the drive. He froze at the sight: a woodcutter's body looming in a long coat, scarf and hat; a terrible Russian face in shadow, blunt, idiotic, belonging to the kind of man who might answer favourably to the questioner from the Directorate of Special Tasks: 'Comrade, you look like someone of unusual strength. Do you think you could break a skull with one blow using this iron bar?'

The figure watched him for a moment longer then walked. Petrov skipped the car and went straight for the house. Had he really seen it? The odd-job assassin? The one-time clean-skin—favoured method of disposal abroad? It made sense. Someone had broken the street lamp. That would be standard procedure.

Evdokia was sleeping. He went to the sideboard in the hallway and made sure the Nagant was loaded. The bullets and their dull sheen. The thought suddenly occurred to him that someone might have changed them; switched them for duds. He tapped the six shells into his hand, then reloaded using the box behind the cereals in the kitchen.

Outside once more, he crept along the southern fence. There was a gap in the hedge here, and he crawled across the neighbour's yard, behind the house, until he was in the bushes on the edge of Lefroy Street.

Footfalls? He was listening. He expected to smell cigarettes. He expected to see discarded Soviet cigarette butts strewn over the ground. Nothing. The cars here he knew: the two dark Holdens, the white Dodge.

He shouldn't have come here. This bloody country. He knew some secrets. Perhaps some eagle-eyed fourth-floor analyst, spurred by Lifanov, had figured that out. The killing of the Chinese governor in Sinkiang was enough by itself. Frinovsky and Voitenkov, two of the operation's chiefs, had long been purged.

He knew Moscow had killed Trotsky. He had seen the file in the reading room of the Committee of Information. There were photographs of the Mexican villa from their agent inside, photographs of Trotsky's beard, Trotsky's bedclothes, Trotsky's dog. There was a photograph of the assassin, Mornard; detailed and labyrinthine plans for putting cyanide in the villa's water and for setting explosives in the floor.

He knew that they'd disposed of their own ambassador in Tehran. He knew the identities of Soviet agents in America, Sweden, Japan, Britain, Egypt, Spain. He knew that the cellars of 11 Dzerzhinsky Street were the killing rooms. That the weapon used was an eight-shot Tokarev. That the resident executioner lived always at 5 Komsomolsky Lane.

Back indoors, he opened the refrigerator door, reached above the back shelf and twisted the light globe until it went off. He opened and closed the door a few times. He turned towards the figure in the hall.

'Why are you carrying your gun in the dark?' Evdokia said.

'I'm going to put some bullets in a block of butter. Hide them in the fridge here, in the door.'

She stepped forward. 'Where's Jack?'

'Outside where he'll bark.'

'Is something happening?'

'We're being watched, I think, by a Russian.'

She walked quietly to the window, looking out. 'You're scaring me. Put the gun away.'

'It was a Russian man in a wretched-looking coat. I can recognise these things.'

'Maybe an émigré,' Evdokia said.

'No. I know every Russian in Canberra and this man tonight was not one of them.'

'It's Generalov. Making you paranoid.'

'Paranoid!' He laughed.

'Well, afraid then. Hysterical.'

He let her take the Nagant, watching as she opened the latch. 'I can't sleep in there with you out here,' she said. 'It's like living with a nervous wreck.'

'Hmm.'

'Do bullets that have been in butter even shoot?'

Two days passed and still no word from Security. Howley probably thought that Bialoguski wasn't serious about leaving. Well, he'd demonstrate. He was fed up with haggling over money. Fed up with Security's incompetence, their general weakness. He had Petrov drunk, compromised on a growing number of fronts and ready to burn. No action. ASIO simply stood by, limp. What he needed was a serious client. An agency with nerve.

The American consulate was inside the MLC building at Martin Place. He passed through its doors, finding himself in a foyer of wood grain and granite. Clocks everywhere. He went to the third floor, US Consulate General, and pressed the bell.

He liked the Americans storing themselves in a building like this, where the floor tiles were polished by machine and the corridors screamed deep focus.

A woman waved him in. An eagle was set into the panelling of her desk. Bialoguski asked for Harry Mullin, the vice-consul, whom he'd met once at an orchestra reception. The Americans walked by him, a flash looseness in the fit of each man's suit.

Harry Mullin wore thickly framed brown glasses and looked twenty years younger than a vice-consul ought. He showed the doctor to a chair. They chatted in a small way about the orchestra, Bialoguski's practice, little zones of context. The man's accent was plain American. He offered the doctor a cigarette. Eventually Bialoguski said, 'My reason for calling is that for a long time now I have been an agent for the Australian Security Organisation.'

'The Australian Security Intelligence Organisation?' asked Mullin.

'Yes . . . that might be a surprising thing for you to hear?'

Mullin drew on his cigarette.

'As part of this service,' the doctor went on, 'I have been engaged in activities of international importance. Activities, I think, that would be of interest to the United States.'

Mullin lifted a hand. 'They know you're coming here, do they?'

'Who?'

'The Australians.'

'No. The connection we had has been broken.'

'Broken.'

'I'm a free agent now.'

The doctor liked the idea of Americans as straight talkers. He felt as if he should put some kind of deal on the table. A take-it-or-leave-it-bud.

'If there's an American service here,' he began, 'an operating service that might interest itself, I'd be prepared to cooperate on two conditions. First, I won't under any circumstances reveal details of the Australian Security Organisation. I'm a naturalised Australian and a patriot. Second, as such, any US organisation interested in my services would need the direct permission of the Australian government. These would be the terms.'

Mullin leaned back in his chair. The view behind him was towards Darling Harbour: rooftops and cranes. 'Well, it's really beyond my scope,' he said, producing a notebook. 'Let's back-track. Get at the details. I thought the body politic here had you firmly marked as Red?'

'That's cover. In truth I'm a reliable citizen.'

'Truth,' Mullin said. 'The truth is an interest of ours. There's some guys here who undertake studies of truth using protractors and little bits of tape. They tell me some crazy things.' He looked up and down, pen suddenly to paper. 'Listen, as I say, it's not my field. I'll just report your offer up the line.'

'B-I-A-L-O-G-U-S-K-I.'

He left the building feeling happy—so happy he rang ov at the embassy. 'Vladimir, it's about time I met this wife

DOCUMENT Z

of yours. Why don't I drive down tomorrow? There's some business in Canberra I have to attend to.'

He was in the capital just after midday the following afternoon. He considered at first staying at the Kurrajong, but that wouldn't do lest he encounter one of his contacts from the unions. Instead, he drove down Commonwealth Avenue and turned into the Hotel Canberra, impressed by its squared gardens and hedges, brilliant in their rigidity and control.

It was just after two o'clock by the time he arrived at Parliament House. He walked up the steps and stood in the lobby. There was no one on the desk and so he took the opportunity to walk up the inner stairs and into a large open hall. Men in suits walked past him briskly. He saw a sign that said 'Government Party Room' and went towards it down a corridor. Outside the room he stopped, looking for more signs. A man with a briefcase and a coat over his arm approached and told him he looked lost.

'I'm after the prime minister,' he explained.

He was directed further down the hall. At its end, another man was coming out of an office holding a newspaper.

'Can I help you?'

'Yes, I'm here to see Mr Menzies.'

The man looked at him. 'I didn't think he had any appointments this afternoon. Can I ask your name?'

'I'd prefer not to mention.'

'Not to mention?'

'The matter I wish to discuss. My name may not be something that Mr Menzies will want to know.'

The man stared at him oddly. 'I presume, then, you haven't arranged an appointment?'

'No, but the prime minister will want to see me. It's a very important concern I need to raise.'

'Have you checked in at the front desk?'

'It was unstaffed.'

The man smiled faintly. 'Well, we have processes here, you see. We have trouble with what we call WPCs—Walking Persecution Complexes. Madmen, you know. People who are being deliberately and callously done in by some arm of government. They come seeking Mr Menzies' salvation.'

Bialoguski spoke with a deliberate clarity. 'The matter I want to discuss concerns the national security. I should ask your name, in fact, for the record.'

'*The* national security?'

'That's right.'

He gave the man a letter he'd written on the Hotel Canberra's stationery. Marked *For the Attention of the Prime Minister Only*.

'My name is Mr Yeend,' said the man. 'I am deputised to read mail addressed to Mr Menzies. I'll open this quickly if you don't mind?'

Bialoguski gave a nod. The note explained that he was a secret agent of the government. That he needed to raise with the prime minister an urgent issue regarding the national future.

Yeend looked up. After a pause, they went into the small office from where he had emerged.

'You're a secret agent?' said Yeend.

'I'm an advanced agent. This means I live my part. I am engaged in it around the clock. Nothing by way of distance between this life and my own.'

Yeend placed the letter on his desk. He asked Bialoguski which service he worked for.

'Can I not speak to the prime minister?'

'I have the authority to help you.'

Bialoguski cleared his throat violently. 'ASIO,' he said.

'Oh,' said Yeend.

'That is right.'

'Who is the head of ASIO these days?'

'You are testing. It is Colonel Charles Chambers Fowell Spry.'

'Hmm.'

'My handler's name is Michael Howley. I have no objection to you ringing them to confirm.'

'Okay. Go on.'

'The service and I are momentarily at odds.'

'Loggerheads?'

'In conflict of a kind.'

'Concerning?'

'Respect or the lack thereof.'

'Respect.'

'They don't understand the effects of their policies on the individual.'

'On the advanced agent?'

'Yes, on the man who must walk and talk and inhabit himself constantly.'

Yeend paused. 'I'm not certain I fully understand.'

'What I mean is there are policies that create enormous strain. For example, they refuse to answer hypothetical questions. Let's say I rent an apartment. Let's say I take time away from my employment to meet with left-wing individuals. Will I be reimbursed? There's no predicting! It is the unexamined life trying to operate in the modern and scientific world. How is an advanced agent supposed to proceed?'

Yeend leaned back in his chair.

Bialoguski went on. 'I operate in the dark, entering into obligations, courting personal and financial embarrassment. There is no sympathy displayed by Security. They are distrusting. They are suspicious beyond need. They want their agents to be timid. They want them to follow the path of least resistance. Listen, I am in the orbit of those who would subvert this nation. I don't mean ragtag communists. I'm talking about outside influence. The menace. What we're obsessing about. People might sleep soundly in this country if they could believe that men such as myself are out there. Well placed and vigilant, keeping watch on the Russians. What I'm bringing to your attention should be embarrassingly elementary. Terms and conditions of employment. But it breeds larger questions. What is Security doing in this country? How professional and proficient can ASIO be when a prime asset reduces himself to begging in the office of the prime minister?'

Yeend reached for a pen.

Bialoguski straightened. 'This is about money, but at the same time it isn't. It is about internalising a bureaucracy and the bitterness that provokes.'

'I'm sympathetic.'

'When I say I'm at odds with the organisation, in other words I've threatened to resign.'

'Is that right?'

'You'll pass on my concerns?'

'I'm surprised to hear this. I'm startled that such a situation could arise.'

'You're deputised. You can relay to the PM what you've been told.'

'I could do that.'

'I'm not here to create trouble. I'm seeking resolution in these affairs.'

'I suspect I'm being drawn in.'

'Let me assure you, it's a limited intrigue.'

Bialoguski reached forward, extending a hand. Yeend shook it. Bialoguski presented his business card—black print on white cardboard and a square hole at its centre where his name had been cut out.

They both stood. Bialoguski said, 'If you need to, you can reach me on this number.'

'Ask for?'

'Ask for Jack. Tell the prime minister he can use the name Jack Baker in any discussions he has.'

The neighbourhood at evening with a dying lustre. He drove down Mugga Way. Homes here that were mansions. The time was right on dusk, Red Hill glooming. The houses sat on the upslope, dark hedges fortressing those longer established.

At 7 Lockyer Street, the porch light was on, making a starkness of the front step. He supposed this was Petrova who had answered the door.

'Michael Bialoguski,' he said.

She wore a blue skirt and a grey knitted top, a thin apron over both. 'I thought perhaps you were him,' she said. She took him to the lounge. 'Volodya is finishing at the embassy,' she explained. 'Will you have something? A drink?'

He thought the room austere. Furniture chipped and falling to bits. He accepted a glass of beer.

They moved to the kitchen where she was cooking. She was attractive, he thought, though not in the stunning way Petrov stressed in his darker moments, overcome by drink, guilt and effusion. They talked about his surgery, how business was, how doctors in Australia made their living. They discussed Marxism, whether or not Australia was supplying arms to the French in Indo-china. He realised he didn't really know where he stood with this woman, what Vladimir had told her, what kind of things she knew. She suggested that he was acquainted with Lydia Mokras, the young girl who came to the embassy, tall, light-haired and striking.

'Yes,' he said. 'That's right.'

Was she going to ask about his marriage? Luckily, Vladimir came waddling through the door, briefcase and cigarette in hand.

'Doctor,' he said. 'It's just us tonight.'

'What happened to the Kislitsyns?' asked Evdokia.

'Philip has gone to Melbourne. The Generalovs have demanded that Anna dine with them.'

They ate with the radio on. Potatoes and mushrooms. His helping was the size of a small planet. The radio played popular songs. Vladimir seemed to be enjoying himself, smoking cigarettes throughout the meal, his apparent duty to top up everyone's glass.

Evdokia wanted to discuss an explosion that had occurred, a couple's home in Armidale that had been attacked by a five-pound bomb.

'Really?' said Bialoguski.

'Oh, yes,' she replied. 'Their bedroom wall was blown in and jagged pieces of glass were buried inches deep in their walls.' Evdokia wondered about the ordnance: gelignite and a twenty-foot fuse. Was this something the general public could gain access to and use?

'I doubt it,' said the doctor. He changed the subject, saying he'd run into an old friend, an oboist, in the bar at the Hotel Canberra. A complete lie, and he marvelled at the ease with which he produced it, how simple it was to create an oboist from nothing but setting, a shared brandy and a glass of wine. At his story's conclusion, he dropped the name Pakhomov into the conversation, for no other reason than to see how it would run.

'Pakhomov,' said Vladimir. 'Doosia, tell Michael to steer clear of Ivan and Anna.'

'I did not know they were friendly,' said Evdokia.

'I wouldn't say friendly,' said Bialoguski. 'I am the family doctor. The relationship is I treat them as patients.'

Vladimir questioned the rate he charged. 'Whatever it is, it could easily be doubled. The embassy reimburses our medical expenses. Evdokia herself handles it.'

Bialoguski smiled. How many scams did the man want to run?

Talk of the embassy changed the mood. Vladimir began grumbling about the treatment they were getting. Evdokia threw more salt on her plate and said that the embassy was run by vicious dogs.

'Generalova,' she spat. 'This is her new portfolio.'

'Obviously it's getting to you.'

'I think it is Lifanov's influence in Moscow. We don't know where he is. What department. Whom he can badmouth us to.'

The doctor was making a mental engraving of everything she said.

'The burden is immense,' said Petrov.

His wife laughed then and tried to inject some humour. 'Oh, it's alright. We are being badgered by jealous *mujiks*. They're toothless and not very creative. There have been worse occasions in our lives.'

Vladimir went to open a bottle of wine he'd been presented by the Russian Library in Sydney. He screwed the cork and held the bottle against his stomach, pulling. Bialoguski tried to pass but was forced to drink.

Dessert was a cake from the Highgate Café. Much later, the doctor drove home warily, consciously looking for policemen and trying not to crash the car.

In the morning, a phone call. He stumbled out of bed.

'Yes?'

'Jack Baker?'

'And to whom is he speaking?'

But he knew already. It was Michael Howley, an edge to his voice. 'This isn't a good time,' Bialoguski told him.

'No?'

'No.'

'Stay by this extension, will you. Mr East is going to call.'

'Who is Mr East?'

'Colleague of mine.'

'Mysterious.'

The line went dead. He put down the receiver and waited and the phone rang. The voice was still and heavy. 'My name is East,' it said. 'We haven't met but I'm a close follower of your case.'

The doctor foresaw what was to come. The man began with the Americans. He said that someone of Bialoguski's name and appearance had paid them a visit, offering to contract as a spy. Interesting. The Americans had notified the protocol office at

External Affairs. This was how everyone in the foreign bureaucracy knew that Security had a highly embarrassing former agent on the loose. The senior leadership of the organisation wanted to break him into little bits.

Bialoguski jumped in. 'No, no. I approached the Americans because I had resigned. You people. I told them I would work only with consent.'

'With consent?'

'That's right. Of the government. I am a citizen of this country.'

'Bullshit.'

'What's that?'

'What you're saying.' The man went on. 'We had a call last night from Geoffrey Yeend. On top of everything already. "Would you believe it, what Jack Baker's up to?" Colonel Spry nearly died.'

'Dramatic,' said Bialoguski.

'Spry says he is in charge of Security, not the prime minister.'

'Yes, but who is in charge of Spry?'

'Personal message for you. He is in charge. You're sacked.'

The doctor laughed. 'Sacked. I've resigned already. Don't you recall? Maybe the system of memory employed by your bureaucracy is broken.'

'That was you resigning us. This is us resigning you.'

'Clever.'

'M-letter,' said East. 'Appended to the last sheet in your file.'

'Remind me.'

'Termination.'

'Oh,' said the doctor. 'Terminalia.'

Neither man spoke for a while. Bialoguski began to wonder how they'd known that he was at the hotel.

'If this is the case,' he said, 'you'll need to stop keeping tabs. What will I do without my shadow?'

East said nothing.

'Do security know what they're throwing away?'

East said he thought they had a fairly good idea.

'Wait,' said the doctor. 'How irrevocable is this?'

'I don't believe that particular word comes in degrees.'

Bialoguski put the phone down hard and sat on the bed in his pyjamas. His alarm clock was about to ring. He turned it off and collected his towel for the shower. He'd been looking forward to this shower. The bathroom was spectacular, huge mirrors like dishes on the walls.

He fumed as he soaped. Americans. You couldn't trust them. Bloody empire of bloody new suits. Insurance executives. Maybe they knew how to wear their watches and sport their haircuts but none of them gave the slightest thought as to why.

There was an electric dryer for women's hair. He got out of the shower and tried it on his skin.

He went to breakfast and smoked a cigarette, ate scrambled eggs, put milk in his Earl Grey tea. What happens to the secret life when it loses its confessor? He ate a pork sausage and pondered. He dabbed at breadcrumbs with a piece of bread. He looked at the sunlight burning the lawns.

Was he secret because of them, or was he secret because this was the practice he lived by? Could you choose a secret life, or did it have to be officially sanctioned? He drank fresh orange juice, two glasses, and it was good. He ate bacon, a rasher with a line of mustard, mulling over the answer in his mind.

Get Petrov to defect, he decided. That was the best and

most meaningful course. Get Petrov to defect and threaten to shop the whole thing to the papers. Use the papers as the other. Use them as the secret church. He'd bring Security to their knees, have them ruefully begging for his return to the fold.

11

Skies heating. Skies blue like an illustration, cloudless. September 1953. Generalov announced that his entire staff was entitled to a four-day holiday. They were even granted permission to leave Canberra, as long as they travelled in groups.

There was a scramble for the cars. The Kislitsyns booked DC 141, a black BMW sedan, and invited the Petrovs to Sydney. Evdokia asked Masha to fill the spare seat. On the Thursday morning, they drove past yellow paddocks, hills and dirt, kilometre upon kilometre of the same idea, fence lines, Hereford cattle, union after union of dusty sheep.

They stopped in Mittagong for pies and beer, and a few hours later Sydney appeared on the horizon, terrific buildings with a gravity that altered light. They checked into the Buckingham Hotel. Volodya seemed rushed, nervous to find everyone their room. Evdokia had the impression that he didn't want them here.

'This is your city,' she said.

'My city? Don't be absurd.'

'You are anxious. Why?'

'It's just the car. My arms are buzzing.' He held them out: a shaky grip on an imagined wheel. 'Where should we eat?' he asked. 'Where would you like to go?'

They stood outside the Buckingham on the street, stepping into the idea of the metropolis. Two years Evdokia had been in Canberra. She looked at Masha and Anna, both grinning uncontrollably.

They went in the direction of the restaurant. The men walked a distance in front, somewhat swallowed by the crowd. There were distant city rumblings, currents, noises heard for the moment but which your mind soon disappeared. The restaurant was plain but the meal good. They observed an unspoken rule: no talk of home. No derisive comparisons, no jibes against the capitalist west. They would be here for three more days, almost unburdened by who they were, and they could fall out of their situation for a moment, pretend that the holiday wasn't a precious, hourly disappearing jewel.

They told anecdotes about clothes. Philip Kislitsyn said he'd once had a suit fitted on Savile Row, every piece a different colour of bone, and no way he could afford it. The tailors had taken his picture—more accurate than a mirror, they'd said—and he'd used that as his out, declaring that the shades weren't as he'd hoped, maintaining this line over the photographer's protestations that the image being judged was black and white.

Volodya lamented his old and trusted leather jacket, needlessly lost when the submarine struck them en route to Sweden because Evdokia had howled that it would sink him.

After the meal, they went to a café on Darlinghurst Road, where they listened to a violinist playing with a cellist. Evdokia paid for everything of Masha's: another unspoken agreement in accordance with the weekend's rules. Two bottles of champagne came to the table. The night was laughter and friendly jokes, the warmer notes of the cello murmuring as second thoughts in the wooden floor.

The Russians separated in the Buckingham's lobby, wishing each other happy dreams. The room Volodya had picked on the second storey faced the street, a suite with two windows, both left open, the room dark but an orange tint invading, some entirely urban glow. Evdokia wanted them to make love. She wanted to engage in a cosmopolitan act to the sounds she could now hear, just another intrigue in a city, humming. She put her hand inside his shirt then undid the buttons. His hair smelled like cigarettes, like hair should smell in the Big Smoke. The shirt came away. She kissed his shoulder, surprised to find it tense in a way unexpected. She took hold of the other shoulder and turned him. She sat on the edge of the bed and unbuckled his belt and made sure that he held her eyes. His breath was heavy with alcohol. Thick fingers fumbling with her blouse; she held them with one hand and undressed herself with the other.

A car's horn blared, jammed against the sounds of revelry nearby. The hotel itself had a sound. A heating system, perhaps. Pressure in the walls. He reached to draw the quilt over them but she stopped him. There was no breeze in the room. The windows open but no air moved.

The arcades had chequered floors. Shops that sold Hollywood cosmetics, women's clothes, babies' clothes. Whole stores just for chocolate. They walked through the laneways between the arcades. Every store had a doormat bearing its name. The windows were elaborate; window dressing, it was called. Lights and little platforms, small altars, spotless glass. She thought of Marx. *The mystical character of commodities*.

Anna tried on a hat in a basement that was full of hats. Hats on stands and tables, hats in boxes and on ceramic heads. The shop assistants came running. They saw your interest in a thing and it was their job to rush and help. Simple economic relations. Still, you felt included in a genuine way.

They ate at a place called Dawson's. Masha refused to use her poor English because she didn't want it upsetting their day. Across the road was His Master's Voice. A cleaner stood at the window with a cloth, removing lipstick kisses from the glass over a picture of Johnnie Ray.

They went into Her Majesty's Arcade, 'The Arcade Women Prefer'. There was a fur shop and a tobacco store. There was a man operating a chair that balanced your body weight against a brass dish bearing small discs of varying load.

They were exceedingly aware of themselves: whether they looked different, what they said, how crazy they appeared in relation to these people in the arcade. Masha pointed and smiled. If she did speak it was hushed. She looked tranquil and happy but, underneath, seemed nervously afraid.

They went into a boutique. Anna bought a dress and walked out wearing it. She looked stiff, not exactly comfortable. Around the corner was a second boutique selling the same dress and she refused to go into the store.

They smiled when they paid for things. They tried to look comfortable while wondering whether these people were blind as to who they were.

They came to rest on an indoor bench. Prams going past, people carrying parcels. Evdokia saw for a moment the world of social hieroglyphics. The act of exchange. The reflex of the real. She tried to glimpse the labour of the individual asserting itself, part of the whole labour of society. Max Factor (Hollywood/London). Kayser Sheerest Nylon.

They went back to the Buckingham, ate their evening meal at the hotel, and the next day got up and did it all again.

On the Monday morning, Lavrentiy Beria was arrested. Evdokia was filing papers when Prudnikov brought the shattering news.

'Evdokia Alexeyevna, where is the ambassador?'

The cypher clerk was puffing, having sprinted down the stairs.

'At the French embassy,' she said.

'When does he return?'

She shrugged: he-doesn't-tell-me.

Prudnikov frowned. 'Look,' he said.

It was a formal note to all foreign stations. *Lavrentiy Beria, head of the MVD, has been found to be a bourgeois degenerate and an agent of international imperialism*. The note was on the Foreign Ministry's letterhead. She looked at Prudnikov, a sick feeling welling in her stomach.

'When did this come?' she asked.

'This morning with the cables.'

'Priority?'

'No.'

He was looking to her, as part of the MVD clique; searching for some kind of indication as to how to react.

'We need a staff meeting,' she said.

'What does it mean?'

'Nothing.'

'Petrova.'

'Let's not worry, Prudnikov. Let's wait and see.'

'I have been a good worker for you.'

'That's right. Very good.'

'Loyal to the MVD.'

'Yes, very loyal.'

'Beria! This is bad news.'

She sought out Volodya. He and Kislitsyn were together in his downstairs office. The news caused a silence. The two men looked at each other and after a time they looked at her.

The staff meeting turned into a meeting of the Party. Kovaliev stood and read the charges, stale in his delivery, flanked by Generalov.

Lavrentiy Beria was working for British Intelligence.

He was working for American Intelligence.

He was working to re-establish capitalism within the Soviet state.

Lavrentiy Beria was a saboteur of Soviet industry.

He had undermined Soviet agriculture.

He had circumvented the presidium's authority.

Lavrentiy Beria had lost the character of a communist.

He was attempting to elevate the MVD to a rank above the government and the Party.

He was caught red-handed plotting attempts at ultimate power.

Lavrentiy Beria was a traitor.

He was guilty of the vilest, most abominable crimes.

He had subverted the police and the security forces and forged a terrorist organisation.

He was a terrorist without ideology or principle, a covert fascist fixated by treacherous ideas, intent on national betrayal.

His hypocrisy was monstrous.

He had tried to steer the GDR away from the course of socialism.

He was a friend of Tito and Rankovich.

He was an agent of external influences, guilty of espionage and high treason.

Spittle edged from Kovaliev's mouth. He sat down and Generalov rose. The ambassador said he was shocked by the scale of these charges. Who knew that the chief of the MVD was such a murderous reprobate? The magnitude of his crimes was sublime.

Vislykh, the new man in the economic section, said in a low voice that he'd heard rumours. Sexual deviance concerning forced liaisons with young girls.

Generalov nodded. 'We must be vigilant,' he warned. 'Only because he has been arrested are we now aware of Beria's corruption. It seems his influence has been pervasive. There are likely to be spies and loyalists in his organisation, men and women who pursue his ends even now, labouring in the shadows, unmasked.'

Evdokia looked at Prudnikov. He was watching the ambassador. She could tell he wasn't breathing. His shoulders were forward and his neck low between them. She'd seen the look before. Someone held frozen by new and hardening fear.

Volodya seemed indifferent, staring blankly into space. Whether he was playing at ignorance or simply believed Generalov's remarks were ordinary tedium, she couldn't say.

***

Philip Kislitsyn walked the Petrovs home.

'Malenkov and Khrushchev,' he said. 'Malenkov and Khrush-chev have had the marshal deposed.'

'You said Beria was destined to take control.'

'Well. Who knows? How would I know?'

'We should get *Pravda*. See how they're reporting the news.'

'We're hearing about this now. It's likely he has been under arrest for days.'

'What about those around him?'

'Sparta.'

'Sparta has been unusually quiet.'

'We've had no messages for a week.'

'Is it possible we've been marooned?'

They reached the corner of Lockyer Street; street lamps hazing in the diminished dusk, no cars on the empty road.

'We shouldn't worry,' said Kislitsyn. 'Realistically, how close are we to Sparta? We're a project on his books, that is all.'

'The question is, how deep will it go? Any purge. How significantly close to the close do you need to be?'

Kislitsyn shrugged. 'Our work is distant to the nth degree. We're discussing a high-level event. Curtained movements of the powerful elite. We stand at the fringes, uselessly, trying to comprehend events that probably even they do not fully understand.'

'How deep is too deep?'

Evdokia interrupted them. She noted that Prudnikov was afraid.

Kislitsyn looked at her. 'What does he have to fear?'

'He walks a fine line,' she said, 'between his loyalty to us and to the ambassador.'

'It is not possible to opt out once you have joined. He knows this.'

She crossed and uncrossed her arms. 'I'm saying we should be careful with him. That is all. Offer him our reassurance.'

'No,' said Kislitsyn. 'Reassurance is the final giveaway that one hasn't got a leg to stand on.'

The three talked until a car went by. Kislitsyn departed for his dinner. The Petrovs went into the house, surprised to find that the kitchen light was on. Both swore it should have been off. Volodya stood at the switch, flicking it back and forth, listening intently to the click. He checked the back door's locks and came and stood again at the switch and listened to its click.

Evdokia put water in a saucepan and began boiling it. She watched while her husband flicked the switch to hear the sound.

The remainder of the week was quiet—tabulations, cypherings, walking Jack in the mornings. On the Friday, preparations began at the embassy for a Sunday lunch. The women were commandeered by Generalova. Evdokia was assigned to the kitchen, alongside Anna Kislitsyna and Pipniakova. The menu wanted meat pies. The three went to work, shopping in Kingston, then arranging the kitchen as a factory, Anna and Pipniakova working on the fillings, Evdokia manning pastry and assembly. Pipniakova's radio set gave them Bing Crosby's voice to work to.

Generalova walked in and out of the room, staring, overseeing the operation in magisterial fashion. When the woman was out of earshot, Evdokia made snide comments about her shoes.

Anna chopped onions and sifted flour. Pipniakova gave herself a burn. They sang along to Bing together. Evdokia rolled the pastry and shaped the pies. She set the pies in rows, a queue for the oven. Generalova came and stood next to her, invading. Hot breath, fatness and germs.

'Must you?' said Evdokia.

Generalova looked at the pies, then put her hands on one and reshaped it. Evdokia scowled. Generalova prodded the crust of another with her thumb.

Evdokia filled a pie, laid the pastry on top. Generalova sighed, lifted the pastry and rearranged it.

Evdokia broke an egg violently. She set the next pie the way she wanted and glazed it heavily. The pie went shunting across the bench top. Generalova eyed it as if she might still dare.

Anna dropped a metal spoon, a crashing sound on the concrete floor. The other two women were watching as if they weren't. Generalova turned and saw them. She made some inaudible comment, walked to the door and didn't return.

The truth behind events. Volodya was outside, working on something in the garage. Evdokia rounded the hedge, her feet crunching down the driveway.

'Doosia,' he said. He was holding a small wrench, hands greased and black. He wore blue overalls, round at his tummy, grease marks on his nose. 'What has happened?'

'You are repairing the car? That is Sanko's job, repairing the car.'

'The pie,' he said. 'What happened?'

She stared at him. 'The *pies*,' she said, 'are cooling.'

He shifted his stance impatiently. 'Doosenka,' he said, 'Kislitsyn rang me. You threw a pie at Generalova.'

She felt herself looking stunned. How to react? Volodya wiped grease onto a cloth. They stood in the driveway, afternoon light casting her shadow down the line. Incredible.

'That bitch,' she said. 'That bitch is twice the bitch that Lifanova ever was.'

'Why did you throw the pie?'

'I didn't throw a pie.'

'The pie missed her narrowly. It broke up in flight and parts of it have stained her dress.'

'I wish I had thrown a pie. I wish now that I did.'

'You quarrelled with her.'

'The pies were in dishes. Is she suggesting I tried to kill her by hurling ceramics at her brain?'

'She says she won't go near you. She's afraid of what you'll do.'

'Who is it she's talking to?'

'Kislitsyn heard it from Sanko who heard it from somewhere else.'

'Sanko! Why are you repairing this car?'

He raised an open palm. 'Generalov's scheduled a meeting. He wants a Party reprimand hanging over your head.'

She groaned. 'I have witnesses,' she said. 'Anna and Pipniakova.'

The call came that night from Kovaliev. A Party disciplinary session would be held in the morning at eleven o'clock. Volodya thanked him gruffly, not allowing Evdokia anywhere near the phone.

The meeting was convened around a large table in the embassy's formal room. Generalov was in his uniform, medals boasting on his chest. The curtains were drawn, smothering the daylight, and the artificial lighting, Evdokia thought, made the room seem airlessly enclosed.

Generalov spoke first, pausing occasionally for Karasev, the service attaché, who'd been assigned to record the minutes. He told them this meeting was for a special purpose that would soon be made horrifically clear. Certain things had come to his attention—various undercurrents in this embassy, which, as ambassador and a communist, he could no longer allow to proceed. He had considered declaring this an open forum, such was the weight of the problem.

Evdokia shifted in her seat. She had Anna's testimony in her pocket, ready to declare Generalova's accusations false.

The ambassador droned on. He had his knuckles pressed to the table. 'Serious charges are to be made,' he said. 'Shocking behaviour that deserves to be ruthlessly exposed.' He glared at Kislitsyn, the second secretary toying with the pencil in his hand. 'Let us begin.'

Evdokia stood up. 'I will speak,' she said.

Their eyes fixed on her, necks craning one by one.

Generalov cocked an eyebrow. 'Nothing has yet been said, Petrova.'

'I wish to make it known,' she declared, 'that outrageous lies are circulating with intent. Pie throwing. What lunacy. It is an infantile falsehood whose fabricator evidently lacks the courage to appear at this meeting and must therefore stand condemned.'

She had expected the ambassador to sit and hear her out. He stayed standing. She declared quickly that she had witnesses. People in direct contact with the time and the place and the personalities around which the incident revolved.

'Evdokia Alexeyevna,' Generalov interrupted, 'your insolence towards my wife is not our concern today.' He gestured that she sit. 'True,' he said, 'you are an expert at splitting the collective. Causing divisions. Encouraging dissension. You are loud-mouthed, which some might dismiss as merely an unfortunate element of your character, not realising the cold and calculated scheming it truly is.' She moved to protest but he silenced her with his finger. 'It is apparent, now,' he continued, 'that your outbursts are not innocent but deliberate and contrived. They are the plottings of a sinister miscreant. Part of a subversive agenda to which you,'—he turned slightly—'and your husband hold.'

She looked to Volodya whose arms were hugged to his chest.

Generalov went on. 'Many have wondered about anti-social behaviours in this outpost, failures to fit with the collective, antagonisms exhibited. Always these have been believed to be conflicts of personality or some such benign thing, vacant of political content. But suddenly we find ourselves enlightened. We charge that they are part of a campaign. A crusade to ruin the good working order of this station, to disrupt and dislocate our functioning parts. An action of sabotage. It has its political motivations: a Beria faction. That is right. A cancer in this very embassy, seeking to usurp the power of the Foreign Ministry and to establish an order headed by the MVD.'

Kovaliev's head bobbed, his eyes pinned to Karasev's notes.

'We must name the perpetrators,' Generalov declared. 'We will out them and hope they die of shame. The Petrovs— Comrades Vladimir Mikhailovich and Evdokia Alexeyevna, who are far from comrades at all. We say they are saboteurs. Husband and wife; organisers of a Beria group; conspirators with the aim of elevating the MVD to a position above myself as the ruling authority of this outpost.'

'Ambassador—'

'From the outset they have attempted to destabilise us, pursuing the reactionary aims of their treacherous former head!'

'You are wrong,' Evdokia half-shouted. 'That is slander. Groundless! Beria must answer for his crimes! It is nothing to do with us.'

'On the contrary,' said Generalov. 'It is everything! Who here will speak?'

Kovaliev jumped to the call. He rose from his chair, half-stuttering as if the words had jammed. 'I . . . Ah . . . It is true! Your mission has been to degrade us, to disparage Stalin, may he rest in peace. We have witnessed your theatrics and orchestrations, your derelictions and their subversive intent. These have been your outward behaviours, trying to bend the collective to your will. But who knows what has happened in secret; what influences you have peddled behind the scenes? Shall we ask? Will you furnish the truth? You are a danger. You have made intrigues against the proper lines of control. Ambassador Lifanov understood your deleterious effect. He may not have known your motivations, but now your treachery, long suspected, is exposed.'

Volodya was sitting in his chair, arms crossed. Evdokia waited for him to interject as Kovaliev sprinted on.

'Beria loyalists,' the attaché shouted. 'Loyalists to the core!'

'These are lies, Nikolai Grigorievich!' she said. 'You are fabricating at such speed you can hardly keep pace with yourself.'

Suddenly, Kharkovetz, the press attaché, was on his feet. His mouth was dry and it clicked as he spoke. 'I agree with this process.'

'What process?' she asked.

He ignored her, addressing the ambassador. 'If these two are a Beria faction, they must be heartlessly unmasked.'

'Who else?' said Generalov. 'Who supports this charge? Vislykh?'

'Yes,' said the secretary. 'If they are guilty, I support it.'

'But we are not guilty,' said Evdokia. 'The charge is convenient and absurd.'

'It is serious,' said Kovaliev, still stammering.

'Oh, desperately.'

The ambassador called on Kislitsyn. The MVD man leaned back in his chair and gave no reply. Still Volodya was silent. His eyes were on Karasev, whatever it was he was writing down.

Kovaliev rambled on with another indictment, footnoting various incidents, incitements to unrest.

'This is not a hearing,' said Evdokia. 'This is an ambush. We are not followers of Beria. We are respected Party members with long careers.'

Generalov laughed. 'Evdokia Alexeyevna, we know your record, the black stains on your Party history.'

'The Party knows who I am and is comfortable, Ambassador. I think there are men in this room with questionable histories who should be the last to throw stones.'

Kovaliev went to protest but she cut him off. 'This charge is a falsity,' she said. 'Let us dismiss it and end this meeting.'

'If the Petrovs won't admit their betrayals, we must test them by formalising the charge,' said Kharkovetz.

'That's right,' said Kislitsyn, putting the pencil behind his ear. 'This is all hearsay. If the ambassador believes it, let him command the charge and afford a proper prosecution and defence. If he believes it.'

Generalov glared at his second secretary.

Kovaliev lifted a book of protocol from his bag. 'There are rules,' he said. 'Without Moscow's permission, no process can be made. As secretary, I can take an agreement to petition them. If the Petrovs won't admit the charge, this is the only way we can begin.'

'Now you are being ridiculous,' Evdokia said. 'You know Moscow will grant you no such thing.'

'We must follow the regulations. I am secretary. This is what the regulations state.'

Generalov called on Prudnikov, who was sitting quietly at the end of the table. 'Petr, what is your opinion of all this?'

The cypher clerk looked fearful. He muttered about the regulations, taking refuge in them, saying there should be a strict observance of the rules.

'Alright,' said Generalov. 'Kovaliev will petition Moscow. He will collect signatures from those who support the charge.'

'We will include a protest that what is alleged is nonsense,' Evdokia said.

'You cannot protest a petition,' Kovaliev told her.

'We will protest it.'

'The rules are plain. You may protest at a later stage.'

Evdokia went to speak once more, but Kovaliev and Generalov stood, declaring the meeting closed. Karasev packed his minutes into a satchel, which Kovaliev took.

'You must write to Moscow,' said Kislitsyn, when everyone had gone.

'All this writing,' said Volodya.

'The facts may make no difference, but then again they might.'

'He's thought hard about this, the prick.'

'Two pricks. Scheming.'

'Is this the kind of thing that makes it them or us?'

'What do you think?'

'We are completely untenable. How is Doosia supposed to work?'

'Shoulder to the wheel. Follow the rules.'

'Six feet from bedlam.'

They looked to her. She wasn't talking. She pulled the strings on the nearest curtain, struck by nausea in the sudden bright light.

Anna Kislitsyna broke away. Their walks and shopping excursions stopped, Evdokia's telephone calls went unreturned. Evdokia understood, or thought she did. Theirs was an ordinary friendship and what was an ordinary friendship when you had a family to protect? It was an intellectual understanding and it didn't help the hurt. If they saw one another at the embassy, Anna gave her a distant smile and nothing more.

Masha wasn't afraid. They ate their lunch together at the end of the orchard in the shadow of the hedge or out of it. An hour in the afternoon sun; the smell of citrus and the cigarettes they smoked.

Others sniped. Karaseva spat into the garden if their paths crossed. Someone made pig noises under her office window then disappeared. Someone wrote 'whore' on the roster by her name. When she left a room, she stood outside the doorway, quietly hovering, listening for laughter or any comments made.

Volodya stayed a week in Sydney. She wanted to know what they were going to do about this, the situation. He rang her once and wouldn't discuss it.

Ethel Rosenberg was executed. President Eisenhower rejected her last-minute letter requesting clemency. She made no statement before dying. There were riots in Rome and Paris.

Generalov demanded to be told what was wrong when Evdokia rang in sick. 'Fever,' she said. 'I won't bring it to the embassy.'

She stayed in the house for two days, the curtains drawn, sleeping with the lights on, not bothering to watch the street.

She cooked soup and reheated soup and fed some soup to Jack. The dog tongued the bowl across the floor, upended it and licked the spilled liquid from the lino.

The hum of the Powerhouse was one of those distant things— could she really hear it or was she listening to the wind?

She was sacked, finally, which was something she had seen coming. The ambassador called her to his desk and closed the door.

'Evdokia Alexeyevna,' he said. 'I am terminating your work as my assistant. You are dismissed as accountant. You will make sure your records are in order and hand them to me. Vislykha will take the role.'

'You don't have the authority,' she protested. 'Moscow assigned me the position. I follow the regulations and the rules.'

He looked at her in silence. He told her she would bring him the records in an hour.

She cleared the photographs from her desk. She left the whittled pencils and the notes and sums she'd scribbled. She wanted Vislykha to realise her intrusion, to know that the space she was inhabiting was not a vacant, nullified place. You are profiting from a casualty, the desk said.

She went upstairs to tell Kislitsyn what had happened. The door of his office was locked. She hovered for a time before collecting the MVD channel from Prudnikov. She asked whether Kovaliev's petition had received a reply. 'Not yet,' said the clerk, though she wondered whether he would tell her, whether things were now so lost that he had chosen the ambassador's camp.

She took the MVD cables to Volodya's room. Easy to lose herself decyphering, running like an automaton, vanishing her conscious parts. Subtract this column from this. Substitute the codewords. The messages uncovered felt as though they were spoken in a godly voice. The way the words were housed inside themselves, secretly bound up in reassortments unbreakable to anyone else.

Moscow Centre wanted Kislitsyn to track down a military man named David Morris, an undercover communist and a tank researcher once on the general staff in Melbourne. They wanted the current address and living circumstances of a lawyer named Finnard, graduate of Sydney University, interested in questions of Marxist philosophy. They sought information on one Fitzhardinge, a librarian at the National Library and a consultant to parliament whom they thought might provide useful advice.

She felt reassured by this humdrum noise. The mundane rattle of intelligence work, pedestrian and routine questing of the unremarkable kind. Disarmed, she was midway through the last instruction before she realised what her decrypting had made. It was an order to Volodya: *Return to Moscow. Brief us here, directly, on the progress you and your detachment have achieved.*

She felt ill.

They wanted him on a plane via London and Zurich at the earliest. Unthinking, she picked up the phone on the desk and asked for a trunk call. The Buckingham Hotel told her that a Mr Petrov wasn't registered. Were they sure? She described her husband physically: not short but short-looking, not fat but somewhat round. 'Glasses,' said the clerk. He knew of the chap referred to but he was certainly not booked in.

She tried Bialoguski. The doctor answered the phone out of breath, and was elusive about her husband's whereabouts, telling her that if he saw Vladimir anywhere he'd tell him to call.

Ivan Golovanov was below the window, pushing the mowing contraption and swearing. Evdokia went home in the mid-afternoon. The phone was ringing as she walked in. It was Volodya.

'I've been sacked,' she said.

'What do you mean?'

'Generalov has dismissed me as his assistant and the embassy accountant.'

She told her husband about the Moscow cable, avoiding the word 'recalled'. '"Come to Moscow as fast as possible"—instructions to that effect.'

'He can't sack you! Who does this man think he is?'

'He is at ease, as he tells me. He looks like a man who is safe.'

'Well.'

'What about Moscow?'

'Is Kislitsyn there? What does he say?'

'Everything is falling apart.'

Silence.

'My eyes are deteriorating,' he said. 'Quite suddenly. I am having medical attention and the doctor says it is not a sensible thing for me to fly.'

'Oh?'

'We'll cable this opinion.'

'A delaying tactic.'

'Moscow won't send a man blind.'

She listened to him breathe. 'What would we be stalling for?'

'Oh, anything. Something. Let's not be fatalistic.'

'I don't know.'

'I've done some good work up here, Doosia. We can smooth things over with the Centre. Get them behind our cause.'

'Smooth things over. Delay things. What do you think is going to change?'

'It is a good country this, don't you agree?'

'Where are you?'

'The Oriental Hotel.'

'Are you coming home?'

'I'll go to the doctor.'

'Go to the doctor and then come home.'

'Yes. Okay. Alright.'

'I'll continue going to work,' she said. 'Upstairs.'

'Alright. It will be alright. This is a good country, isn't it?'

'Come home. Be careful.'

'Yes. Yes. Alright.'

12

Bialoguski rang the *Sydney Morning Herald* from a phone box on Victoria Road, asking to speak to any journalist with a special interest in world or national affairs. They put him through to a man named Clean. He listened closely to the man's voice, trying to make a political assessment.

'Listen,' Bialoguski said. 'Are you a man of the left or the right?'

'What's that matter?'

'Answer.'

'Left, right—I'm too bloody busy.'

'Left or right?'

'Let me refer you. We've got both kinds of bastard here.'

'Look, I need a journalist who's not a communist.'

'If there's one thing I'm not.'

'Alright.'

He told him he was a Security agent, recently retired. He wanted to write an exposé based on his penetrations. He wanted to forensically describe the activities of the New South

Wales communist front, its various organisations, the Peace Movement. There were respectable doctors and lawyers and scientists sinking in the shit of Marxist philosophy. People having their pockets cut open and their cash funnelled in unsavoury directions. He had documentary evidence. Hard facts. Names. He would write these articles anonymously and he would be paid. If they needed proof of his Security connections, he could provide the names of men who would vouch for him. The best idea, he thought, would be to pen the articles under a pseudonym, something suitably heroic and metaphysical: T.J. Shawl or K.K. Ghost. The articles could be used as the basis of news stories, but the articles themselves had to be the magazine type with illustrations and a hard, black edge. There were further options. A series of articles on the Soviet embassy. He had a direct connection to revelations about the activities of Soviet diplomats and embassy personnel.

'Who am I speaking with?' asked Clean.

'For the moment I'm just a man calling from a phone box.'

He mentioned the name Petrov; the names Pakhomov, Vislykh, Generalov. Said there were underhand goings-on he could expose. Front-page news.

'Hold on,' said Clean. 'How can we meet?'

'I'll call you,' said Bialoguski. 'For the moment I am simply interested in your interest.' He disconnected.

Arriving at Cliveden, it was a shock to find Petrov on the doorstep. The Russian looked drunk and sulky, mostly wretched. The weather was much too warm for an overcoat, but Vladimir's hugged his body all the same.

'I need to see Beckett,' he said.

Bialoguski felt his dark mood. They went upstairs. He poured them drinks and they sat.

'Bastards,' Petrov spat.

'What's wrong, Vladimir?'

The man jerked a newspaper from his pocket and thrust it under Bialoguski's nose. 'Look at this,' he said.

It was an article. Life in Russia. The day-to-day starvation of the masses; the overbearing fear of the purge.

'Lies?' suggested the doctor.

'No,' said Petrov. 'It's all true. Except really it's twice as bad!'

Bialoguski looked at him carefully.

'Come on, Doctor,' the Russian went on. 'I think you know. You are clever enough to realise we are suffering terribly. Maybe you believe in dialectical materialism, but about the ruthless conditions in the Soviet Union you are smart enough to know.'

'What is this, Vladimir?'

The man pointed to Malenkov's bulbous, dual-chinned face. 'This man and his clique, they live like the czars. It is as plain as day. Their cars and their food and their houses. But you go to Russia and say something against them, they'll cut your head off.'

'Go on!'

'They will. Just see what they will do to this bastard Beria! And how many people did Beria kill?'

'You're drunk, Vladimir.'

'The Russian people are ruled at bayonet point.'

'A Soviet diplomat saying this.'

'It's true, Doctor. Power-thirsty bastards at the helm and anyone who stands up gets shot. That is the Russian way.'

Bialoguski refilled his glass, doing his best to feign surprise.

Petrov went on. 'And who do they think they are fooling? Conditions in the Soviet Union—the foreign diplomats see things for themselves. Why don't we just live and let live? Open our frontier to all comers!' He breathed heavily, shook the ice in his glass and snarled. 'Doosia has been sacked,' he said. 'Generalov doesn't have the authority but that doesn't stop the prick. It's no good. You try to be honest and good and not put people in, but that is exactly the display of weakness that makes you the target. We should kill ourselves and save them the trouble. Doosia is making an attempt to fight back, but they want blood. You can't argue truth to power. There is no case. This is how we live. It's madness. We can't beat the determination of this pack of bastards. They have long since forgotten what they even had against us.'

'You know what you're talking about,' Bialoguski said. 'You know more than I.'

Petrov looked at him. 'I've been recalled. They want me to book air tickets home immediately. I need to see Beckett about my eyes. Can you book me in with him?'

'Of course.'

'I tell you. Better to work in Australia on the roads than to live daily in fear for your life.'

'A cigarette?'

'I'm jealous, Doctor. You go wherever you want. Do whatever you like.'

'Oh.'

'You must think I am an atrocious drunk.'

'I don't know the pressure you are under.'

'You're a friend, Doctor. We honest types have the worst of it.'

Bialoguski struck a match. 'Do you mean that?' he asked. 'You would rather work on the roads?'

Petrov nodded, not meeting his eye, looking at the Poynters' floor.

Bialoguski told him the roads were for dimwits. 'There are better opportunities,' he said. 'As it happens I'm scouting at the moment for myself. Business investments. I've had some Ampol exploration shares that have come good. Eight or nine hundred pounds—more if I hold on. I might buy a share in the Adria. No joke. There's also a farm I'm looking into. A chicken operation that's on the market at a good price.'

'A chicken farm?'

'That's right. I don't know anything about farming, not like you, Vladimir, but we could partner. Much better than the roads.'

He had the man's attention now.

'Investments?' said the diplomat. 'You've never mentioned this.'

'I've only just found out about the shares. Listen. Someone in your position, Vladimir . . . with a plan and the right contacts . . . I imagine it wouldn't be too hard to hang around.'

'Hang around.'

'That's right.'

'Well.'

'If it's so bad, bugger them.'

'I don't know.'

'If it's so bad.'

'It might take some organising.'

'You could show them. Tell the truth. Explain how it is first-hand.'

'That would really put them in it.'

'That's right.'

'We'd need to be careful.'

'Tight-lipped, you mean?'

'That would be it. Getting the process right.'

'The process, exactly. I could be your agent, Vladimir. If you trust me. In truth, I don't know much about your country. I went through Moscow once. I don't tell people that fact but I'll tell it to you. It was 1941 and it was snowing. Maybe it is unfair to judge, but my impression of that city was huge buildings looming over a populace that couldn't see them, such was each individual's concentration on their own affairs. That was what it was. Grand architecture and grey-coated ghosts. Two cities, completely separate. One city for the rulers and the other for the starving hordes. Nothing in between.'

The Russian was filling his glass again. 'I am in between,' he said. 'That's who's in between. Doosia and I are the Soviet middle class.' He laughed.

Bialoguski thought they were getting somewhere. How hard to push it?

'With the right contacts,' the doctor said.

'They'd shoot me. The Russians. Quick as look.'

'You could just disappear.'

'That's right. Disappear.'

'Something to be arranged.'

'They'd kill me. Not give it a second thought.'

'You'd be gone. We can talk to the people who can turn you into a ghost.'

Petrov gave a nervous laugh.

'What about Evdokia?' Bialoguski asked.

The diplomat looked at him. 'This might be the problem,' he said.

'Oh?'

'Convincing her. She suffers here. I have no family in Moscow, you see.'

'I could talk to her.'

'No. I will do it. It would have to be a delicate thing.'

'The farm.'

'Yes, the chicken farm. That would be a life!'

'That's right. You wouldn't have to put much down. Managing and part-owning. Maybe you buy me out down the line.'

'These people? These contacts?'

'I think I know how to get in touch. It might be a process. Perhaps we should start now so that the whole thing is not dramatic.'

Petrov pushed his cigarette into the ashtray. 'You don't know about Russia, Michael.'

'No, of course not. I'm a theoretical socialist so in reality I have no idea.'

'The horrors that happen.'

'I'm prepared to believe whatever you say.'

'You would be a good bridge. With these government people.'

'I could negotiate. I think they would see me as a realistic person. A Macquarie Street doctor. I could see what they are prepared to put on the table. Not even use your name.'

'A chicken farm.'

'That's right.'

'Let me think about it.'

The Russian stood up with a sudden jerk, headed for the bathroom. Bialoguski sat for a moment, thinking. It took him some time to realise that Petrov's small suitcase was sitting on the floor. He eyed it. He thought about its contents—what Vladimir might secret in there that he couldn't fit inside his wallet. Letting the impulse carry him, Bialoguski hurriedly ripped some phenobarbital from his medicine chest. He crushed a tablet and sprinkled its powder into the Russian's drink.

'Let's eat here tonight,' he told Petrov when the man returned. 'I'll drive over to the Adria. Get us something.'

Petrov swilled the liquid in his glass. 'Alright,' he said, finishing it in a gulp. 'But afterwards, I have to go.'

'Go? Where to?'

'I need to be back in Canberra. Things keep happening while I'm not there.'

'I think you should stay, Vladimir.'

'I'll have dinner with you but I have to go. I need to get out of this city.'

13

Darkness, loud and punched out. The highway everywhere like an echo. Petrov slowly came to realise that he was in it. *On* it. No longer inside the car but sitting here on the road, holding his knees, the Skoda in front of him and on fire. Engulfed by flames. Ablaze.

He felt damp. What time was it? His right arm touched all the parts of his body, searching for blood. There was blood—dark shrieks of it on his clothes.

Was it someone else's blood? Had he hit someone on the road?

The smoke carried the choke of burning oil. He went from sitting to lying flat. He'd crashed, that much was obvious, but he couldn't remember anything, his body numb from the impact, his feelings about things darkly void.

How did he get to the hospital? The doctors put him in a room and one of them asked, 'What hit you?'

'A truck,' he replied. 'A truck out of nowhere.'

He sat on the bed while a nurse attended to his face. She told him there were bits of windshield embedded in his skin.

He couldn't remember the car going over. Perhaps something *had* bumped him. Hadn't he passed a panel van at some point? Or had something mechanical failed in the car?

This was a way they might think of to end his life! The thought was like a cold nugget and he held it in his hand.

Doosia came and took him home in the afternoon. She was good to him, his wife. He thought they were at their best together whenever catastrophe or heartbreak struck. Irina's death. The series of operations Evdokia had endured in Sweden. They might not have the most tranquil of marriages, but he thought they were experts at bonding through crisis.

She made him an early dinner and cut the chops so he could eat them with a fork in his one good hand. They sat on the back porch. She went to the bathroom and while she was gone he got the Nagant and put it behind the cushion of his chair.

Kislitsyn came with Vislykh. They stood over him as if he was an invalid. Vislykh asked where the wreck was. The police wanted the embassy to contract a tow truck, but he thought Sanko could use the utility. Petrov looked at him sadly. He told him the car was completely melted. He doubted it still had tyres.

Kislitsyn accepted a glass of lemonade. He said that Generalov was asking about the Skoda's insurance.

'The papers are in my desk,' said Petrov. He realised almost immediately that he might not have renewed the policy for 1953.

Later, Doosia ran a bath. The water felt good against his bruises, whole muscles in his legs the colour of a plum. He drifted, waking with a stiff neck to add to his physical complaints.

The police couldn't charge him with anything. He was a diplomat. He could be as rude and evasive as he liked. He told them he'd been fishing. They seemed fixated on the question of what he'd really been doing on that particular stretch of road.

He telephoned the Mutual Life and Citizens Insurance Company. He told them of the accident and they checked the policy. Expired, they said. But he'd sent a cheque! June or maybe July. They hadn't received it, they said. Which bank and what cheque number? Was he sure? The file showed that they'd sent him two reminders.

He walked stiffly from his upstairs office to the downstairs toilet. What was a two-year-old Skoda worth? He lit a cigarette and sat. What fresh havoc would Generalov be permitted to unleash?

Howley looked at the photos of the crash. The cauterised ruins of a Skoda on a road siding. He read the notes of interview with the driver, Third Secretary Vladimir Petrov, Soviet Embassy, Canberra, by W. J. Osborne, senior constable at the scene.

Subject claims to have been clipped by 'red truck'; will not divulge origin or destination; states reason for travel as fishing trip; cuts and abrasions, severely bruised buttocks and legs. I have made close inspection and there is no evidence of damage consistent with Skoda having collided with another vehicle.

Howley rang the senior constable and introduced himself. Osborne said the car had been towed. The scene was empty space now. Not worth the visit.

'Special interest in Petrov?' he asked.

'No.'

He stood at his window to think. Intelligence analysis. Soviet spymaster destroys his Skoda at about sunrise on the Sydney to Canberra road. Assess the security implications and file a report in point form.

He needed the inside story. The doctor would know by now. He was coming around to the idea that perhaps cutting Bialoguski loose hadn't been the brightest plan, when the phone rang, confirming it.

URGENT
Telephone message for: Director General, ASIO.
From: Michael Howley
Copy to: B2, HQ,
ASIO RD, NSW

Bialoguski has informed that Mrs Petrov has got the sack from her job at the embassy and that she and her husband wish to defect. He is willing to assist and bring them to us if we will take him back into his former work, otherwise he will take them to the newspapers.

14

'There's some kind of edge,' Evdokia had said. 'There's some kind of invisible edge out there and I think we are going over.'

She told him about the crash. Told him that, in the aftermath, Petrov was suffering bouts of anxiety, his hands shaking.

'I don't know what to say, Evdokia.'

'You're his doctor, Michael. Can't you supply him with something? Medication?'

'I'll give him a check-up.'

'He wants to visit you,' she'd complained. 'One day out of hospital and straightaway he wants to get on a train.'

Bialoguski was reporting this to Michael Howley, sitting in the Security man's Austin, parked in a street alongside Centennial Park. 'Petrov is teetering,' he said. 'He's worried. Paranoid. Given the right circumstances, I can convince him to defect.'

'The right circumstances,' Howley repeated.

'You have to understand, you're dealing with a man who's

only known totalitarian rule. He can't approach you. He can't know how you'll react. You're a security institution so he thinks you'll probably kill him. That or leave him in place, which he doesn't want. He won't be able to stand things as a double. What he really wants is out.'

'What are you suggesting?'

'Let me take him to someone. A public figure for whom he has respect. This person will be an intermediary, someone who will vouch for your organisation and whom he can trust to broker a deal.'

They had just arranged Bialoguski's claim on his backlog of expenses. It was only fair, Howley had said, when the doctor had continued his work in Security's absence. It was clever too, Bialoguski knew, giving him a lump sum as an apology without setting a precedent.

'I've got him interested in a chicken farm,' he said.

'What's that?'

'A plan for his future. Something that appeals to his under-developed Siberian brain.'

Howley was wearing a jacket that the doctor quite liked, brown, and with a brown tie. The Security man lit a cigarette and said, 'There are some conditions. Under no circumstances can we be seen to provoke. We can't push buttons. We need proof he's coming freely. It's got to be a political defection.'

'Highly political.'

'I chose freedom, etcetera.'

'Proof can be very complex. Did you ever study mathematics? This will be something you'll need to consider ahead of time.'

'He tells you things, does he? His intentions?'

'He attempts to mask them but they're peeking through.'

'Can you record him?'

'Yes.'

'I'd like to have his innermost thoughts on tape.'

'Okay.'

The Security officer reached over Bialoguski's shoulder, retrieved a small satchel from the back seat. 'This is a device,' he said.

'A gadget?'

'It engraves soundwaves onto wire spools.'

Bialoguski put the device in his lap. It was a cream box, six inches by four inches by two inches thick. There were wires, a small microphone and a metal button. There was a small linen bag that looked as if it attached to a belt.

'It works as follows,' said Howley. 'Pin the microphone behind a button on the inside of your shirt. These leads run to the microphone. The unit hangs tightly against your right groin. Its range is good. You switch it on and off here, with this button by the microphone.'

'Ingenious.'

Howley raised a finger. 'The unit makes a noise, a soft humming sound. For this reason, be careful how you use it. Cars are best. The target won't hear anything over the engine.'

'I'll drive him somewhere.'

'Lead him onto the subject. Don't press too hard but find a way. We need evidence of his sincerity and the voluntary nature of his action.'

'The recorder straps to the groin. Why?'

'You have forty-two minutes of wire. If you're going to change spools, be sure the recording head is up. Press the new spool onto the spindle until you hear the click.'

'Get his intentions. Etch them onto wire.'

'Don't bait him. Just lead him there. Most importantly, understand that the government won't be providing political asylum unless the Petrovs are brought to *us*. *We* give out the tickets; not the newspapers, certainly not the Yanks. The Petrovs must come directly to us so we can keep them safe. If bad things happen between their defecting and their reaching us, those who had vouched custody will be held to account.'

'Is that right?'

'There might be a bonus in it,' Howley suggested slowly. 'Something in the order of one thousand pounds.'

Bialoguski went home after their meeting and paced the flat wearing the gadget. He practised walking and standing, casual movements of the type one performed during conversation. He stood in front of the mirror. The gadget was a tool and a mental alertness, an opportunity to better understand one's physical self. It felt like a book under his balls. It posed questions about who he was, what his voice was like and how his body worked. It gave him beyond-normal powers and it asked him to perform himself.

After a few hours' rehearsing, he thought he had its wearing pretty much under control.

According to the map the chicken farm was twenty or so miles from Sydney, near a place called Castle Hill. Petrov agreed to visit. He wanted a glimpse of things as they might be.

Bialoguski drove. The day was patchy, clouds blowing across the face of the sun. Bialoguski was looking at him strangely and he realised he was fidgeting, unclasping his seatbelt then clipping it up again.

'Let's have a beer,' he told the doctor, opening the two bottles he'd brought for the journey.

'I've told these people your name is Peter Karpitch,' Bialoguski said. 'I've said you are inspecting the farm's condition because I am not experienced.'

The farm was called 'Dream Acres'. The owners were Eleanor and Max, the doctor's former wife's sister and her husband. Bialoguski said that Eleanor had a low opinion of him, but that Max, a Sydney dentist, still repaired his teeth at cost.

A dirt road led to the farmhouse from the front gates. Bialoguski parked and they got out. Petrov wanted a cigarette straightaway. The country looked good. Every other breath, he dragged its smell through his nostrils.

Max turned out to be a slight man who looked nothing like a farmer. They toured the farm first, all five acres, accommodation, Max said, for five hundred birds. Not much was being maintained. Bialoguski leaned against a fence and the fence came down.

'It's the dentistry,' said Max. 'With a job in the city it's just too hard to keep up.'

They walked and looked, going boundary to boundary. Petrov began to see things—new sheds for the birds, a small run for a horse. Eventually, they returned to the farmhouse. He was happy to see there'd be a good view of approaching cars.

The furniture indoors was heavy and old. Eleanor told them that meat, milk and groceries could be delivered to the house.

'That's good,' Petrov joked. 'You could stay here and never leave.'

Bialoguski asked Max what terms he was thinking.

'Oh,' said the dentist. 'Four thousand pounds. Three thousand cash.'

'Three thousand, eight hundred,' the doctor shot back. 'Two five in cash.'

Petrov saw Eleanor wince.

'Well, that would be alright,' said Max. 'If you're prepared to do the deal.'

The doctor turned to him. 'What do you think, Peter?'

Why did Bialoguski want to go so fast? Petrov said nothing and shrugged.

Later, in the car, he told Bialoguski that Max was useless; that with a few months' hard work the farm could be made to deliver a return.

'Let's make an offer then,' Bialoguski said. 'I'd be buying but it would be your project. We can make a deal between us.'

'Let's wait a while. Let's just see,' he said.

'It's a good prospect though, isn't it? It's good land. It meets the criteria.'

Petrov didn't say he was interested in a second set of criteria: what kind of refuge it made.

'Tell Evdokia,' said Bialoguski. 'It would be a good life, I think.'

Petrov got into the ophthalmologist's examination chair. It was important that he convince Beckett to make a ruling against his travel.

'I am having trouble again with blindness,' he said. 'Perhaps the macular star is back?'

Beckett put the pen-light to his eye.

'Oh, and I have a flight booked. Would you advise against flying in such a state?'

The surgeon swung an apparatus across the chair, adjusting

the machine's chin rest so his patient could comfortably peer in. 'I'm not sure I see anything,' he said after a time.

'Oh, I assure you, it's like an explosion on my vision.'

Beckett toyed with some settings on the instrument. 'Are you going back to Moscow?'

'I am scheduled.'

'I don't know that I would want to go back. With all the changes taking place there. Beria.'

Beria? Petrov sat still. What did an Australian ophthalmologist know about that?

'It is my duty,' he said.

'Don't you like this country?' Beckett's tone was calm and seemed naive. Petrov couldn't see his face because the penlight was back in his eye.

'It is a fine country,' he said eventually. 'Plenty of food. Plenty of everything.'

The surgeon brought another instrument from the far side of the room and changed its lens. 'Why don't you stay here?' he said as he worked.

Petrov was surprised. He stiffened warily in the chair. 'It is my duty to go back,' he said.

The surgeon shrugged. 'If I were in your place, I'd stay here.'

He examined the eye again. Petrov sat thinking about whether the man's words were scripted. Whether this was innocence or some type of structured plot. After a time, he told Beckett that something like what he was proposing would be very hard.

The surgeon reached for a pair of glasses and gave them to Petrov to sit on his nose. 'Not if you know the right people,' he said. 'It is traditional that the diplomatic corps look after other diplomats who are in difficulty.'

Petrov said nothing.

Beckett told him, 'I have friends who know about these things. You just need to be helped by the right people.'

He switched the glasses for another pair. Petrov stared at the eye chart on the wall. He wasn't sure what this was. Some kind of trick? An entrapment? Surely Beckett wasn't secretly left wing? He looked like a conservative, spoke like a conservative. No, this couldn't be a provocation. It was a lone anti-communist trying to sway him; a religious man or a naive liberal. That, or this actually was a rehearsed and orchestrated sounding, a Security agent testing him out, giving him a way to fly the coop. Beria! That had been a savvy thing to drop.

'What do you think?' Petrov said. 'Should I fly with these eyes?'

Beckett sat the pen-light in his coat pocket. 'If you still have the complaint, we shouldn't risk it.'

Petrov asked for a note to that effect. The surgeon gave him one, as well as another round of pills. He put both slowly in his briefcase, waiting to see if the man had anything further to say. It didn't seem so.

On the street, he examined the parked cars. If Beckett was a Security agent, maybe one of these cars would have a man inside, someone to follow him on his way out. He couldn't see anyone. After a time, a taxi came slowly down the street and he hailed it. He asked the driver every now and then to make a wayward turn, looking back to see what traffic followed. Nothing seemed in pursuit.

He examined the taxi itself, searching for irregular markings. It wasn't an improbable idea: the Security service fashioning a cab and putting it in the right place to pick him up. The car was a Chrysler Plymouth. They wouldn't even need to fashion it. Easier to hire a real taxi and switch the driver. The man was middle-aged with a moustache, staring at him in the rear-view mirror. Perhaps it was the way he was behaving. Perhaps it was the scratches on his face from the car crash. He smiled to himself, but at the same time the situation was deadly serious.

He stopped the cab four blocks from the hotel. There was a pub on the corner. He sat at the edge of the bar, drinking with his back to the wall.

Later, he sat on the bed looking at the articles from his suitcase. He'd just now unpacked them, one by one: his shirts, his toothbrush, a comb, some slippers, his razor, his gloves. He was having a strange feeling about them. It felt as if they were sudden impostors in his life, his personal belongings, resting before him on the bed. The toothbrush had bent and yellowed bristles. The comb had scratches at one end. These might have been intimate markings, engravings of his. But they weren't. He'd lost his connection. That, or these objects had lost their rapport with him. They belonged to someone else. Anyone else. They weren't just unfamiliar but ominously so. He sat there wondering seriously whether it wasn't some product of capitalism. These were Australian things: these cufflinks, for example, bought in Melbourne almost two years ago. But perhaps not. The Russian things—his camera, his watch— these had the contagion as well.

The city beckoned at the window. He refilled his scotch and stared out. The bodies below were easily seen: night walkers, couples glowing with confidence, a father and son, two women crossing the street, coming too close to his window and disappearing from view.

He thought about changing hotel rooms. He thought about changing hotels. He needed a heavy dose of the erratic. If there was a corollary to the idea that your world was being organised by outside forces, it was that random, fitful turbulence could re-establish reality. If you moved fast enough, you reinstituted the sanity it took to judge things by appearance alone.

Shadows like fluid. He rammed the whisky bottle in his coat pocket, went downstairs and darted from the front entrance of the hotel. The first pub he came to had a side door and a back door and he used both in succession. This led him to a laneway. He made a complete circle back onto the street and got into a taxi that had just emptied.

'Kings Cross,' he told the driver.

He alighted outside a dimly signed pub and went in. He fished out coins for beer. The pub smelled more than was ordinary, bitter, a fog of cigarette haze. Men wore overalls, hadn't shaved, looked like weather-hardened, dependable types. He sat this time at a table, ignored.

Perhaps Doosia would die. She sometimes became ill; sudden frailty striking that body of hers. Loyalty was an awful feeling, uncomfortable. Acid under his skin. Were he alone, he could be on the farm in a week. Leave the embassy a suicide note, put together a new life that was simple, sunstruck, dirt-laced. But even without Evdokia's blood ties—her mother and sister—he wasn't sure reasoning would convince her. She was too proud; the revolution's child.

He thought about Beckett, musing on the identity of his contacts. Men of secret authority who could be trusted. The noise in the pub was men in conversation, no music, no radio.

Men talking and joking with one another. Relaxed. At rest. Not caring what they said.

He stared deeply into the near space, trying to imagine Moscow at this time of year. He couldn't.

15

Summer declared itself, a week of warm stillness, shocking almost, the sun's heat and the way the suburb became a thing for catching it. In the evenings, hoses appeared in front yards and on the nature strips, black snakes with fountain heads. Evdokia took Jack for dusk walks and the dog drank from leaking taps at the new housing development, a paddock overtaken to house government workers, dirt and sand in mounds. The fridge at Lockyer Street made terrible noises.

At the embassy, everyone complained. Generalova carried ice blocks in a towel and made sure that all the curtains were drawn and the windows shut. On the secret floor, she delegated the task to Prudnikov. The gardeners put off their work till the evenings. From the third day onwards, the embassy children were taken to the swimming pool at Manuka, a facility that was open air but hidden inside a building that looked more like a library or a government office.

Generalov was still threatening to make Volodya pay for

the Skoda. Hundreds of pounds. The car was technically owned by the Foreign Ministry, but the ambassador must have known it was secretly an MVD asset. They knew that Vislykha, as Evdokia's replacement, would do everything she was told; there would be no hesitation in making deductions from Volodya's pay.

Husband and wife had a strange conversation. Volodya told her there were farms on the outskirts of Sydney, good places where the earth could be worked, places not so far from the great city and the centre of things. He talked about farming practices in Larikha, before the collectives, how his father had been the slaughterman, known in the district for his deftness with knives. She looked at him carefully and asked why he was telling her this; what did he mean to suggest?

'Nothing,' he said.

'Your hands are shaking.'

'It's just nerves.'

That Saturday, Masha told her that Pipniakova was saying amongst the women that Vladimir had been drunk when he crashed the car. It was not a ground-breaking piece of analysis. Evdokia went to bed alone that evening and woke with a sudden determination to turn things around. She worked all Sunday, an electric fan going in the lounge room, poring over her handbooks of Party rules. She laid out their defence against the accusations that were destroying them: the Beria faction, the splitting of the collective, the petition of support for the charges that she knew was doing the rounds. She stood and read aloud their testimony. She was at some imagined hearing, a Party meeting in Moscow that followed official procedures, where they would be allowed their fair say. She called Generalov jealous. She said Lifanov was a pitiful, vindictive fool. The staff at the embassy were cowardly, afraid to engage in opposition to the ambassador's hopeless rule. She wrote these things on paper and spoke them aloud until she had committed them to heart. She hoped that the MVD would intervene. In fact, she began to trust that it would. No matter who controlled it, she thought, the fearful implement of Felix Dzerzhinsky, faced with her declarations, would simply have to save them.

Moscow's continuing silence was altogether uninterpretable. At times she was convinced they properly saw the goings-on as trivial. Then she was certain they were preparing a prison cell or worse.

Volodya had sent his cable, asking for a delay in his travel for the sake of his poor eyes. She saw Prudnikov every afternoon and each time he shook his head.

Lemon or chemicals approximating the idea. It was a Sunday morning, weeks later, and she had her hands in soapy water washing the breakfast plates. There was the noise of a vehicle in the drive. She listened. Volodya was in the lounge with the newspaper and, as things stood, she expected him to jump up to check with paranoid vigour who had arrived. He didn't. He must have known which visitor was at hand.

Bialoguski. He was wearing a suit and looked sweaty about the face.

'Doctor,' said her husband falsely. 'I didn't know you were in town.'

Beer and biscuits. They sat first in the lounge but quickly shifted outside.

'I'm just visiting a specialist,' Bialoguski said. 'A cardiac man who sees patients of mine.'

He produced a white handkerchief and wiped his brow. Opening a bag, he gave Evdokia chocolates and Volodya cigarettes. He told them he'd stopped at Civic. He had a habit of tapping things. He made adjustments to his tie. She knew there was a purpose behind his presence. They talked and she waited for the agenda to emerge.

'Vladimir says you have lost your job, Evdokia. As a result of this clique at the embassy?'

'Yes,' she said, unable to prevent herself vilifying Generalova, complaining that the woman couldn't dress and was piggishly overweight, an uneducated and dimwitted peasant unfit to represent the Soviet Union at a children's picnic. She said the women at the embassy were envious of her own personality, her confidence with fashion, her ability to socially interact.

'Perhaps they fear for their husbands,' the doctor said, and smiled.

'Their husbands are bastards,' said Volodya.

Evdokia took the spare cigarette the doctor was offering, lighting hers from his.

'And perhaps you will be called home?' he said. 'That must be a frightening thought?'

She looked at him. He and Volodya had obviously been speaking.

'Frightening? No.'

'You aren't afraid? My impression is there is some uncertainty.'

'I don't know about that. I would look forward to going back even if they were to hang me.'

The doctor gave the appearance of surprise. It was the appearance of surprise because she was certain he was the type of man for whom the emotion was impossible.

'You don't like this country?' he asked.

'It has been bad for us.'

Volodya stood suddenly. He hoisted his belt and whistled to Jack. The dog came and both went mysteriously inside.

Bialoguski was forward on his seat, fingers locked. 'Why don't you stay here?' he said.

For an instant she thought he was talking about the porch. When she realised he meant Australia, she was taken aback. She felt a touch of anger. She hardly knew this man. Why would he come to their house and suggest such a thing?

'You shouldn't talk like that,' she said. She wanted the rebuke to be stern but it came out like a whisper, her voice weak and almost consoling.

The doctor gave a half-shrug. He asked about her family's health. It was a tactic, she knew, but she talked with him for a time about her mother and sister.

'What of your father?' asked Bialoguski. 'He is well?'

'He is,' she lied, wanting to kill the topic.

Bialoguski was nodding, eyebrows arched. What was Volodya doing, leaving her out here with this man? She ashed her cigarette and decided, for safety's sake, that she must leave Bialoguski in no doubt. She began by telling him that the capitalist imperialist system robbed its workers, that its heart was dark and corrupt, that it enslaved its inhabitants and its fellow nations, warmongering to satiate its consumptive lust. The peaceful coexistence of the capitalist system and the socialist system was an impossible dream. Even in the face of what she had seen in the west, the ideas of Marx, Lenin and Stalin held true. Peace was propaganda pushed by the forces of capitalism as cover for their inexorable aggression. History's march was as inevitable as death. Marx had repaired Hegel's dialectic and she believed in this triumph like others believed in God. She told him that war and capital were one and the same.

He was staring at her. This type of speech was a deeply harboured impulse that she could easily set off. She thought she had impressed on him her loyalties. Not left him in the grip of any ambiguous ideas.

Volodya came back. He sat between them on a chair, opened another beer. She thought it a safe assumption that he had been somewhere close and listening.

The doctor stayed for lunch and left for Sydney mid-afternoon. She followed Volodya to the writing bureau. He shuffled papers as they spoke.

'He should be more careful, the doctor, about what he says,' she told him.

'Oh, he's alright. He's clever.'

'Tell him it is dangerous, such talk.'

'He's ours. An agent. He is discreet.'

'Tell him not to visit anymore.'

'I don't control him, Doosia. I don't tell him what to do.'

'Was that a provocation on the porch just now?'

'I've forgotten what I'm looking for. What am I looking for?'

'Volodya?'

'Have you seen that child recently? What is her name? Mirabel.'

She put her thumb in his belt and tugged. 'Are you listening? I'm trying to talk to you. What if he's asking Pakhomov these same things? Probing where he shouldn't. Everyone at the embassy knows you and he are close.'

'They don't.'

'What do you suppose the cable to Moscow will say if someone overhears that kind of talk?'

He was flipping through a receipt book, playing at being absorbed.

'Well?' she pressed.

'I'm going to walk across the street. The father will probably be repairing something in his garage. The people in this place have it good but they are still resourceful. I'll ask him about Mirabel.'

'Why are you being like this?'

He turned to leave.

'Volodya,' she said, emptily.

'Why am I being like what?'

Moscow sent their reply. The first paragraph said his immediate recall was off. All air travel was cancelled on account of his health. His heart pumped in his neck. The second paragraph said they were dispatching his replacement, Lieutenant Colonel Evgenii Kovalenok. He was coming by ship and would arrive in April. There would be a two-week handover and, following this, the Petrov residency would end. He and his wife were to purchase tickets from the Orient Line for a date in keeping with these plans.

He lit a cigarette using the lighter from the burn tray. He read the letter again and then vomited. Matter hit the desk edge, went somewhat in his bin. The cigarette fell to the floor, still smoking. He sat doubled over for a time.

When they had been told to leave Sweden, Evdokia had cried. She'd loved Stockholm, had friends in the embassy. He had been more concerned about what might happen to them upon their return. Workers stationed in foreign places weren't ever quite trusted again. To his surprise, they were promoted. Better jobs and a better apartment. This time, who knew what might occur. It wasn't only the Beria accusation. He had a firming sense that Moscow Centre had been following him somehow, seeing for themselves what he was up to in Sydney; that they knew of the money-making practices that he engaged in. There were people who could organise his shadow. Kislitsyn, most obviously. Pakhomov as well. How sure could he be that Kislitsyn hadn't betrayed him? The man was on their side against the ambassador and Kovaliev—was this because he knew of some awful fate and had MVD orders to keep the quarry calm? How were he and the Centre communicating? A special channel somewhere? A direct line to Kislitsyn at home? The man was a bastard. You couldn't trust a soul.

He sank into his chair and wiped his mouth with a handkerchief.

His wife's voice sounded in the corridor. She was speaking to Prudnikov; in the next few seconds she'd be with him in this room. His eyes met with the MVD safe against the wall. It was locked, the key with Prudnikov, stuck in an envelope pressed closed with the MVD's wax seal. A much smaller strongbox sat on top of the safe, used to store odds and ends as well as the MVD's cash float. Two keys existed for this second box. One was carried in Evdokia's pocket, one was carried in his own.

An idea was slowly dawning. He looked at the filing drawer where they kept the blank destruction certificates. It was almost time to destroy 1952. This was a security practice for stations abroad: burn all traces of everything after the passing of one year. Moscow's orders, lists of agents, anything incriminating that had fallen into operational disuse. As MVD chief resident, the destruction of the documents was his job. Incinerate them in front of a witness, provide receipt of the act to Moscow in the form of a certificate of destruction.

He looked at the first safe and at the strongbox. Evdokia was just outside now and he tried to prepare himself for the transmission of the news.

Bialoguski had a small tin mug, army surplus from his time with the Auxiliary Medical Corps. Each day, shaving, he filled the mug with boiling water to clean the razor blade. Today, furious again with Security, he had to concentrate hard not to let the blade cut his skin. Michael Howley had just told him about Beckett. That the ophthalmologist was suddenly ASIO's man.

'What do you mean, your man?'

The conversation had taken place in Howley's Austin by the rear fence of a fuel station.

'We took your advice,' his controller had said. 'Looked to recruit an eminent Australian. Beckett put the idea of defection to Petrov more or less directly. By the Soviet's response, Beckett doesn't think the chances are too bright.'

'Beckett!'

'That's right.'

'Beckett's a fool.'

'He's eminent. We think he's an obvious contact for Petrov to trust.'

'When I said eminent, I meant public profile.'

'We know what you meant.'

'I should be consulted in these things. Better the connection comes through me than Beckett! What's Beckett?'

'We thought it best.'

'We-we-we.'

He did cut himself. A dash of blood appearing and the searing touch of cream. Of course, he knew why they'd gone with Beckett. He was one of them: a WASP. Unlike Russian-speaking Polish emigrants, who were on a basic level untrustable and more or less enigmatic when they did succeed, Security were able to picture in their numbskull minds Beckett's competencies and where his loyalties would lie.

Damn this country. Ten years he'd been here and he'd never asked for charity. He'd roomed at the YMCA, sold his shirts to pay the rent, slept in Hyde Park when the shirts ran out. He'd found himself session work playing music for the ABC; attempted to join the army, was rejected as a non-British subject, was accepted a year later once the war was looking bad. At Cowra, the boys called him Bill for Bialoguski and knew he was more than prepared to fight. The army saw his intelligence and got him sent to the 113th General Hospital, Concord West, where he mopped floors for a month before applying for medical training at the University of Sydney, which was the one thing Australia had given him for which he felt he owed something. In retrospect, those had been good days, living hand-to-mouth on his repatriation subsidy, studying nights in a small room, separate and locked away, working under an electric lamp, sleeping at dawn with an eye mask and rising for breakfast at 4 p.m.

'Is Petrov as keen as you've attested?' Howley had asked.

'He's right on the edge.'

'I sat near him in the Buckingham's bar.'

'And how did he look?'

'Anxious.'

'To use one of these phrases,' Bialoguski had said, 'I think he is showing obvious signs of strain. I should lead him harder. Why don't we use against him some of the things we know?'

'That's a political mistake.'

'It doesn't have to be public. What's the use of your organisation if you can't do the secret things we don't need to see?'

'You may have to let him go. Develop a distance. Let Petrov do this on his terms.'

'First you don't know if he's keen; now you're talking about terms.'

'Stay close but distant. Provide the room he needs.'

'How long do we let it take?'

'It's not up to us.'

'The timing is a necessary concern.'

Howley had given him spare reels for the recorder. 'There's a view amongst the heads that this should be your last operation. After this defection, the idea is that you and the organisation go in separate, friendly ways.'

'The bonus you mentioned.'

'That would be a facilitating step.'

'I keep detailed diaries. I write everything down, and this will aid my recall. I'm going to be called upon to discuss this. I want to become an elemental part of this event. This is my ticket if we're going to end on happy terms.'

'Let's concentrate on now.'

'Why don't we start by keeping me informed.'

'Where is he now?'

'He arrived yesterday. He's in bed.'

'Sleeping unaided?'

'What's that supposed to mean?'

'People are questioning your methods. It's my job to relay the message that you're not to produce bodies by unethical means.'

'Petrov is my patient. I'm his doctor, bound by an oath I take seriously.'

'Take him to the farm again.'

'Perhaps. It's rather up in the air now as to what is the best way to proceed.'

He dried the razor using paper towel. In the kitchen, Petrov was at the refrigerator, wearing pyjamas.

'Vladimir,' Bialoguski said, 'we should pay that deposit today. On the farm. On Dream Acres. What do you think?'

Petrov looked at him, holding a dish of butter. 'That can wait,' he said.

'They want a date, Max and Eleanor. We should be careful. We don't want them looking for another buyer.'

The Russian put the butter on the bench. 'The third of April,' he said. 'That would be the best day to effect the sale.'

Bialoguski opened the bread bin. He looked at the way Petrov's belly hung low, almost out of his clothes. 'The third of April? That is a very specific date.'

'I have been told my posting is to end,' the diplomat explained.

'In April?'

'That's right. Doosia and I are scheduled to return.'

'Oh,' he said slowly. He suddenly wasn't sure what to add; went to say something but lost it on the tip of his tongue. Howley's fault. All these instructions were ruining his natural game. 'Is this helping Evdokia with her opinions?' he eventually said.

'You must come again and talk her into it,' Petrov pleaded. 'It's no use coming from me.'

Bialoguski decided that he was tired of this. It was time to throw Security's caution to the wind, make a move and force something.

He stood by the front door with his jacket and satchel. 'I have a patient now at the surgery, but I'm seeing Doctor Beckett at his home this afternoon. I think you should join us.'

'Beckett?'

'Yes. We meet every now and again. We're colleagues. Really, I insist. Actually, he might be someone who can help you. He has friends in important places. Important government people.'

He left Cliveden without waiting for Petrov's response and drove straight to Darling Point Road. Beckett's mansion was at the top end, a white structure with a hedge that was browning in places, an incredible spot to live really, the view towards Blackburn Cove and Double Bay. He caught the man in the front yard, just getting into his car.

'Michael,' Beckett said, surprised.

'Doctor.' Bialoguski extended a hand. 'It's a beautiful morning, is it not?'

'It is.'

'I believe you've lately met a friend of mine. A Mr Howley.'

Beckett looked at him blankly. Surely, Security hadn't told Beckett about Petrov without filling in the nearby blanks?

'Startling, isn't it?' said Bialoguski. 'I suppose you thought I was a man of the rabid left?'

It was a relief to see Beckett eventually nod. The ophthalmologist took him indoors to a small library where medical texts and volumes of poetry adorned the shelves. They sat and Bialoguski gave a briefing on Petrov's state of mind: fearful, mutable, haphazard. He said he would bring Petrov here this afternoon. Beckett would openly suggest personal and financial protection.

'Here?' asked Beckett.

'Yes. It is important for you to present yourself in a certain way. As a Russian, he responds to strength and boisterousness. Be a kindly man of broad tolerance. Talk to him of your friend in Security.'

'Shouldn't I speak with Mr Howley about this?'

'No. We can control this situation. Petrov and I are close friends, as you know.'

Beckett seemed uncertain.

'It will be alright,' said Bialoguski. 'Right now he is in a terrible spot. He has been recalled for April. He can't trust a soul at his embassy. I assure you, it is not a paranoid situation but very real. You and I will be the men of his salvation.'

'Well.'

'We won't use the word "defection". We will tease him out with the idea of "asylum" instead.'

'I'd prefer to speak with Mr Howley.'

'There's no time. I'll bring Petrov this afternoon. What alcohol do you have in the house?'

'Are you sure, Michael?'

Bialoguski stood. 'This is agent work, Doctor. This is the fundamental difference between men such as Mr Howley and men like you and me. The spymasters and the spies. Our actions are the real world. Theirs are something else. Abstractions. Literatures. Our relations are lived while theirs are theoretical. Do you understand? You are new to this, but already I see great talent.'

Beckett said nothing.

Bialoguski went on: 'When he arrives, greet him firmly. We will sit here in the library. I will make play of asking for your discretion. You are his doctor and we can explain the rules about that.'

'I'll use the word "asylum".'

'That's right. That's exactly the idea.'

'What else?'

'What else? You're a gambler. Use the racetrack as a preliminary base. Chat about your winnings. Tell him you have wealthy and influential friends. Ask him what he might turn himself to, vocationally, should he stay. Use his own fantasies of freedom against him. Don't mention anything about his wife.'

16

Sydney and its lunchtime crowd. He felt nervous amongst this blended array. He crossed from Macquarie Street into the Botanic Gardens. The grass was spongy underfoot. He wore his long coat and hat. He went and sat on a bench by Governor Phillip's statue, pigeons gathering at his feet, the sun high overhead. Thoughts of the car crash haunted him: metal lurching with that sudden, surprising momentum that comes of no control; pictures in his mind of the car's flip. Negative images, half-witnessed. He couldn't be sure if they were invented or real. He wanted them to be true. It upset him to think his near death could occur without conferring on him a memory or some form of life-altering insight, however small. Caving steel, breaking and rippling glass. There had to be something there to seize on and use.

He wasn't going to the gulag. He knew that much because he knew what happened in those prisons and it wasn't a fate he would stand. For two years when he first arrived in Moscow, he had helped manage the messages for the camps. Hundreds of installations across the Soviet Union, communicating in code, humming with corrective noise. They called it 'the zone'; names such as Vorkuta and Norilsk, the people's collective dread. He sat listening to the voices: the camp administrators wanting more guards, more help, reporting their progress in economic terms—lengths of railway, tonnages of timber and rock; reporting the names and numbers of the dead, prisoners starved, shot, beaten by guards, prisoners stabbed, beaten by one another. It was Petrov's job to supervise twelve cypher clerks in the tiniest of rooms. They encrypted notifications about impending arrivals, timetables and schedules, changes to camp regulations. The worst traffic was the lists: manifests of names, numbers, birth dates, years served. Only the most common of names had a shorthand in the codebook. The rest, cyphered, had to be onerously enclosed in a spell/endspell. It wasn't their job, as clerks, to ask if securing the transmissions was really necessary. Personally, Petrov suspected it was simply a quiet statement, a nuance on top of the terror. One of the clerks was Byelov, a large Ukrainian who was sent away to replace an operator at one of the camps. He telegraphed his colleagues a note about the ferocity of the winter there: *Ground so frozen no one is buried. Stacked instead like wood. Waiting for thaw to be given SPELL G-R-A-V-E-S ENDSPELL.*

It was this message that Petrov recalled now, walking from the gardens to the chemist, buying a packet of aspirins, taking three. The sun had him feeling queasy. He started thinking about Beckett. Should he go on this visit? Maybe he would ask Beckett about his helpful friends. Would there really be any harm in asking? Couldn't he ask just to ask? If Moscow got word of things—though he couldn't see how they would—he could simply say he was exploiting Beckett for counter-espionage information. Of course! He should have seen that all along. Wasn't it the genius of his position? That he could play at being as interested as he liked? It would be comforting, in any case, simply to know where Beckett lived.

Bialoguski drove them to the house after lunch. He was surprised at its size, an enormous place, two storeys with a veranda and balcony, and he felt suddenly that Beckett was a more important man than he'd given him credit for; perhaps the ophthalmologist's associates really were the 'right people'.

Beckett met them at the car. 'How are you chaps, alright?'

He was wearing a white shirt, shorts and sandals. They all shook hands. Bialoguski fished four bottles of Bell's Special from his Holden and made a display of giving them to Beckett. Petrov thought Beckett's foyer bigger than all the rooms in Lockyer Street combined. The house had a private library. They sat there and quickly drank beer to knock some of the heat out of themselves before switching to things harder.

Beckett talked keenly about sport. Petrov nodded along, not understanding the specifics but following each tale's gist. The man owned part of a racehorse with a syndicate. The syndicate had gone sailing down the coast to Merimbula last Christmas. Christmas off Merimbula wasn't quite the frozen affair that Christmas in Russia presumably was, no?

He laughed where he was supposed to. He accepted a gin and tonic. He accepted an English brand of cigarette. Bialoguski and Beckett chatted. Their various discussions seemed to end always with a friendly jibe against his country,

its leadership, its struggle. They were inviting him to partici-
pate, he knew.

Eventually, Bialoguski said, 'Halley, did you know that Vladimir
has been given his final orders? He is to go home soon.'

Beckett looked across at Petrov. 'How are you feeling about
that, Vladimir, your tour coming to an end?'

His tour.

'I'm still in contact with some friends, you know,' Beckett
went on. 'Very much so.'

Petrov was careful not to respond directly. 'Let's have
another of these gin and tonics,' he told them.

An hour passed before the question arose again. They'd
talked music, they'd talked movies, they'd talked new surgeries
that Beckett wanted to pioneer.

'What do you think, Vladimir?' said Bialoguski. 'Should
Halley give his friends a call? It could be something best done
in business hours.'

Beckett nodded. 'Yes, that would likely be convenient for
them.'

'Let's wait,' said Petrov. 'Let's keep drinking first.'

They filled his glass.

'I suppose it's a serious thing, isn't it?' said Beckett. 'It is a
difficult step to take.'

'Not so difficult,' snapped Bialoguski. 'Possibly, the easiest
thing.'

'I mean the decision,' explained Beckett. 'The step itself is
simple, but the decision must be grim.'

'Liberating, I'd say,' the doctor countered. 'Quickly so.'

Petrov felt himself getting increasingly nervous as the men
talked. The ice in the gin licked his lips and the fumes filled
his nostrils. He found himself a cigarette and had to clamp his

hands hard over the lighter. Bialoguski's voice seemed to be dominating the whole room.

He knew he was going to do it. He was going through with the phone call whatever happened. It's just so I know whether I have an out here, or no.

He waited for silence. 'Maybe we will call your friends, Doctor Beckett.'

'Do you mean now, Vladimir?'

'Yes, why not.'

The man leaned forward in his chair. 'There's one friend in particular who I think could help you. A Security chap. A good man.'

'Yes, let's call him.'

Beckett nodded. He went to a bureau against the wall, lifted a handset to his ear and dialled a number. Petrov and Bialoguski sat watching.

'Hello. I would like to speak to Mr Howley, please.'

They waited. Howley, Petrov thought. Not a name that rings a bell. He tried to picture the faces of the men from Melbourne, the followers, wondering if one of these was Mr Howley. Or was he somebody else on the borderlines of the familiar, the man across the room at any of the cafés he frequented, the man smoking in a hotel lounge, the man posing as a repairman, a council worker, anyone.

'It's Halley Beckett. Listen, I have two friends here who want advice. One is a doctor friend of mine. Can you, quite unofficially of course, give me some advice as a gesture of our friendship? They want to get certain assurances of protection and security in connection with a serious step one of them is considering.'

They weren't able to hear the other voice on the line.

'Yes,' said Beckett. 'He is quite serious in his intention.' Beckett listened and then looked at Petrov directly, curling the handset from his mouth. 'Do you want to see this Security chap officially?'

He didn't say yes, but he nodded.

'Yes, he wants to meet a Security man officially. He will want credentials, and assurances as to safety, security, protection, etcetera. He wants you to understand that it is a most serious step he is considering taking.'

Beckett listened again. He said that the Security man was prepared to meet and asked Bialoguski, not Petrov, what time was best and where.

'Ten tomorrow morning,' he told Howley. 'Flat number nine, twenty-two Wolseley Road, Point Piper. That's right . . . Yes . . . Yes, I suppose there's no harm you knowing the doctor's name. It's Bialoguski. Yes, he has a phone number. What is your number, Michael? Yes, it's FM 3940.'

And the phone was cradled.

'He says he will meet you there, Vladimir. And he will keep his knowledge of the appointment completely confidential.'

They drank on for another hour. Petrov knew they were trying to settle him. His arms were hot. He felt short of breath. He ran water over his face in the bathroom. He believed it but still it was somewhat unbelievable, what he'd just done. The clock reached six and he didn't feel at all like eating. He asked for beer. He said he was tired of these sticky drinks and wanted something plain.

Bialoguski told him to relax. Said he'd find it easy tomorrow morning, told him he'd be there to be sure it went alright.

Manna from heaven. Howley rang B2 and informed him of the news. B2's voice betrayed his excitement. They read the protocol sheet together—insurance, Howley supposed, and a guarantee they were on the same page.

Colonel Spry was notified. Cabin 12 was put into immediate effect. The two fresh safe houses Howley had scouted went on the activation list. All calls were to be logged and minifon spools checked and archived.

The night outside was a collapsing wall of heat. Howley armed his briefcase with a draft request for political asylum. He and B2 had small debates about questions they'd been dreaming of for years. Should he wear a minifon to the meeting? No; tell Bialoguski to wear his instead. Should he take cash with him? No; make the offer; tell Petrov the final amount depends on what he can produce.

Howley rehearsed what he might say. He pictured himself photographed by the surveillance team that he was considering bringing along to surround the flat.

Beckett called again. Petrov and Bialoguski had just now left for the doctor's flat.

'Describe the mood,' said Howley.

Beckett told him Petrov was a certainty. He was anxious, breathing with a brick on his lungs and in a cold sweat. He'd been drinking heavily. On his way out he'd told Beckett, 'They could easily shoot me,' then delivered a bullet to his temple by means of an imaginary gun.

Howley disconnected and gave a moment's thought to ramifications. If Petrov was genuine, they were talking the world stage. An international shockwave heading from the west to beyond. A political and intelligence victory of as yet undefined proportions.

Bialoguski rang from somewhere, his voice hushed and somehow out of Petrov's earshot, saying the recorder would be available for collection that night from the boot of his car.

Howley went to Cliveden and stood in the darkness. The underground garage had the smell of metal, concrete and oil. He pocketed the wire from Bialoguski's recorder.

The next morning, John Lynd and Leo Carter came to Howley's office. He briefed them and they drove three cars to Wolseley Road. The morning was calm and the sky open, and the men took position around the building, watching a group of women and children walking to the bus stop at the end of the street.

They were in place when the taxi arrived at 9.46 a.m. Petrov appeared from the underground garage, walking for the cab while still getting into his coat. The car drove south. Lynd and Carter stayed on guard while Howley went upstairs.

'What's he doing?'

Bialoguski had opened the door still buttoning his shirt. 'Embassy business,' he said.

'How's that?'

'I don't know. Something about obtaining Italian visas for couriers. I told him you were an important man. Not someone to disappoint.'

'Is he coming back?'

'Twelve o'clock, he said.'

They waited outside. An hour passed. Howley sent Lynd in one of the cars to the Italian consulate. A minute later, Bialoguski came down.

'He's called. He says it's unlikely he'll be back in time to meet. He has a plane booked to return to Canberra at three. He is not sure whether there will be time before then.'

Howley looked up and down the street. 'He still wants to meet?'

'I think so.'

For no reason they could name, they waited another ten minutes, staring up at Cliveden. Then every Security officer in the city went looking for Petrov, putting a watch on Pakhomov and visiting pubs one by one. Where was he? Howley made phone calls from the office, keeping B2 up with the news.

At 2.53 p.m., FM 3940 called. Bialoguski's voice said that Petrov would be back in Sydney on Friday, could he meet with Mr Howley then?

Howley paused. Someone was speaking Russian in the background.

'Is that Petrov who's next to you?'

'Yes. That's right.'

'Will you ask him something? Will you ask him whether he is treating this matter seriously?'

Further background conversation, rapid and intense. Bialoguski said, 'Mr Petrov just told me he is quite serious.'

'Okay.'

'He wants to meet you Friday. Here, at this flat.'

'Alright. Tell him I will meet him then.'

Hours later, Leo Carter rang from Mascot. He'd followed Bialoguski's car to the aerodrome, where he'd seen Petrov hastily board ANA flight 53 to Canberra at 6.10 p.m. Seat 12, according to the waybill.

'How did he look?' asked Howley.

'Fast.'

Bialoguski collected Petrov from the airport the following Friday. 'Beckett says that Mr Howley worries about you,' the doctor told him. 'He is concerned that you might be harmed.'

Petrov tried to suppress a nervous laugh. When they arrived at Cliveden, Bialoguski asked him if they should call Security straightaway.

'Is there any scotch?' he said.

He turned off the lights in the lounge room and paced there for a time. He kept thinking of the things that could go wrong. He tried to sit. He walked from one side of the room to the other, realised his face was sticky with sweat.

It was they who had betrayed him. It was they who had done the betraying and the consequences were theirs to bear.

'Alright,' he said. 'Let's ring him.'

Fifteen quiet minutes elapsed before a dark car pulled up in Wolseley Road. It sat silently before a man in an overcoat got out.

Bialoguski opened the door. The man was standing with a briefcase. He said his name was Michael Howley. He shook Bialoguski's hand, then Petrov's. Petrov attempted a greeting. What came out was a low cough.

They sat looking at one another. Bialoguski turned on the radio. They listened to the racing results from Flemington. Howley—if that was his true name—opened a leather pouch on his knee. 'Well,' he said. 'Should we establish something?'

Petrov had decided the appearance was perfect. The face, the blandness. Exactly the image of how the enemy Security man should be. He felt himself wanting to trust Howley already.

'Let's establish a certain fact,' Howley said. 'You want to see me officially. You have asked to see me. You are doing this voluntarily.'

There was no harm now. Just sitting with this man in this room had put him well past the point.

'That's right,' Petrov said. 'An official meeting. The reason is in connection with my staying in Australia.'

The man passed him the pouch. It was an identity document. 'I am authorised,' he said. 'I am empowered by the Commonwealth to deal with these matters.'

'Alright.'

'I think you should say it. It's best that you say it directly.'

Petrov kept hold of the pouch. He looked at Bialoguski and then back at the man. 'I want to stay in Australia. Can you tell me, what would be your country's position?'

The man gave a nod. 'I am authorised to offer you political asylum.'

'Asylum?' He laughed nervously again. A thing that just came out.

'That's right,' Howley said. 'Physical protection. A new identity. A sum of money to get you started.'

'How much money?' interrupted Bialoguski.

'No,' said Petrov. 'How much protection?'

Howley told him arrangements were in place. Safe locations prepared, trusted men who could be relied upon, deliberate men armed with guns and experience. Protection for as long as was needed. Years if that was the case. If he asked for asylum he would have it. He would be provided with money to start himself in business. To purchase for himself a house and a car. He and his wife . . . presumably his wife was seeking asylum as well?

Petrov grimaced.

'Oh,' he said. 'My wife is uncertain. She has her family in Moscow to think of. I would say she is fifty-fifty.'

Laughter once more. When he said fifty-fifty, he sounded like an Australian.

'You have discussed it?' asked Howley.

'Oh, yes. She knows the dangers of returning. I think perhaps I can bring her round.'

'Would she expose you?'

'Expose?'

'To your ambassador. Your embassy.'

He shook his head. 'That is unlikely.' He hesitated. 'Though not impossible.'

'What would happen?' asked Howley.

'If she told them?'

'Yes.'

'If they knew anything of this, they would shoot me.'

Silence.

'How much money?' Bialoguski said again.

Howley looked at him. He said it was difficult to say. It might depend on the nature of any business Mr Petrov wanted to start. Perhaps somewhere in the orbit of ten thousand pounds.

The doctor nodded. 'And the costs for protection? Of course Mr Petrov is not expected to pay for these.'

Howley leaned back. 'Tell me, Bialoguski,' he said, 'what is your involvement here? In our files you are listed as a communist sympathiser. You are associated with the left wing in Sydney. With the peace movement and other radical groups. That is dangerous. Should we trust your discretion in matters as important as this?'

Bialoguski looked shocked.

Petrov laughed. 'I will vouch for him,' he said. 'I will say he is alright.'

'Are you certain?'

'Yes. The doctor is a good man. He is just looking out for my rights.'

Howley smiled. 'Alright,' he said. 'Now, of course, in return for asylum . . .'

'Yes,' said Petrov. 'I know what it is you want. I will tell you about the Soviet government. The work in this country they are carrying out.'

'That will interest me greatly.'

'Yes.'

'That is what I would like to know.'

'And I will tell you. After I have come.'

'Can you give me any idea of what I can expect to learn?' Howley asked. 'I may have to make special arrangements if your information or story is of great importance to me.'

Petrov knew the underlying question was whether or not he was MVD. 'I know your position,' he said. 'I can tell you what you want to know.'

Howley pressed: 'Can you tell me whether you know of any Australians who have passed on to the Soviet people information about their country that could affect its security?'

Petrov smiled. 'I don't know them all. No one does. But I know some. I will tell you what they do. Not yet, but once I have come.'

Bialoguski got up to make sandwiches. He said there was salami and cheese and no one objected. While he was in the kitchen, Howley gave Petrov a number he could ring: FL 2962. They would use codenames. Petrov would be Peter and Howley, George. Petrov took the number and placed it in his shirt.

'When will you come?' asked Howley.

'Not for a time. My successor arrives on the third of April in Sydney. I will come here to meet him. I won't go back.'

'I have the request here. The letter you can sign. Your application for asylum.'

'Hold on to it.'

'You can do this now. You can leave tonight if you would like.'

'Not yet.'

'It won't be dangerous, staying on?'

'It will be alright.'

'You're certain?'

'It will help you. In the meantime, I will get all I can for you. Things that will interest you. Physical things, documents to confirm what I have already in my head.'

The man seemed pleased. 'Of course,' he said. 'Proof.'

'That's right.'

'But you know the risks. You must decide what you will do.'

'The risks, that's right. It will be careful work. The systems are complex but there are certain weaknesses to exploit.'

'What will happen? What will your embassy do once you're across?'

He was feeling better, the nervousness departing. Control was taking its place. Really, defecting was just like running an operation, only this time he'd succeed.

'They will report it to the police,' he said. 'They will tell the police I am missing and ask their help to find me.'

'The police won't find you. We'll make sure of that.'

'Generalov will see your Minister for External Affairs and perhaps write to Mr Menzies asking where I am. The embassy will suggest I have suffered an episode of mental weakness. They will mask their attempt to locate me behind concern for my safety, an unbalanced man, sick in the head and in need of help. Once they conclude I have defected, they will accuse me of some offence. They will say I have stolen an amount of money. I have embezzled funds and am on the run. They will do anything not to make it a political event.'

'We might prepare a statement for you: "I no longer believe in communism", something to that effect.'

'Alright.'

'Can we meet tomorrow? Should we see each other somewhere and make sure the doctor isn't there?'

The voice from Flemington announced a pause for the news. Petrov's gaze went to the kitchen. 'Yes,' he said. 'I think the doctor is just looking out for me.'

They agreed to meet in the morning. When Bialoguski returned, the Security man stood to go. The doctor showed him to the door, and Howley wished them a good evening. Bialoguski killed the radio and they watched him leave from the window. The car passed beneath them and disappeared.

'Sandwiches,' said Petrov. 'We should go out. The Adria perhaps.'

'Always the Adria! Why not the Roosevelt?'

The next morning he was beset by a strange sense of unreality. Of two realities, perhaps. He was a loyal MVD officer and a loyal husband. Then he was a defector and a traitor, and now a hero to new friends. Bialoguski was the only bridge. Heading for Kings Cross, it didn't occur to Petrov that these two worlds had inevitably to meet.

The Potts Point post office was part of the Cahors building on Macleay Street. He sat in the park opposite, well back under a tree. He looked for surveillance and convinced himself that a man on the far side, who was reading while two children played in front of him on the grass, was a Security plant. Someone in the windows as well, perhaps, the Cahors building stretching nine storeys high, modern curves, a photographer with a good lens, marking him out. He felt a sudden pang of fear. What did they already know about him? What catalogue of photographs of his behaviour did they have? A rush of distrust pulsed through him.

In the very next moment, Michael Howley appeared from behind him. Completely disconcerting that he was able to sneak up. The man crossed the street, stood for a moment outside the doors of the building and went in. Petrov followed.

Surfaces of wood veneer. The lobby carpet was tan-coloured, a pattern of interlocking leaves. Howley had ascended the stairs. The two men stood silently on the first-floor landing, waiting at the shaft for the lift.

The flat on the seventh floor had a minimum of furniture. Petrov assumed there were microphones in the walls.

'Drink?' Howley asked. He was holding a fresh bottle of scotch.

'Yes, alright.'

There was no ice. They sat on a lounge and Howley handed Petrov a soft leather bag.

'Five thousand pounds,' said the ASIO man. 'I would suggest you put four thousand in the safe at the house where we will be staying, and that you keep one thousand to purchase clothes or other personal things.'

'This is for when I come?'

'For the moment you break from the Soviet Union.'

'You have that letter?'

'I'll be carrying it at all times.'

'I return to Canberra tonight.'

'Alright. I'll come with you. I'll stay there until you defect.'

No. He didn't want them on him. 'It will be alright,' he said. 'I'll come to you in Sydney. April third.'

'If your embassy becomes suspicious . . .'

'It will be alright. I can manage.'

'Won't you need a quick way out?'

'No. They are idiots at the embassy. I will get what documents I can and then I will be done.'

The man refilled their glasses. It was Bell's Special, Petrov saw. Howley pressed him again about the spies. He asked whether Petrov was prepared to say anything now.

'Yes, I will tell you something general,' he said.

'Can you tell me two things?' Howley said. 'Who are the persons in Australia who give secret information to the Soviet government? Will you be able to show me copies of the reports?'

The man's face was compelling. Petrov felt the need to confess; a divulging force taking hold in the room, microphones in the walls, an honest face wanting to know. He could see himself now. Months of this. Years. Men questioning him in solemn and eager tones, alert to the utterances and the inferences that lay behind. How long would it take them to unravel him—a life that was his life but also one of secrets that they dearly wanted to hear? He would need to form some kind of strategy for the way he would play along.

'Yes,' he said. 'I do not have the names of all of them. I know some of them. I will get copies of the reports.'

'Tell me. Who are they? Where do they work?'

'Later. Details later.'

'Are they in government departments?'

'Some,' Petrov said. 'I would say that during the war there was a very serious situation for you in the Department of External Affairs.'

225

'External Affairs men giving reports to the Soviets?'

'Yes.'

'Are they still doing it?'

'Not much now. They are very frightened.'

'They are still there?'

'One is there.'

'You know who he is? You know what he was doing in the war?'

'Yes, I know.'

'You know the Soviet official who received the reports?'

'I know.'

'Was the local Communist Party active in this?'

Petrov paused. 'Yes,' he said.

'You know the Party members involved?'

'Yes, I know.'

Howley's face remained bland. Petrov wondered whether this was news to the Australian, or did they have their own sources and so already knew? Parts of the Communist Party were Security and vice versa. The organisations leaked into one another. Unknowable. Impenetrable.

It occurred to him to ask just how many men in Security knew of his plans. Howley said it was himself and his boss, the organisation's head and a few trusted men.

'Alright,' said Petrov.

He looked at his watch, wondering if he should get an earlier flight. The other world. There was a second-hand car in Acton that Generalov was insisting he buy. He stood to go.

'My wife,' he said on his way to the door. 'If she does not stay, there can be no publicity for my story. Not until she has left Australia. They might kill her here if it is published.'

Howley hadn't moved. Was watching him from the chair.

'Do you think there will be a war soon?' he asked.

Petrov smiled slowly and opened the door.

'No, not yet,' he said, and made his exit for the hall.

17

She crossed the park between the Melbourne and Sydney buildings, Civic noticeably unpeopled, green expanses, dirt expanses, commerce in stasis, and she walked towards J.B. Young's. It was the beginning of March and the idea of home was taking on physical dimensions. Moscow. A hammered-out feeling in her stomach. She tried to picture the new apartment where her family had moved: Varsanofievsky Pereulok, dom 6, kvartira 6. Two rooms, Persian carpets on the floors. The old furniture that would be unfamiliar now, pulled from the arrangements and zones that identified it, given new and strange existence. She was bracing herself in a way. Preparing for this inconsequential shock in preference to contemplating her and Volodya's fate—a thing so arbitrary, she'd decided, it could be anything from death by vanishing to a promotion and letter of congratulations.

She stood looking at the kitchen utensils. Peelers, cutters, articles for washing up. She was putting together a chest of these items. Gifts for the most part, but also a supply of their own.

She thought about unlucky friends and colleagues, the state they'd fallen into once ejected from the Party and the ruling systems, the squalor that beset them, the manual jobs, the queuing and the struggling for basic things—shoes and eggs and an hour to sit down. Was she really going back?

She sat in the front passenger seat of Volodya's new car.

'What about Jack?' she said.

'Jack?'

'What will we do with Jack?'

'Oh.'

'You could give him away. Give him to a boy on the street.'

They were crossing the river, bending a way through Parkes.

'You don't seem worried,' she said. 'Don't you care what will happen to your dog?'

King George Terrace, parliament going by. 'Yes, I am worried for Jack,' he said. 'Jack is the most innocent victim of all.'

She looked at his hands on the wheel and the gearshift, the nervous grip she thought she saw there, the concentration etched on his face. 'Maybe you could give Kislitsyn the dog,' she said.

'I'll ask him.'

'That is what Jack needs. He's a dog for a man. It is in his breeding and demeanour. The way he thinks. How his impulses are wired. Philip will make him have more respect for things than you.'

'I'll ask.'

'He'll take him.'

'He may refuse. If he won't take him, we'll just set him free.'

She laughed. 'Set him free! We're not talking about a wolf. You think he can fend for himself?'

'No?'

'No. Impossible. If you drop him in the bush, he finds his way home. If you disappear without warning, he just waits at the house until he dies.'

That night she burned her magazines. It was a bonfire of *Home Beautiful*, the plastic smell of the thin film, wasting. The first magazine flamed and went out. She tore pages from the next, gave the flames air and they took off. Two dozen editions of *Australian Women's Weekly*. Lift-outs she'd saved from the papers. All burning between four bricks, dark and oily smoke staining the sky. She had intended to take them home, a kind of record or a history of the country over three years. But it wasn't worth the risk now, transporting contraband literature. Not much point compounding the trouble they were in.

Inside, Volodya was drinking beer, listening to the radio. She opened each of the drawers in the kitchen, trying to recall what was the ministry's property and what was theirs.

'Furniture,' she said.

'Hmm.'

'Should we sell the furniture? The things we own.'

'Give them to the Golovanovs.'

He was right. Ivan and Masha deserved everything that could be gifted. She made the list in biro.

Wool hearth rug
Small mahogany coffee table

Blue lined curtain and rod
Two-bar electric radiator
Cork tablemats
Condiments set
Brass dish and red glass dish
Pewter teapot
Waffle iron
Two asbestos mats
Stove towel
Glass nutcracker
Bed rug
Table lamp and shade
Clothes basket
Axe
Hand axe

'The things in the garage?' she said.
'What?'
'The stepladder. The pick. The shovel. The rake.'
'Those things aren't ours.'
'The hurricane lamp. The box of tiles.'
'Box of tiles?'
'The wheelbarrow and the garden hose.'
'Not ours.'
'A hand fork and a pair of shears.'
'Isn't there a catalogue? A manifest?'
'The fuel bin. Pieces of wood.'
They went to sleep late. Or she went and he stayed listening to the radio. She woke when he came to bed, the mattress sinking away, pale light like the moon on the walls. She put

her hand in his but he removed it. She listened to his breath and her own breath. It was hot under the sheets and he tossed them away. The darkness was a half-darkness. The room was the same as it had always been, but the night felt weathered and unordinary. Patterns in language and in the world.

'Volodya,' she said.

'Yes?'

'You know we will turn out like the Rosenbergs if we stay.'

Sunday. He stood on the landing in the secret section, listening for sound. Nothing. He walked to his office, unlocked the door, stood there. He went to Prudnikov's office and opened the door. The man was there, seated at his desk, staring at the mouthpiece of his telephone.

'Vladimir,' said Prudnikov.

'Hello, Petr.'

Prudnikov waved the telephone receiver. He put his finger to his lips and they walked into the hall.

'The phone,' he said. 'I have become suspicious of it.'

'Oh?'

'It drops volume at unexpected times. On other occasions, I'll be sitting there working and I swear the receiver emits a low humming tone.'

'Bugged?'

'What can we do? Can we test it?'

'Tomorrow, we'll take it to pieces carefully.'

'Okay.'

'Meanwhile, don't have conversations in your office. If it is bugged, it is more useful not to let them know we know.'

'Good, Vladimir. This is what we will do.'

The MVD chief nodded. Then he asked Prudnikov to fetch the safe key. The man went into his office and came back. Petrov told him he might be some time. Why didn't the cypher clerk enjoy the afternoon, not sit here locked up like the damned?

In his office, Petrov worked for twenty minutes before he opened the safe. The 1952 letters were kept in a marked paper sleeve. He took them to the desk and flipped through them as if looking for something. Names. Instructions. Plots and paranoias. He weighed the pages in his hand, went to a drawer, drew out a notebook and removed the covers and the spiral. He took the pages from the notebook and sat them inside the paper sleeve. He took the 1952 letters and put them in an envelope. Then he put the sleeve in the safe and locked it.

He was relieved at how calm he could be. Now you are spying, he thought. Death right here in front of you and yet your hands have stopped their shaking.

He put the envelope in the strongbox. Shoved it at the very bottom, underneath everything else in there.

This is what it means to get your life back. Documents in the wrong safe. Proof of the old life for a new life. Five thousand pounds. What was that? A farm, a car, appliances and a little left over to live.

In part, he knew it wouldn't be that simple. In part, he was certain it would be the simplest of things.

He closed the strongbox and returned its key to his pocket. Prudnikov came out from the back room looking groggy. The clerk resealed the safe key, the two men standing in silence, saying nothing for the sake of the phone.

***

He woke late the next day and had a shower, feeling lighter. He went to the back porch to dry himself and took a huge, comforting breath of garden air. It felt good to stand there naked. He sat in the chair and smoked a cigarette. He'd bought a packet of Turf, trying a new brand: 'The REAL smoke with the true tobacco taste'.

Generalov called him to his office just after 10 a.m. The man was affecting his commander's look, standing in the centre of the room, serious and domineering, as if a battalion of lives rested on his shoulders, maps of the battlefield and theatre of action on the walls.

'Comrade,' the ambassador said.

Petrov stood there silent. Soon—perhaps just a week from now—he wouldn't have to listen to this prick.

'I have received some information,' the ambassador went on.

'Information?'

'It concerns you.'

'Oh?'

'Yes. A matter of security.'

A wave of blood suddenly crossed his body.

'Someone has written to me,' said the ambassador. 'It's a note in Russian. Here. Read it.' Generalov passed the letter over.

Parts of your maps or plans are being known or disclosed, it said. *Zalivin is a very big foolish man. For this I congratulate you. With regards, KH*.

'What do you make of that?' asked the ambassador.

Petrov read it again. Zalivin, big and foolish? He had a sudden sense that it might be a code—a reference, perhaps, to him.

'I don't know,' he replied. 'Do you know this KH?'

'I have no idea,' said the ambassador. 'I think it is an anti-Soviet letter. It concerns me. I think perhaps it is related to you.'

'I don't know.'

'Maps and plans. What does that mean?'

'I would be guessing.'

'It sounds like something to do with you. Things to do with your secret work.'

'I doubt it,' he said. 'The congratulations wouldn't make sense.'

'You must take it as anti-Soviet. I think the sentence means to be ironic.'

'Perhaps.'

'More evidence of ineptitude.'

'What?'

'Maps and plans. I think your intrigues are a laughing stock, widely known.'

Petrov said nothing.

'Tell me,' said the ambassador. 'Who are the MVD's contacts in this country?'

'Who says we have any?'

'Let's not be rude.'

'I won't tell you.'

'You are trying again to be difficult. This is the function of you and your wife. Tell me who the contacts are. I may be a long time here. It is important that I know.'

'You want me to help you?'

'That's right.'

'Yet you sack my wife and turn everyone against us.'

'They turn against you by free will. Tell me the names. I can make things a step more difficult.'

'I won't tell you. The MVD is not that cowed yet.'

The argument actually relaxed him, banishing thoughts of discovery. Generalov was staring. He had one hand splayed on the table and the other behind his back. An odd position, crooked and tilting forward.

'That's all,' he said suddenly.

By the tone, Petrov knew the man was surprised. He had expected to win. He had expected Petrov to betray the names. He left the office feeling victorious. And the bastard's biggest surprise was yet to come.

He was sitting with Kislitsyn at the bar of the Kingston Hotel when he saw Michael Howley and another man come into the room. The Security men took seats on the far side of the bar and Petrov glanced at them while Kislitsyn spoke about an article he was reading on the Russification of Latvia. The two men were careful watching him, cautious about where they looked. His impulse was to join the two tables, introduce the rival services and get everyone a drink. When Kislitsyn went to the toilet, Howley gave a direct glance. Petrov acknowledged him, bought a bottle of wine from the bar, and when Kislitsyn returned he left. It was hot out, darkness coming.

Evdokia was in the lounge room with Masha, reading aloud a letter from Masha's daughter.

He opened the wine and drank.

'I'm taking Jack for a walk,' he said.

He got the dog and lit a cigarette. He walked along Lockyer, saw the man at the wheel of a car, walked up Lefroy. When the car pulled alongside, he opened the back door and Jack leaped in.

They took Blaxland Street, crossed Captain Cook Crescent and then took La Perouse.

'The outskirts,' said Petrov, joking.

'That's right,' said Howley.

Jack's huge nose sniffing at their ears.

'You're visiting Canberra?' said Petrov.

'We're worried about you. We've taken a room at the Kingston, number eight.'

'Close by.'

'Yes.'

'Who is the second man?'

'That's Mr Carter.'

'Carter should stay away. I want to be near you only.'

'Alright.'

They turned onto Carnegie, a projected road, the dirt somewhat flattened and gravelly, shifting beneath the tyres.

'How's our confidence?' asked Howley.

'I've prepared things.'

'That's good.'

'Yes, but there is one problem.'

Petrov told him about Generalov's letter. He saw Howley stiffen.

'Let's get you out now,' the man said. 'I have the request for asylum and the money in the car.'

'No, we wait for Sydney in one week.'

'Are you sure you've told no one of your plans?'

'Beckett. Yourself. The doctor.'

'What about your wife?'

Jack's breath smelled of rot. Petrov didn't answer.

'I'll drop you back,' said Howley.

'Room eight,' said Petrov.

'Yes. Ask for George.'

Stealing what didn't exist. He burned the paper sleeve marked 1952 and Evdokia signed the certificate of destruction. The real letters stayed in the strongbox. This is easy, he thought. This is something I should have done a long time ago.

He knew Evdokia was under increasing strain. She was running low of Australian pounds and he was buying all the basics.

There was another meeting of the Party. He sat there thinking, *This is the last Party meeting I'll ever attend.* Kovaliev put forth a motion commending the work of the Party women. The ambassador moved an amendment removing Evdokia from the list.

Howley met him at the corner of Blaxland and Frome, bugs and moths running derelict orbits around the street lamp. He gave the man his rifle. He wanted to bring the Remington across with him, to the other side of the curtain. He couldn't very well carry it on the plane to Sydney.

Three days to go.

Friday morning, he went to see Prudnikov about the phone.

'Comrade Petrov,' the man said strangely. There was both worry and austerity in his face. 'Last night a raid was conducted.'

'A raid?'

'Yes. The ambassador and I made a raid on the safes.'

He stood as still as possible, trying to ward away whatever was about to change.

'In your safe we found documents that should not have been there,' said Prudnikov.

You are a failure. Whatever you do, you drag yourself further towards death.

'Comrade,' Petrov whispered.

'You should be more careful, Vladimir. You've committed a bad breach of regulations.'

'Regulations?'

'Yes. Generalov waits in his office.'

He hardly moved. 'What documents are you speaking of, Comrade?'

Prudnikov shrugged. 'Oh, some memorandum you received from the Australian Communist Party. Some cables you were writing that should not be kept in a consular safe.'

Consular safe. They had raided the downstairs office. The upstairs strongbox was untouched.

He went to the ground floor and to a bathroom and wiped his face, staring at himself in the mirror for a long time.

Generalov looked smug. 'Comrade Petrov,' he said, 'keeping secret files in the wrong places?'

'An accident, Ambassador.'

'I will have to report it to Moscow.'

'Yes. Of course.'

'You admit the charge?'

'If you bring the charge, I will sign it.'

'The penalties can be severe.'

'I admit the charge. I am not afraid. I admit to charges when they are true.'

The man shrugged and Petrov left the room. He drove to the TAA office and collected the air ticket for Sydney. Kislitsyn approached him upon his return and they sat in his office, discussing the fallout of the raid.

Evdokia burst in. He saw in an instant how furious she was. It was the frustration of someone angered and then injured, a weakness shaking her voice.

'Volodya,' she said. 'Is it true?'

'It's a small breach, Doosia. A small breach and that is all.'

'A breach is a breach. And now of all times!'

'It's nothing. Moscow will see it as such.'

'Are you trying to have us destroyed? Look at you. Holding that stupid air ticket. This charge is all they need!'

He gazed at her, but not.

'You understand, then,' she said. 'Or perhaps you are trying to help? Are you finding us a better camp in the gulag by adding to the charges? You know all the best ones.'

'Doosia.'

'What do you have to say, Volodya?'

'You're angry. Alright. But don't be so loud. Don't be too loud because that is a victory and they will hear.'

She opened the door, stepped outside. Slammed it.

He got the latest copy of *Pravda* and wrapped Moscow's documents in its folds. He undid his shirt and shoved the newspaper inside, twisting his torso. No noise. He walked downstairs, passing no one. The hinges of the back gate whined. At the house, he lifted the mattress and put the newspaper underneath. It was an obvious hiding place, he knew, but he wanted to put them out of sight as fast as he could.

He opened a scotch bottle and drank. Jack was trailing him.

'What are we going to do with you?' he asked the dog. Jack said nothing. Petrov boxed his ears.

He and Evdokia did not speak when she came home. It was a hard silence and he didn't break it. Had he planned on asking her one more time? He wasn't sure. Her yelling had got to him and now he was happy to just sit and wait.

He transferred the documents to his satchel.

Next morning, Sanko was early to collect him for the airport. He dressed and wondered about things to say. He felt nothing. He ought to feel something but he didn't. He looked at Evdokia eating breakfast. Suddenly, walking out the door was the simplest of affairs. As if he was going to buy cigarettes in Manuka. Back in five.

Sanko honked from out the front. He looked at his watch, standing in the hallway with his luggage. For a moment, he almost walked into the kitchen to say goodbye. But he was afraid. Scared that whatever this confidence was, it might falter. He closed the front door behind himself and set out across the grass. Sanko lifted his things into the Zim, and he got into the front seat and the car started and Sanko did a U-turn. He dared a last glance at the house. She was standing on the porch with Jack, still in her nightgown, holding something, he couldn't be sure what, standing there watching with Jack as the car pulled away.

18

Mid-morning, but the light had an afternoon hue, wrong-shadowed and washed out, she thought, mysteriously connected to an apprehension that was lurking, a sick feeling in the house she was trying to expel. She was sitting at the small table in the kitchen, chain-smoking. A fourth cigarette and a fifth. Irina was the last time she had done this.

Someone knocked at the door. She stood slowly and stepped quietly into the hall. Two columns under the door sill. She didn't answer and the someone walked down the side of the house. Golovanov, whistling. Tending to his vegetables, she supposed.

When she woke up it was dusk. The phone was ringing and she went to answer but was too late and she would never in her life know who that was.

Friday, 2 April 1954. She made a stew with some remaining beef, some potatoes and peas from a can.

It was a restless night, passing half-dreamt, the kind of nervous sleep that suggests maybe you are becoming ill.

On the Sunday morning she met their successor, Kovalenok. The Sydney plane had arrived early, a tail wind, and she got to the embassy to find him in the MVD office. They began the process of the handover. Kovalenok was perhaps ten years her junior, dressed in a good suit, wearing thin-framed, rudimentary glasses, intelligent-looking, a courteous man, seemingly competent and at ease. The first task was to cable Moscow Centre notification of his arrival. They wrote the message quickly, using the cypher that was then signed over to his control.

Kovalenok signed for the contents of the MVD safe. They counted the money in the strongbox—two thousand, two hundred and fifty-five pounds, all correct—and he signed for this as well.

He said, 'In Sydney, your husband asked me to say he will be delayed.'

'Oh?'

'He said if he is not back today, then it will be Monday.'

'It's not surprising. He is always busy in Sydney. Likely the city will occupy you as well.'

'Yes.'

'You are taking Lockyer Street?'

'I am.'

'It is a good house. The night duty officer has a vegetable plot in the yard. Let him keep it. His turnips are good. I'm sure he will give you some in return.'

'Alright.'

She pointed to Volodya's latest reports. Kovalenok said he'd read most of them in Moscow.

She watched him examine the contents of a drawer. 'At the Centre,' she asked carefully, 'did you hear about the campaign against us?'

'Yes,' he said. 'I wouldn't worry about that. Your husband is a good man. Moscow understands the situation. They will be needing people of experience to guide things. Don't worry about any of that.'

She ate the remainder of the stew for lunch, feeling relieved, wondering whether it had been Volodya who had made that call.

Masha's daughter had had another baby. At the Highgate Café they read the letters once more. A woman at the next table muttered something about the English language, and for a few moments drinking Schweppes soda water, Evdokia looked forward again to the journey home. She was completely out of work now, having signed away the MVD responsibilities. She and Masha went to the Capitol Theatre, but found the matinee was a children's film.

The next morning, she wandered the house, not quite aimless, but unable to fix herself to a certain thing. The phone rang.

'Evdokia Alexeyevna?' It was Ivan Golovanov.

'Yes.'

'This is the duty officer,' he said.

'Ivan? I know who you are.'

'Yes, Evdokia. Listen. Have you heard from Vladimir?'

'No.'

She listened to him breathe. He sounded tired. 'Well, Generalov needs to see you. Come to the embassy. Alright?'

The ambassador was holding a copy of the *Canberra Times*. She stood in front of his desk and he asked the same question. Where was her husband? She knew Vislykha, in the antechamber, was listening. She tried to look Generalov in the face and remain composed.

'I don't know,' she told him.

'Isn't he late from Sydney?'

'Late? I don't think so. Timetables change quickly in our work.'

'He told Kovalenok he would return Sunday.'

She shrugged. 'Now it is Monday. It's one day. That is all.'

She went home and sat and thought and asked herself when he had said he'd be home. Sunday? Monday? In truth, she couldn't be sure. She picked up the phone and called Doctor Bialoguski. No answer.

Don't have killed yourself, she thought.

Masha spent the night at Lockyer Street. The next day, Evdokia was in the ambassador's office once more.

'I am fearful now,' he said. 'Vladimir is past overdue and I worry that something has occurred. Of course I remember the crash. Do you know I have premonitions? I have a foreboding. I must report your husband missing. Has he contacted you?'

'He will be back, Ambassador. Something will have him waylaid.'

'The first step, of course, is to notify Moscow. We will also ask the Australians. We will ask their government's help to find him.'

'Aren't you overreacting?'

'He is two days missing, Comrade.'

Kovalenok came into the room.

Generalov said, 'I do not want to alarm you, Petrova, but it is possible your husband has been kidnapped. We must protect you from this fate. Kovalenok will escort you safely to collect what you need, then you must stay here in the embassy where no harm can reach you.'

'Ambassador—'

'Do not argue, Evdokia Alexeyevna. We must take these precautions until your husband is found. Do you know of his plans in Sydney?'

'No, I do not.'

'We ask that you cease your enquiries.'

'What enquiries?'

'Do not attempt to locate him. Tell us what you know and we will find him.'

She got into the Zim with Sanko and Kovalenok. They drove the short way to the house. The MVD man said, 'What was his mood when he left for Sydney? Was there anything unusual?'

She replied that her husband had been happy. The man could make of that what he would.

They waited in the front yard while she went inside. The house was suddenly a strange zone, an odd smell in the rooms, particles hanging brightly in the air. She collected her clothes and toiletries, hardly thinking, grabbing at drawers and shoving things into a bag. She heard the cut of a shovel and realised Ivan Golovanov was in the backyard. He came to the window of the kitchen.

'They are taking me to the embassy,' she said.

'What do you mean?'

'I think they are making me a prisoner.'

'A prisoner?'

'Tell Masha.'

'I will.'

She needn't have appealed. The room they put her in was Ivan's—the duty officer's room with its desk and equipment cupboard. She stood and thought. She went to the telephone in the consular office and called TAA. She told them it was the Soviet embassy speaking and asked whether Vladimir Petrov had a flight booked for Canberra. He hadn't. She called ANA. The woman there knew her but said her husband wasn't listed.

Kovalenok told her Moscow had sent some questions. She sat with him in the ambassador's office and the ambassador did the asking.

'How was your relationship with your husband?'

'We were on good terms. Happy terms. There was no indication that anything was wrong. A good man. A strong man.'

'Did he pack extra clothes?'

'No. Only the usual. The ordinary.'

'What money did he have?'

'I don't know.'

'Has he ever suggested suicide?'

'I think he could easily commit suicide. That was the state he was in. Over the edge.'

'Was he looking forward to returning to Moscow?'

'We were making preparations. He was ready to go back but he was afraid of lies that were circulating.'

'Can you help locate him?'

'No. If I knew where he was, I would tell you.'

When this was done, Kovalenok took Moscow's cable and asked the same questions again, his tone slightly more comforting than the ambassador's, but she gave the same answers, too strong for the moment to slip up.

'Where is your husband now?'

Good question, she thought, trying to arrange certain facts in her mind.

'What about this Bialoguski?' said Kovalenok. 'He is friends with this man, is he not?'

'Yes.'

'Plaitkais has spoken to him. He has not been of much help.'

'I might speak to him,' she said suddenly. 'Perhaps he has seen Vladimir and will tell me.'

They booked the trunk call. Bialoguski answered. He said that Petrov was probably somewhere in Sydney, busy and somehow occupied. He would turn up. A man is not a needle.

She returned to the duty room and sat. The room had a musty, boarding-house smell. Women were outside on the lawn, talking, Pipniakova and Koslova amongst them. Were they meaning to tease her? Let's poke fun at the animal in its cage.

She drew the curtains. She felt a searing hate for everyone.

In the morning, Kislitsyn came to the duty room. They didn't have much to say to one another, him sitting there idly toying with his watch. He told her he was going to fly to Sydney. An on-the-ground search: Moscow's brilliant idea. He didn't ask about Volodya. She didn't volunteer a word.

She was hungry. Wasn't anyone going to bring her something to eat?

Not if it wasn't their job.

Koslova stopped her at the door to the kitchen.

'Evdokia Alexeyevna, are you authorised to be here?'

'I have a right to eat,' she snapped.

The woman eyed her as she cut some cold meat.

Masha brought the newspapers: the *Canberra Times* and the *Sydney Morning Herald*. Evdokia took them to the edge of the orchard and read them cover to cover, searching for anything of bearing. There had been two car crashes. In the first, a child had been dragged three hundred yards in a pram when a drunk hit a family of five. The drunk had been caught—a metal worker. In the second accident, a single car had veered from the road outside Sydney and struck a tree. Holiday-makers, husband and wife. There was a murder also, but the names of the victim and the perpetrator were known.

She looked up to see Kovalenok standing over her. He told her politely that she might be kidnapped from this spot. It would be much safer for all of them if she were to remain inside.

In return, she asked for a radio set. Sanko and Chezhev brought one and placed it in the corner of the room. She listened to the news broadcast and a drama, falling asleep on the sofa, and it was dark and raining when she woke.

Ivan Golovanov was sitting on a small chair in the hallway.

'What if I escaped through the window?' she said.

If it wasn't Golovanov guarding her, it was Chezhev. If not Chezhev, then Sanko. They sat in the hallway, a twenty-four-hour watch. She had nothing to do but read and listen. Three days passed before Generalov came. He arrived holding a pipe. She had never seen him smoke before.

'Comrade,' he said, 'I am now certain that your husband will not return.'

Stress on his face. She thought of the pressure that Moscow must be bringing to bear.

'Is that an opinion or a fact?' she asked.

He remained silent. She was half-convinced he was about to announce that Volodya was dead.

'Have you received something?' she questioned. 'Have you heard where he is?'

Generalov's gaze dropped to the floor.

'What's happened?' she demanded.

But the ambassador turned and left the room.

Later that night, Ivan Golovanov told her he'd seen a booking slip. She'd be leaving for Russia by aeroplane on the nineteenth.

19

Their first gifts to the defector were a pair of binoculars and a chessboard. At 2 a.m. he was on the couch in the lounge room of the safe house, listening to the sound of three men—Howley, Gilmour and Saburov—conversing below him in one of the downstairs rooms. He was happy with the house. It sat on a rise; a house with a rooftop veranda with cast-iron railings that looked out over a series of other roofs and then to the water. At the back of the house was a kind of uphill reserve, a darkness of trees and grass. An open area for escape, he thought. He'd spent some time that afternoon viewing kookaburras with the lenses.

He was tired now but could not sleep. It wasn't the voices of the men but those in his own mind. In truth he felt awful. The elation had long vanished and his chest was tightening.

There was a man with a gun at the front of the house and a man with a gun at the back. He wanted a gun himself but they said the government could not do that.

Kovalenok seemed alright. He'd shaken Petrov's hand and said, 'Don't worry about this rubbish with the ambassadors. When you get back to Moscow, across the frontier, every-thing will be fine.' Which Petrov understood to mean he was doomed.

His first job in the safe house had been to fake his death. He had written the note fiercely:

I have put an end to my life because in our environment the leaders, mainly, have proved themselves to be slan-derers and liars who invented various stories in order to dishonour the life of honest people. The chief slanderers were Comrades Lifanov and Kovaliev who described me as an enemy of the Soviet people. Let them bathe in my blood. Let Mr Generalov, who confirmed this, also enjoy my blood. It is a pity our collective has cringers. It is a disgrace. Against the rules etc. Let them bathe in my blood and enjoy the fact that I am not among the living.

Gilmour had taken it to Kings Cross to post and then they had given him five thousand pounds. He'd handed some over and tomorrow Gilmour was going to bring him some clothes. The rest was in the safe in the corner of this room and he had the key. Two thin bundles of notes.

Saburov was reading aloud in Russian. Petrov was worried about the translator's background: that he might have an attach-ment to the Russian Social Club. Howley had assured him he did not. He made out the word 'Sudania'—the codeword for Australia. Saburov was reading Moscow's letters. Probably they would trust the letters, come to believe in them more than in him. That was alright.

On the table in front of the couch was a beer glass. He considered going to the fridge. His first act as a defector, a free man, had been to drink two beers in a hotel bar before walking to meet Howley. By that stage he had already signed the asylum request and handed across the documents. He'd snoozed in the ASIO flat in the Cahors building. He'd met Colonel Spry, the head of Security, who had impressed him: a soldier, a leader with a sense of humour and a directness that made him want to divulge everything he knew. Which, of course, he wouldn't. He had settled on that already. He knew that to be useful, he needed to remain useful. So that afternoon, when the questioning had begun, he was helpful but also helped himself with specific failures. Errors of memory, pauses to think and correct himself, leaps backwards to change names or dates that in the conversation were an hour or two old. It was part of the process and they would learn that. Easy to confuse July '52 with August '53. Best to keep asking because the answers will change.

He thought about Bialoguski and Dream Acres. Could he see the doctor again? He would have to be careful but he didn't see why not. Give it time. Caution was important.

He had told them he wanted Jack. He wanted Gilmour to send some agents to Lockyer Street to nab the dog in a car. The security men said no. If Jack disappeared, the embassy would know that their third secretary was alive. He supposed it made sense.

He was talking plainly about Evdokia now. Telling them that she was an MVD operative with field experience and a long intelligence career. He was hinting that they should approach her directly. If they let her know what he had done, she would have little choice but to come across. He wasn't afraid. He thought he could account for this path he had been forced to take. She would understand and she would forgive. He had thought it was possible to do this without her. Why, then, did he want her here?

He sat up on the couch, listening, and then he stood and went to the window. Street lamps. Lamps on the sides of houses. A car was coming towards them. He watched the lights prime the nearby walls and roofs.

He was certain the assassin would come from New Zealand, probably by a flying boat via Rose Bay. He had to believe in Howley. He would put his life in the man's hands for now and a long time. If Howley said Saburov was alright, he was alright. If he said, do this, move now, he would.

They were ready to interview him again first thing the next morning. In his imaginings, he'd thought the process would involve microphones in the walls, but the microphone was in front of him on the table. They gave him coffee and an ashtray.

Howley said, 'Why don't you quickly go over your history once more?'

He gave it again as he'd written it scrappily the day before. Larikha. Joining the Party. The navy. The cyphering training and the various stations he'd worked in, who his bosses had been, how he'd come to Australia, who in the embassy was MVD.

They told him they'd put Kislitsyn under full-time surveillance. Howley was wearing a tiepin.

Petrov asked, 'What about my wife?'

'She's at home,' Howley said.

'You must talk to her. Convince her to defect.'

'Hmm.'

'It's important. She has information that might be very useful for you.'

Gilmour put a brick of cigarettes on the table and they opened a box and began to smoke.

Howley said, 'Between 1945 and 1948, the Communist Party here had a group of External Affairs officers who were giving them official information—that right?'

'That's right.'

'How were they reporting it?'

'In what way?'

'Yes.'

'Copies of documents.'

'They were handing over copies of documents?'

'That's right.'

'Documents about Australian foreign policy?'

'About many things. America. England.'

'About atomic tests?'

'No, I don't think so.'

'But about other things?'

'Yes.'

'Policy papers?'

'Position papers, yes.'

'Secret documents?'

'Yes. That's right. Documents that were secret to you.'

'Written by us?'

'America and England, also.'

'Who were these men?'

'What were their names?'

'Yes.'

'Some of them I know. Later I will remember.'

'Are those men still there?'

'It's possible. Maybe one.'

'You know his name?'

'I will remember.'

Howley paused. 'But these men were your agents? Inside External Affairs?'

'Maybe.'

'You're not sure?'

'They don't tell me the past unless it is of use.'

'Why not?' asked Howley. 'Why don't they tell you the past?'

He shrugged. He said that in the Soviet Union the past was always secret. The past was a kind of power to be regulated and meted out, and if you didn't know the history, there was nothing to betray.

They threw darts and he drank bourbon. The dartboard rested against a terraced garden bed on the uphill slope. Leo Carter had replaced Gilmour. There were nine people in the world who knew where he was: the safe-house team, these two men with guns, and Colonel Spry.

For a few days, the interviews went on, and in the middle of the second, the phone rang. It was on a small stand in the hall. Carter picked it up. There was a hushed conversation. He rang off and told them that Evdokia had gone to the embassy. Three men had escorted her to Lockyer Street and collected some things.

Petrov pictured Kovaliev's face.

'We must get her a message,' he said. 'She thinks I am dead but she must know I am still alive.'

Howley remained silent. Leo Carter asked how that could be done.

'Bialoguski,' Petrov suggested.

'No,' said Howley. 'The doctor must stay in the dark.'

Petrov went to the window. Trees moving in a slight wind. The midday sun on terracotta tiles.

'Will they take her through Singapore?' asked Howley.

Petrov turned around. 'Yes,' he said. 'If they stick to their regular plan.'

'We could approach her there. That way, you are safe and later she can join you here.'

'We should consider that.' Petrov suddenly froze. He was thinking about Rex Chiplin's man in the post office. 'The telephone here,' he said, 'is it a regular line? A standard line in every sense?'

'Why?'

'Is it orthodox?'

'I'm not sure what you mean.'

'The registration. Is there anything that indicates it belongs to Security?'

Howley was looking at him curiously. 'No,' he said. 'It's perfectly fake. Or perfectly real. Whichever.'

'The communists,' Petrov blurted. 'They have a spy in the post office and he tells them whose feeds you tap.'

They sent for her. When she got to the ambassador's office, Kovalenok handed her a note. It was a message from the Australian government to the embassy. They were saying her husband was with them and was alive.

'What do you think?' asked the ambassador.

She said nothing for a time, then: 'Somehow the Australians must have forced him to stay.'

She surprised herself by finding she could actually believe that. Yes; either he had decided to stay or they had forced him.

The two men looked relieved. She thought this was because at least now they had something to report.

'A forced defection,' said Kovalenok.

'An act of provocation.'

'An ill-adjusted mortar on the landscape of no effect.'

The ambassador looked at her. 'We are going to respond to this note,' he said. 'And then you will ask to see him.'

She went back to her room and found Masha and told her the news and they hugged. Masha looked up and down the corridor. 'Now it is you we must worry about,' she said.

The next day it was in the papers. She knew it was because she wasn't allowed to read them. Sanko came early and removed her radio set.

'What are you doing?' she protested.

'The ambassador requires it.'

Masha sneaked her the *Herald*. The prime minister had announced it to his parliament: Soviet diplomat crosses the curtain—victory for the free world.

She started to laugh at the photograph of Volodya and then she tried not to sob.

Kovalenok came and explained she was to take one last trip to collect her things. He, Sanko and Vislykh drove her to Lockyer Street. There were two men on the road there. Reporters. They made the escort nervous.

When she entered the house, she saw it had been destroyed. Every drawer was open, the sum of their material lives scattered on the floor, boxes blown apart, shoes flung, the fridge door ajar and it still running. She stayed ten minutes, walking the rubble. She packed almost nothing.

Kovalenok came inside, muttering about possibilities for danger. 'We must return another time,' he said.

That evening, they brought her and Volodya's belongings in trunks. Standing over her, Vislykh made her sort what she did and did not want. She might have kept one small memento, but in the end she packed nothing of Volodya's. She didn't want to provide anyone with evidence of intent.

She lay in bed with the lights off. She'd tried to open the window for air. Someone had nailed it shut. She listened to the building creak. Maybe they would murder her. They could do that and there would be no consequences. Tell the world she died of nervous shock.

At the embassy, people began gathering at the front gate. Journalists. Busybodies. A small crowd, pressing the buzzer out there.

Generalov gave out revolvers. Evdokia watched from the window of the commercial section. Kislitsyn crossed the grass to the fence and asked the crowd to leave. Someone booed him. He recrossed the grass and a few minutes later Kovalenok went out. He was carrying a camera, one of the Leica imitations. She heard the voices shouting questions. In response, Kovalenok raised the camera point-blank and shot. She knew what he meant by it—an act of photographic recording would have dispersed a Russian crowd. But on the Australians the message was lost. The photographers in the pack photographed him in return. He made his retreat to the building and no one else ventured out.

She went to bed.

Not too many ways I am getting out of this alive.

Masha delivered a bowl of oats. The prisoner added water to the milk and pushed the oats around.

She saw Vislykh return via the back gate. A short while later, she was called to the ambassador's office.

'Your husband has written a letter to you. I believe it carries signs of being written under duress.'

Volodya's jerky handwriting.

Dear Doosia,

I have read in today's newspapers announcements saying that you think I was forcibly seized. That is untrue. I am alive and well and I am being treated well. I desire to assure you personally of this and I have asked the ambassador to arrange for me to see you as soon as possible.

V. Petrov

What announcements? The ambassador was staring into his desk.

She said, 'I can't tell you whether the words are his, but the handwriting is a definite match.'

'It's very short.'

'Yes.'

'Not many long letters are written at gunpoint.'

'No.'

The ambassador handed her a second letter. It was a prepared reply. She would copy it into her own hand. She read the letter and he watched her.

She said, 'I won't write this. I will write my own letter. Maybe I will borrow from your letter, but I won't sign anything that isn't my own.'

He seemed to be expecting this. He pointed to the typewriter.

She sat and wrote a page that wasn't really for her husband but for the trial she might have in Moscow. She said his letter was forced. She suspected he had been kidnapped. The Australians must have learnt of his imminent departure and decided to act. She hoped they would release him. She hoped the diplomatic efforts underway would have some effect. She told him she was trying to be strong. She needed to reach Moscow, leave this country, go somewhere where she would be safe. She told him to think of her.

Taking her lead from the ambassador's letter, she said that given the circumstances it was not possible that they meet.

Generalov read what she'd written, gave a grunt and she left the room.

Two days later, the ambassador summoned her once more. He and Kovalenok stood each side of the desk. Her letter was there between them, unsent. They said nothing at first. Perhaps Moscow had denied permission for her missive to be dispatched.

Kovalenok put a pen and a page typewritten on embassy stationery before her and asked her to read it. It was another letter from herself to her husband, far shorter this time, just a simple paragraph:

Dear Volodya,
I have received your letter. My meeting with you under the conditions proposed by the Australian Department of External Affairs is impossible, as I am afraid to fall into a trap.
*   E. Petrova*

'No,' she said.

Kovalenok frowned. 'What is no?'

'No, I won't write this.'

The two men looked at her.

'You must,' said Generalov. 'It is not we who have penned this letter. It is Moscow.'

She shrugged.

'What is wrong with it?' said Kovalenok.

'I won't say it, that is all.'

Kovalenok indicated that she should sit. Evdokia refused. He offered her a cigarette and she shook her head.

'Sign the text as it stands,' he said. 'It will reach your husband faster.'

'Do I care when it reaches him?'

'You are his wife.'

'That is not what is at issue.'

Kovalenok put his fingers on the page. 'Captain,' he said, 'you must understand that this is Moscow's text. We simply do not have permission to change it.'

It took her a moment to realise he was addressing her by her MVD rank.

'I have no orders,' she said. 'No orders concerning this note have been given to me.'

'The instruction is implicit,' said Kovalenok.

She shrugged once more.

'I'm sure you have been thinking about the law,' he said. 'There are special laws in these situations and obviously you must know. There will be a trial when you return. Believe me that what happens now may influence the proceedings. What can happen? Camps and possibly even execution if it is judged that your husband, in this affair, has left of his own accord.'

She said nothing.

'You are going home very shortly, Evdokia Alexeyevna,' Generalov put in. 'The opportunities for you to demonstrate your allegiance are vanishing. You should sign and we will testify that you were eager. Alright?'

She looked at the note. 'Alright,' she said. And picked up the pen.

Whole days passed where she hardly left the room. She sat looking through the window, watching the sway of trees in the wind or simply staring into space. Masha brought her some books—novels and biographies—but they sat unread. She began to sleep oddly, snoozing for hours in the afternoons and waking at 3 a.m. Kovalenok started to insist that she walk each day in the embassy's grounds. He escorted her, tried to involve her in a taste experiment he was conducting, smoking his way through different brands of Australian cigarettes. They were careful to keep clear of the fences and the front gate. Soon, she found herself looking forward to leaving for Moscow, regardless of what fate might bring. The solitary days added together and she was ready for anything to give.

Inoculation. A doctor came and she was taken to a room upstairs and given injections. Cholera and smallpox. She needed certification to travel. Smallpox was one shot but cholera was a two-stage affair. 'Next week we will inject you with the second half,' said the doctor.

She looked at Vislykh, who was observing, and said that there might not be time for that to occur.

'That's right,' said Vislykh. 'Can we not simply do it now and issue the certificate?'

The doctor shook his head. He was a white-haired man of about fifty and had, she thought, a successful practice on the street near the hospital. Vislykh appealed to him, saying the travel was an emergency—could he not issue the certificate and she would have the second shot somewhere along the way?

The doctor said, 'No.'

She was escorted by Kovalenok from the room.

Some hours later, a second doctor came. He was no one she recognised, younger than the first, blond near to orange hair and large hands like a farmer's. He delivered the second shot into her opposite arm and on the certificate his signature was an indecipherable mess.

She knew that the couriers had arrived. Vislykh came and said that Kislitsyn, also, would be escorting her home.

Why? She wondered whether Moscow was afraid that the Australians had got to him as well.

It was left to Masha to tell her that the next day would be the last. The two women spent the night in the duty room. Evdokia thanked Masha for everything she had done.

'Don't look so distressed,' Masha said. 'I promise it will be fine in Russia. It will be alright and you will see. Here, now. Write for me once more the address of your family, and Ivan and I will visit and life will have gone on.'

At 9 a.m. on the nineteenth, Generalov called her to his study. She could not tell whether the pity in his voice was mocking.

'I don't need to remind you that the couriers are armed,' he said. 'After Darwin, you will stop in Jakarta, then Singapore.

In these airports, you will play cards and laugh. You will be tourists travelling. This way you will not attract attention.'

'My salary,' she interrupted.

The ambassador stared.

'You must pay my salary. Until I cross the frontier I am still considered as officially on a posting. I am owed my full salary, my travelling expenses and the addition of twenty-five per cent in Australian pounds.'

'Comrade—'

'Pay me these amounts.'

He coughed. 'The instruction from Moscow is that you will receive such payments there.'

'Is that true?'

'Yes.'

'And you did not tell me?'

'I have had more pressing concerns.'

She did not know whether to believe him. Then he told her to see Vislykha. The woman would hand over Volodya's uncollected salary, accounted to the day he left for Sydney. Evdokia thought this a good sign. They weren't trying to say Volodya hadn't been doing his job.

Downstairs, two cars were parked behind the embassy. Kislitsyn and Kovaliev were loading one with her trunks. The two couriers and Vislykh were standing with the other. She was ushered into the second, the Cadillac, and she sat for fifteen minutes before Kovaliev took the first car towards the gates. She didn't see the crowd but she heard them, a small chorus of shouts. She waited in the Cadillac for a further fifteen minutes before Zharkov and Karpinsky got in. They said hello but nothing else. Soon, Sanko started the car and at the last second Vislykh got in beside her and slammed the door. They raced through the gates. She was shocked at the crowd's size, the mob they'd grown to—maybe thirty or more individuals with cameras or microphones or fierce looks. The car bounced over the kerb onto the avenue. The crowd was scattering when she turned to look back.

At the beginning, all she thought of was a car accident. That Sanko might errantly tip the wheel into the oncoming Easter traffic. Vislykh was handing her a handkerchief, offering comforting words that she didn't fully listen to. He put a cup of brandy in her hand, which she drank, and then he was pouring vodka.

How many hours to Sydney? The airport was on the southern side. The road turned and dipped and turned. She looked through the window at the passing country. She knew she was going to be ill before she was. The Cadillac made a forced stop outside Collector. She crossed towards some trees and was sick in a shadow. Then she stood for a long time, holding the cloth to her mouth, her nose filled with the smell. Vislykh watched her, leaning against one of the car's doors. She had another brandy and the Cadillac took off.

The men conferred about the flight time—whether or not they were late. The consensus was they weren't. Even so, Sanko took the road faster. She asked for water but there was none. She asked for the radio and was told it didn't work. She had some idea that there was something public about all this. A sense of apprehension that permeated the car. Most likely, people were angry about the espionage, the undermining of democracy that she'd helped. It wasn't a matter of success or failure but of appearance and intent. They were right to hate her. Who was she to come here and engage in such acts?

The car whistled on the road. She was carrying her small handbag and that was all. They passed the intersection for the Wombeyan Caves Road.

It was dark when they hit Sydney's outskirts.

20

Bialoguski sat in his Holden on a badly lit street, parked at the higher end outside Lydia Mokras's flat. Her light was on, the one that lit both the kitchen and the lounge. He'd seen her shadow just now. She was alone.

He listened to the radio. He saw no reason to be annoyed that Petrov had defected through Security without him. That was their business. That was the official part and there was no reason for Bialoguski to be there. He wondered how the Russian had felt, crossing that boundary, *the* boundary, the world-sized hinge. Like a warrior? A hero? A miscalculating fool?

When the news had broken, Bialoguski had begun to prepare the ground for his inevitable and irrevocable exposure—all the while playing his hand perfectly until the last. When Pakhomov and Plaitkais had come to his surgery searching for their man, the doctor had ensured he was out. When Evdokia called to say Volodya was missing, he'd carefully cultivated the impression that he was leading the hunt himself. He'd dragged Lily Williams mysteriously from a dinner party, demanding that the secretary of the Jewish Council to Combat Fascism tell him when she'd last seen the VOKS representative. He'd whispered the conversation conspiratorially, as if Petrov's absence were a grave secret, hardly known by those who knew. Then he'd got Jean Ferguson of the Australia–Soviet Friendship Society out of bed, in her dressing gown, and interrogated her suspiciously about Petrov's whereabouts, the man's movements and demeanour, the clothing he'd last been seen in. Jean had reacted weirdly, highly uncomfortably, as if he might be threatening her sexually. That pleased him. He'd told her that the embassy was worried. They'd put himself and Pakhomov on the case. Would she put the word out amongst the Sydney left?

It was cleverness on his part. Fooling them at the last. When they discovered the truth, they'd be awe-struck. Which was why the next day he bought a gun, ringing Howley and demanding the permit, fearing either the embassy's or the left's reprisals. Reluctantly, ASIO organised it with the New South Wales police. He went to a pawn shop in Kings Cross and paid forty pounds for a .32 calibre revolver and an ill-fitting shoulder holster. He then registered both with a sergeant at Special Branch.

The meaning behind the gun was that he was officially sanctioned. It was the state saying, you have served us loyally and therefore earned protection from our enemies. He liked to look at himself in the mirror with the weapon underneath his clothes.

Lydia was in the kitchen, her silhouette visible through the glass. He crossed the street carrying a document bag and ascended the stairs at the flats. She wanted to know who it was. He announced himself and was surprised when she asked what he wanted.

'Let me in,' he said.

There was a pause while Lydia took her time, finally opening the door in a pink woollen jumper and, he was fairly sure, no bra. She stood with the door at her hip as if she didn't want him inside.

'What?' she asked.

'You can't invite me in?'

She looked at him. Stepped back.

'I'll have a drink,' he said, taking a seat on the couch.

Lydia took her time opening a bottle of beer.

'He doesn't know anything about you, does he?' Bialoguski asked. 'No compromising information, I mean.'

'Who?'

'Petrov!'

'Oh,' she said. 'The defector.'

'Yes. Are you afraid?'

'What would I have to be scared of?'

'He might have information on you.'

'Does he?'

'You tell me.'

'There's nothing he could have.'

'You're sure?'

'Yes, I'm sure.'

'Only I think Vladimir had the impression you were collecting political intelligence.'

She put a glass of beer in his hand.

'That would be all it was,' she said.

'An impression?'

'Yes.'

'Why?' he asked.

'What do you mean?'

'Why would it just be an impression?'

'Because,' she said.

'Because you're not a spy?'

'No,' she said. 'Of course I'm not.'

'Only you gave me that idea.'

Lydia shrugged.

'Sit here,' he said after a time. 'Sit on the couch.'

She did.

'What if Security believe his story?' he put to her. 'Perhaps Petrov will tell them what he thinks.'

'But will they believe him? The drunk.'

Bialoguski smiled. 'They might deport you.'

'They can't. I'm resident.'

'That won't stop them. At the least, I'd say you'd lose your job at the hospital. I think you need someone to vouch for you. A person whose opinion Security will trust. Perhaps someone who's been given reason to protect you.'

'What are you doing here, Michael?'

He laughed. 'I want to know what it was all about. If you're not a spy. I mean the day at the harbour and the photographs we took.'

'You were there. You tell me.'

'If Security asks, what should I tell them?'

'Asks who?'

'Myself.'

She had slippers on, he noticed. Peach-coloured.

'Where is your boyfriend tonight?'

'I work too much. We broke up.'

'Your wish?'

'I don't know. I suppose so.'

'You know, I'm going to be famous soon.'

She met his eyes, her head slightly angled.

'Yes,' he said. 'I will be in the news. You may hear some things about me that you did not suspect.'

'Have you been charged?' she asked.

He looked at her.

'Your abortions?' she whispered.

He half-grinned. 'They are not my abortions. And no, not that.'

'Why?'

He said nothing for a moment, then reached into the document satchel he'd brought. From inside, he drew a nine-by-six-inch photograph. It was a portrait of himself in a bakelite frame. He'd autographed it, under the glass, in thick pen. He gave it to Lydia. She took it with two hands and held it on her lap. He leaned across to kiss her. Instantly, she put a hand out and began to laugh. Her mirth shocked him and he recoiled.

'What is this picture, Michael? A souvenir?'

The laughter made him angry. 'You're not going to know me soon,' he spat. 'You don't know me already. When you hear the news, this picture is what you will have.'

'Are you aware that you are mad, Michael? Do you know that you aren't normal?'

He took the revolver slowly from the holster and held it flat in his open palm. He was looking at the gun and not her. He waited for her to say something though he knew she wasn't going to. After a time, he stood and collected his satchel from the floor.

The street outside was as he'd left it. Except Lydia had killed the light. He imagined she was watching him, her fingers on the fold of the curtain, using the darkness of the flat to keep from his sight.

A dog barked hesitantly. He put the car in gear and drove. At the first intersection, he touched his hand to the gun once more. The cold metal calmed him. The gun was a cooling secret—a secret that knew everything was changing. Petrov had defected, and the doctor had given his life—his left-wing life—to see it happen. He was supposed to have wanted this all along, coaxing the man across. Why then did he feel so strangely uncertain? And why so hopelessly unenthused?

21

At Mascot airport, the police could do nothing. They were too few, too unprepared. They stood on the apron, cudgels against their thighs, lost men, a row of doomed figures, sweat glimmering on their necks.

Behind them, the BOAC Constellation stood like an idol in the arc light. Before them, the crowd was hundreds strong, a piping sea of night breath, a slowly rising voice.

Two lone placards: WE WANT A FREE CZECHOSLOVAKIA and REDS = PIGS.

Press bulbs knifing at intervals through the darkness, casting white chrome impressions on the terminal's outer shell.

The crowd were becoming bold. A man in a woollen vest was giving a speech from on top of an oil drum, punctuating his oration with karate-chop actions at the plane.

The Russians emerged from the darkness at the edge of the terminal, a gang of five, Mrs Petrov at their centre, grey suit, red bag, white gloves. The men holding her arms looked straight from a piece of anti-Soviet propaganda: brutal, thug-faced killers in long coats, one thick-bodied and dumb-looking, the other a scheming Machiavellian rat.

The crowd thought the men were dragging her, pushing her, physically compelling her to move. They swept towards them, shouting, appealing, a clarity of purpose developing when the violence started to come.

In the Constellation's cockpit, the pilot's radio was saying, *'Speedbird . . . Speedbird . . .'*, and he listened, watching the Russians and the knot of demonstrators around them advance. *'Speedbird . . . be advised of your Soviet passengers approaching . . .'* The towerman's voice was nervous, shaky. The pilot watched two policemen jog towards the plane, shoes shining in the lights. The noise of the crowd intensified. There was a mob behind the Russians, either side and in front. They were coming close.

The steward came into the cabin to say that several people were under the plane, the wings and the fuselage. *'Speedbird, do not start, do not start,'* said the towerman.

The stairs were rocking. The pilot saw them shift, roll, come back into place. The Russians were up or halfway up. In the crowd, there seemed to be a protest within the protest— a group of men, a rough element pushing and grabbing; the majority simply yelling, content to stand by.

The pace of the Russians' boarding seemed a surprise. A few seconds where he thought things might go either way. Then the crowd's noise drifted into a lull. They began backing off. They were walking slowly, but away, only the slightest signs of an intent to linger. Soon, they were where they'd started, by the terminal, and they looked primed by a certain satisfaction, an almost glow, the energy released when an electron falls one level to the next.

'*Clear,*' said the pilot's radio, and he was glad to hear it as he began again his pre-flight check.

Shrinking constellations. As Sydney's lights contracted below them the forces in the plane felt world-shaking.

Kislitsyn was telling her, 'Stop crying.'

She took his handkerchief and kept sobbing. He glared at her, but she had her reasons. Returning to the USSR as a victim. Being punished, horribly, for doing nothing wrong.

It occurred to her that for the last fifteen days she really hadn't been thinking straight. She still wasn't thinking straight. The evidence was she had one shoe, and on the tarmac just now she'd almost been broken into pieces.

The plane was levelling out. She stood and walked down the aisle. The ladies lounge was a small room with an actual lounge chair. It had a mirror and an adjacent room with a toilet. Evdokia looked at herself, the dishevelment, and a voice asked, 'Are you alright?'

It was the hostess. Black-haired with thin features, she wore a uniform with a hat. She was looking at the passenger, concerned.

'I don't know,' Evdokia said.

'Would you like water? Would you like my shoes?'

She examined the woman's feet. They looked big. She tried the shoes on. They were far too large.

The hostess said, 'Keep them. You'll need something when we land in Darwin.'

Darwin?

The woman saw her confusion. 'To refuel.'

She returned to her seat. Incredibly, the couriers were both sleeping. Kislitsyn gave her a beer and four cigarettes. He was looking out the window; just blackness out there. He lit her cigarette and told her it would be alright in Moscow. She would live in her old apartment with her mother and she would go back to her old job, the way things were before. She knew the idea was ridiculous. 'You are always the professional,' she said, and he protested, but she was on her feet again, heading for the ladies lounge.

The hostess was there with the steward. The steward asked her: 'Do you want to stay in Australia?' She wasn't expecting the question. She looked into his face. It wasn't a query born simply of kindness. His tone said, I have the power to get this done.

'I want to see my husband,' she said.

'But do you want to stay?'

She took a small glass of water. 'I am scared,' she said. 'The men who are with me—two of them are armed.'

'They are armed now? On the plane?'

'Yes.'

The steward looked down the aisle.

'They have revolvers,' she said. 'They are dangerous men. They are here to protect me by force.'

'Do you want to stay?' the steward asked again.

'Can you help me?'

'Yes.'

She looked at him and then at the hostess. She began to nod, not totally sure what the nodding would mean.

She returned to her seat. Kislitsyn was now sleeping. Eight hours to Darwin. Longer into a headwind. She made an attempt to sleep. They offered her one of the Constellation's beds but she refused. She wanted something to focus on. She put her mind on Tamara, regretting immediately that she hadn't bought either her sister or their mother new coats. She shook Kislitsyn's arm and asked him if there was time for shopping in Darwin, or did the vendors take Australian pounds in Singapore? He looked at her as if she were a crazy person. Maybe she was a crazy person. If she was, it was because of what they had done to her.

What he had done to her.

The hostess came with a blanket. Evdokia pulled the blanket around herself and shut her eyes. The headrests on the seats were uncomfortable. She ended somehow with her skull bumping against the Constellation's shell.

Later, she woke to find a man in front of her with a camera. The lights in the cabin were low for sleeping, and he had his sleeves rolled up and was taking pictures of her. She was watching and he knew this but he did not stop. He rested his arm on an adjacent chair to steady the shots. Then he disappeared. Was he just a man with a camera or was he a proper journalist, she wondered. If he was a journalist, then people had known she would be on this flight and had been able to get tickets. Meaning that Australian Security men might be on this plane. She turned her head and looked up the aisle. There might be a face. There might be a face that you know.

The plane, dark and rattling. She recognised no one in this other-world of capsular sleep. Again, she drifted. She was occupying a space that was semiconscious. Breathless bad dreams; shadowy figures with shadowy motivations and ideals. She opened her eyes to see Kislitsyn, closed and reopened her eyes to see Zharkov. It was fear and anxiety and this rumbling, high-altitude hell.

Eventually, the sun came: a low-breaking blue light on the plane's side, dimly perceptible at first.

The descent lasted a long time. Kislitsyn sat watching the earth below, waiting. It was over now, whatever the event had been. Still, he wouldn't feel relief until they were airbound for Jakarta.

The Constellation raced its wheels to the runway and lurched. He looked out as the Darwin terminal came into view. There were soldiers. Ten men in uniform, waiting. He said Karpinsky's name and pointed. The man unbuckled his seatbelt and leaned across to look.

'The army?'

'The army or the police.'

They both looked at Evdokia. 'We're not getting off the plane,' Kislitsyn told her. 'We wait here until it takes off again.'

She nodded, looking terrible.

The Constellation slowly came to rest. Stairs were wheeled to its doors. People stood and made their way into the morning sun. The Soviets remained seated.

Soon after the plane had emptied, the hostess asked whether they needed help.

'No, thank you,' said Kislitsyn.

They waited. The steward arrived and requested that they alight. The plane needed to refuel, he said, and it was against regulations for any passengers to remain aboard.

Kislitsyn asked for an exception.

'Why?' asked the steward. 'Is one of your party ill?'

'No,' said Karpinsky.

'Then I must insist that you disembark. The fuel truck won't refill us if you refuse.'

Grumbling, the Russians stood. They started down the aisle, the three men and then Evdokia. Kislitsyn went first. When he reached the forward cabin door, he saw that the soldiers were assembled at the bottom of the stairs. Well, he thought, I hope no one accidentally shoots me.

He started down. He could hear Karpinsky breathing heavily behind him. All eyes were on them. When Kislitsyn reached the tarmac, he purposely moved left, trying to put some distance between himself and the courier.

A uniformed man said, 'Excuse me. Are you carrying a firearm?'

Kislitsyn said nothing.

The man had sand-coloured hair and was enormously framed, wearing loose-fitting green pants with a belt ten centimetres wide. He announced that he was a policeman and that he was going to search Kislitsyn's body. The MVD man didn't resist. He stood while the policeman patted him down, craning his neck towards Karpinsky, who, faced with the same situation, was trying to push his assailant aside. The Australian wasn't having it. Kislitsyn watched as the policeman gripped Karpinsky's arm. The courier reacted fiercely. He swung his cabin bag at the man's body, lunged and played his bag into the man's chest.

'He's going for his gun!' a voice cried out. 'Hold him! Hold him!'

A second and a third man jumped, one moving for Karpinsky's left arm and the other for the right. Karpinsky tossed the first aside easily, launching him hard towards the ground. But the third man was on his wrist and had begun to bend it. Now the courier started reaching, and Kislitsyn knew without question that someone was about to end up dead.

Except the wrestling wasn't over. A fourth man leaped in, reaching for Karpinsky's shoulder, yanking at his jacket. The jacket came down below the shoulders. The man was trying to use it as a restraint, yanking it as low as possible over the arms. Kislitsyn knew the tactic was doomed, but he hadn't anticipated the remainder of the act—the grabbing of Karpinsky's neck. While jerking at the jacket, the man had manoeuvred himself into a position behind Karpinsky that allowed for the application of a rudimentary headlock. Karpinsky offered one twist, but that was all. The man's strength was too much. The man tightened his grip using his other arm and the courier froze.

Overpowered. Bodies leaped all over Karpinsky now. The pistol was held aloft and there was the thin sound of bullets spilling to the ground.

Zharkov stood by silently. The gun that he had been carrying was now held by the Australian policeman at his side.

Evdokia was halfway down the stairs. When she reached the bottom, Kislitsyn watched as a man in a suit approached her and led her to one side.

'My name is Mr Leydin,' the man said. 'I am the Governor of Darwin and I am here to represent the Australian government.'

She looked at Karpinsky in a headlock. She stared at Kislitsyn and Kislitsyn stared back.

'I am asking you whether you wish to seek political asylum in Australia. Do you wish to do so?'

She knew they couldn't ask her this. She knew this was breaking the rules. Why would they do it within earshot of the others? Did they think she could say yes and her family wouldn't die?

She whispered, 'I don't know. I don't know.'

'I am authorised to make you this offer. Authorised by the prime minister directly.'

She began to walk away. Not towards the others, but into open space. Leydin trailed behind. He was a thin man, somewhat gaunt. A minute passed, and then she hit on an idea. 'Why don't you kidnap me?' she said.

'Pardon?'

'I cannot choose. They will kill my father and my mother and my brother and my sister.'

'I'm not sure I understand.'

'If you take me by force, alright. But I must not choose. I cannot choose. Look, they are watching me.'

Leydin gazed back at the restrained party.

'Will you kidnap me?' she asked.

He turned and she read the no from his face.

'Do you know where my husband is?' she asked. 'Is he alive? Is he here? Can I speak to him?'

'Yes,' said Leydin.

'Yes?'

'Yes, he is alive. He has been afforded the protection I want to offer you. He's not here, but you can speak to him. If you come with me I will arrange it.'

'I cannot go with you.'

They stood silently for a moment.

She said, 'Why don't you kidnap me or give me some kind of poison?'

'I have no authority to do that.'

'You have no authority doing what you have already done.'

'Do you wish to seek political asylum in Australia?'

'I cannot choose.'

'You cannot choose.'

Their talk went in circles. She became nervous of the time they were taking and asked to return to the group. Leydin gave a nod and said, 'Alright.'

He came with her and stood beside her.

Kislitsyn asked him, 'You are in charge?'

'That's right.'

'You are breaching protocols here. That is very serious.'

'I am not. I assure you, there is no one here who is not free to walk wherever he should choose.'

'These men want their guns back.'

'They cannot have them.'

'They have done nothing illegal.'

'I believe they have.'

'They are diplomatic couriers and they have immunity.'

'Regardless, the Air Navigation Act mandates that weapons be lodged with the aircraft's captain during flight. You are Mr Kislitsyn?'

'That's right.'

'If you would like to remain in Australia, I am authorised to offer you political asylum.'

Kislitsyn looked surprised. Evdokia could hardly believe it. If the MVD man had been in any doubt about the content of her and Leydin's conversation it was all but erased now.

'Could you arrange that?' asked the Russian.

'Yes. The Crown will make arrangements for your safety.'

'That's interesting. That's very interesting,' Kislitsyn continued, disparagingly.

They made their way to the terminal. Kislitsyn and Zharkov congratulated her, declaring that her behaviour was without fault. They sat in the hall of the terminal. She thought the couriers might be about to produce playing cards.

'You are to be admired, Evdokia,' said Kislitsyn. 'Your strength will not go unnoticed in Moscow.'

She almost cried.

A BOAC worker asked whether they would be breakfasting in Darwin. Kislitsyn told him no. They weren't going anywhere that wasn't aboard that plane.

Evdokia looked at Karpinsky. After the confrontation, she knew his blood was still boiling. He was holding his diplomatic pouch with an incredible grip, quite possibly destroying whatever films and documents were inside.

They sat for what must have been an hour. Others watched them, and every few minutes she looked up and around to see Leydin rushing about. He came into the hall now and again, followed by one or more men in suits. She noticed one particular man watching her intently. He sat in the far corner of the hall with an illustrated holiday brochure, 'The Grand Pacific', open on his lap, but all the time he was staring at them and at her. She thought to point him out to Kislitsyn as competition, but her comrade, she saw, was well aware and was returning fire with his gaze.

The call came over the address system. They were beginning to board the plane. She stood to go.

'No,' said Karpinsky. 'We wait for the other passengers to go aboard.'

She had no idea why he wanted to do that. Kislitsyn made no move and so she sat.

In the safe house, Leo Carter was studying his Soviet charge. Since their return from the disaster of Mascot earlier that evening the man hadn't slept. They'd prepared him a plate of chicken but it hadn't been touched. Petrov's first-line interest was to pace the room. That and water, which he was consuming glass after glass, fuel for the sweat on his forehead and his ceaseless need for the toilet.

The defector was pissing from the back door when the phone rang. Leo answered. It was B2. 'Call Darwin airport,' he said. 'Call a man named Leydin there.'

'Laydon?'

'Leydin. The acting administrator. Tell him you're Spry. Instruct him that western morality dictates that the man in your possession must be put in contact with his wife.'

Leo got an operator and requested an immediate trunk. The operator said she'd see what was possible and rang off. Petrov came inside and Leo told him what was happening. They sat in silence waiting for the phone to ring. The man's hands were covered in grease. Leo supposed it must have happened when Petrov had been shoved under the tarp of the ASIO utility parked in the night shadow of hangar one.

After ten minutes, he rang the exchange again and asked what the delay was. A woman named Myrtle told him there was some kind of tangle in Brisbane. He thought for a moment and then said, 'This is an important call on behalf of the attorneygeneral. I want you to give it operational flash priority.'

'Flash priority?' she repeated.

'Yes.'

'Do I need to take your name for that?'

'No, you do not.'

The phone went quiet and he imagined Myrtle examining her board and deciding what plugs to pull. 'One minute,' she said, and the phone died. When it rang again he picked up. 'You're seeking Mr Leydin?' said Myrtle.

'Yes.'

'He's on another phone.'

'Connect me to anyone.'

'Anyone?'

'Any person at Darwin airport.'

He heard a clunk and then a voice said, 'Edwards.'

'Yes, is Mr Leydin there?'

'I'm afraid he's busy.'

'Tell him it's the director general of Security,' said Leo. 'I have an urgent message to deliver.'

'Alright.'

The handset was put down. Leo heard nothing for a time, and then Leydin was on the phone.

'Carter is my name,' Leo told him. 'I am speaking on behalf of the director general of Security, Colonel Spry. I have Mr Petrov with me and he would like to speak to his wife if you can arrange it.'

Petrov was leaning towards him, staring at the phone, trying to make out what was being said. There was some debate among the safe-house team regarding whether or not Petrov really wanted his wife to stay. Leo thought that his sickened face at this moment near settled it.

'Hold the line,' said Leydin.

It was 7:15 a.m. It took Leydin until 7:18 to come back. 'She has walked halfway to the plane with her companions and has stopped,' he said. 'I will see if I can get her to come to the phone.'

Leo relayed the news. Petrov was uselessly holding a hand-kerchief in one hand.

***

'There's a phone call from your husband,' Leydin said. She stared at him until she was sure he was telling the truth.

'You may take the call upstairs,' he continued.

Kislitsyn and Karpinsky stiffened.

'No,' she said. 'I will take it downstairs. My companions will escort me.'

Leydin opened the door to a downstairs office that held a desk and a phone and asked her to wait while they rerouted the connection. The room had a window that faced the hall and there was a second door leading somewhere else. Her instructions were to pick up the phone when it rang. She stood at the near side of the desk. There weren't words for what was happening in her mind. She concentrated on her face. She would need everything she could summon to control her expression throughout whatever happened next.

When a minute elapsed, she was certain that this was a ploy. But then the ringer fired. She watched the handset, black with a white or bone-coloured dial and brown, looping flex. The bell rattled with a shrill physicality.

'Hello?'

She listened to the voice for a long time before taking in what it said: 'It is Volodya. It's Volodya.'

'Hmm,' she said.

'You must stay here,' he told her. 'I have stayed—I was forced to stay by those pigs. It's me, Doosia. Are you there? Can you hear me? You must stay. If you go back, they will not let you cross the threshold of your house. You won't see your parents. I beg you, not as a husband but as a man. If you want to live, stay here. Trust the Australians. Are you listening? Follow them. Go with them! I am alright. Trust them, and I will come to Darwin and to you. It is freedom,

Doosia! They have promised us a good life and we won't doubt them. Why don't you respond? Doosia? Are you there? Go with the Australians. You must escape the hell that awaits. We will make a new life. I'm pleading this as a man making an honest appeal. Doosenka? Don't get back on the plane. Are you on this line? Hello? Doosia, don't leave. I am here and safe. Stay with the Australians and stay in Australia with me.'

'No,' she said. 'You are not my husband. You say you are my husband but I do not believe that you are him. No. That is all. That's it. You are not my husband. I have listened to your voice but I am afraid you are not him. That is the end of everything we have to say.'

She rang off. The Soviet party stood in silence.

Kislitsyn led them slowly from the office. Leydin was there with two of his staff, holding documents and pens. The administrator asked whether she would like to speak to him.

'She would not,' Kislitsyn snapped. He made in the direction of the tarmac.

'Wait a moment,' she said, though she hadn't meant it to sound so trembling. She made a quarter-turn and gave Leydin a wink.

'Will you speak with me?' he said.

She reached and collected her travel bag from a chair. 'Yes,' she said. 'In private.'

They walked the few steps into the office. It was just the two of them. Leydin was behind her and she whispered quickly for him to shut the door. She kept her eyes from Kislitsyn and the couriers.

'Will you surround this room with police?' she asked.

Leydin's face looked kind, Russian in a way, she thought.

He picked up the phone and got an exchange somewhere in the building and within a minute ten policemen were standing at the glass. Leydin asked her whether she would sign the request for political asylum. She looked first at him, then the police, then the door that led somewhere else. Kislitsyn's voice was protesting outside.

'Get me out of this building,' she said quietly. 'I won't sign anything until you have taken me to my husband first.'

'It's me, Doosia . . .' As husband and wife spoke, Carter began to collect the things in the room. He picked up articles that were Petrov's—a pair of glasses, his lighter, a pair of shoes— and put them in a pile. Then he went to Petrov's bedroom, opened the man's suitcase and packed everything into it that was on the bed or the floor—shirts, trousers, a set of pyjamas. He listened to the defector's voice as he worked, desperate and peaking, rambling almost.

He went and sat nearby again for the final seconds of the call.

'Well?' he asked.

The Russian gave him the handset. The line was dead. 'She says I am not her husband.'

'Oh.'

'She says she does not recognise my voice.'

Leo tapped the cradle pins and booked another trunk. This time he was connected in under a minute. Edwards answered again and told him, 'Hold on.' Shortly, Leydin came on the line wanting Colonel Spry.

'He's not here,' said Carter.

'Is there a means by which I can speak to him?'

'You can speak to me and I have his authority.'

'Alright.'

'Petrov tells me his wife would not believe it was him. He would like to speak to her again if that is possible.'

Leydin said, 'She is with me here. She has said she will stay in Australia, but she won't sign the document until she sees her husband.'

'She'll stay?'

'That's right.'

'If she has said that, I accept responsibility for you assisting her whether she has signed the document or not.'

'She has stated she will stay. She will not sign the document.'

'Then don't worry about the document. You have my authority for that.'

'Carter?'

'That's right. Leo.'

'Alright.'

'Where will you take her?'

'We will go right now to Government House.'

The call disconnected. Petrov was looking at him.

'She's staying,' Leo said.

'She is?'

'They are taking her from the airport now.'

The defector grinned, looking like a man released. 'That is it then,' he announced. 'A new life together, free from the demons and the bastards. Shake my hand.'

Carter did. Petrov burst out the back door and stood looking at the trees up on the hill. Shadows running westerly. He put his hands on his hips, staring.

Leo hit the pins again and found B2. He explained the facts as they stood; heard the relief in B2's voice. He explained that he'd employed flash priority and that Petrov's name had been freely used. As such, they needed to entertain the notion that safe house two was blown. He was already packing up, he said. If required, they were ready to go.

Outside, Petrov was breathing freely, his girth visibly expanding as he sucked on the air. He looked gripped by his success, enamoured of it, in command of it, held high by its promise.

Leo pitied him.

22

Now would the pain begin? Now that she was a murderer of the worst possible kind. She sat on the veranda of Government House, a long, white-painted building with the appearance of a farmstead, set on grass and fronting the sea. Leydin's wife, Millie, was fetching her a drink. They had driven straight here from the airport in a saloon car. Everyone was being friendly, Millie Leydin especially, which she appreciated, a woman helping her out. She was trying to put on a good display—a happy demeanour, suitable to the recently doomed, now saved.

There were children here, the Leydins' and another family's, playing at the edge of the garden, shaded by palms, their voices warm and slow.

This was more how she'd first imagined the country would be.

Millie Leydin sat the drink in her hand. Something dark with ice, a straw and broken mint. The Security man—Barrington, his name was—came from the veranda's end. He told her a plane had been booked for that evening. His superior would be coming up.

'With my husband?' she asked.

'No,' he said. 'Mr Petrov will remain at the secret location.'

She nodded. She wanted to speak to Volodya but at the same time she was happy to avoid it. That way, she could attempt to forget that she was a person who held the souls of others in her orbit and whose choices had consequences. Even now her family were probably being detained. She pictured the chain of events: Kislitsyn to Generalov; Generalov to Prudnikov's office, hastily writing his cable, squirming already to absolve himself of blame; the Foreign Department quickly to Moscow Centre; the Centre to one of its squads and the squad racing by car to Varsanofievsky Pereulok, dom 6; her mother and sister and frail father either at home or not at home; the squad seizing them instantly, or waiting behind the door to do so on their return. The breaking of bones and lives.

'Are you alright?' Millie asked.

'Oh, yes. I am grateful to be here with you all.'

Leydin asked whether she would listen to a news broadcast. At the eastern end of the drawing room she sat by the radio. The voice announced that Mrs Petrov had decided to stay. She had chosen freedom at Darwin and her decision had set the free world cheering. There was an interview with a man who had been at Mascot airport. He said Prime Minister Robert Menzies was to be congratulated. That was exactly how he said it: Prime Minister Robert Menzies. She sat listening to the story of herself for the first time. At each heralding of her bravery, of the triumph of love over cruelty, she became further convinced of her family's fate. What a horror she was. What a reprehensible thing she had done, putting her life above their own.

Barrington came to the drawing room and alone saw what was happening. He asked if she would take some air on the veranda. They went there and smoked cigarettes. The veranda had a series of shutters that opened and closed and he set them carefully, angling out the sun.

That afternoon, Michael Howley arrived. He had brought a letter.

Dear Doosenka,

I am waiting here to see you as soon as possible.

This letter is in the hands of Mr Howley, who is the main man responsible for Australian Security and who is personally responsible for my life here and your life. He is a very good man. We must trust him, and we will trust him for the rest of our lives.

You decided very well. You are very brave. We have to show that Generalov is not a truthful man.

And so, my dear, I wait impatiently for you. When you are with me, we will have a very good and happy life.

I am always yours,

Volodya

The mention of Generalov hurt. What was Volodya doing writing about his battles with that man while her family was in the basement at Dzerzhinsky Square?

She went to bed early and found it vile how well she slept. She put it down to the tiredness, the drama and its draining effect. She ate breakfast feeling guilty. She was glad to feel that way.

Afterwards, Michael Howley approached. He was sorry. His organisation had tried but failed to have her baggage retrieved from the plane at Singapore.

'That is alright,' she said.

She wondered whether his politeness was a prelude to upcoming hard interrogations about her activities and then some kind of trial.

The children played in the sun. Millie Leydin gave her a bag of clothes, mostly tan-coloured. They had tea together and put brandy in it. She became certain that Millie's friendliness was false. It was simply the woman's role to keep her calm.

They went to the airport again at 4 p.m. They wouldn't take her through the public terminal. A car took them over the tarmac to the aircraft.

The plane was another Constellation, in all appearances the same as the first. Howley stood one side of Evdokia and Barrington the other. They had given her a low-fitting hat and driving glasses. Everyone on the plane knew exactly who she was.

The noise inside the plane was conic. She watched the country out the window. The hostess was offering chicken sandwiches.

She asked if they were going to Melbourne. Howley said they were going to a safe house near Sydney.

'Welcome to Operation Cabin 12. There will be a woman there,' he told her. 'We've already assigned her to the house.'

She wanted to know when Howley had first met her husband.

'Oh,' he replied. 'That might be a question best discussed with him.'

Formal but friendly, she thought. Was that how these people had decided they ought to be?

They landed at the aerodrome in darkness and she slept through the descent. A few minutes after they'd awakened her, she was sitting in the rear of a large black limousine.

The woman from the safe house had come to meet her, a thin woman with a small mouth and lines around her smile who introduced herself as Elizabeth or Lizzie.

The drive was north, over the Harbour Bridge. Evdokia thought the car was moving unnecessarily fast. On the far side, they swapped vehicles in an underground car park behind a picture theatre. The house they eventually pulled into was double-storeyed with a twin garage at the front. They zipped into the space and the doors came down.

She climbed the stairs and the first person she saw was Volodya. He was standing in the centre of the dim room, his form lit scarcely by a lamp.

This is a film, she thought. This is a film and it is going to end.

He came towards her and she struck him. It wasn't something she had planned. She just swung. Her fist connected with the skin of his neck and made an impotent slapping sound, infuriating in its lack of effect. Volodya raised a hand, protectively, anticipating further attack. She launched at him again. She thought the feelings of betrayal were going to turn her inside out.

He was gripping her arm. She withdrew it, yanking herself off balance. He tried to hold her but she wasn't having that.

'Let go,' she snarled. 'Let me go.'

He said something.

She pulled herself away, yelling. 'Coward. Bastard.'

She tripped over, fell in front of everyone to the floor. On her knees, Volodya's hands under her arms. It took strength to stay down.

'Fucking coward. Fucking defect.'

Volodya wasn't going to let her go. She wanted to be left

alone to lie here on the floor, but he wouldn't let it happen in front of them all. She stood, pushed his hands away, asked where the basin was.

Elizabeth led her there. The woman gave her a small towel, wetting it first under the tap.

'What do you think of me?' Evdokia asked.

Elizabeth presented a box of tissues. 'I think you are very brave,' she said.

Why did everyone believe that?

'Are you an intelligence officer?' Evdokia asked.

'Actually, I've been seconded from the secretarial pool.'

The woman suggested she have some rest, recuperate after the plane flight. They went to the bedroom. Twin windows faced the ocean. On a chair, one of Volodya's shirts.

Evdokia sat on the bed.

'Will you fetch my husband?' she asked.

The woman closed the door as she left. She might have nodded but Evdokia purposely kept her head down, avoiding the pitiful, sympathetic gaze. It wasn't rudeness if you did it to save yourself. Any look of condolence would have had a crippling, near-unbearable effect.

The questions came in volleys: questions that he didn't want to answer; indeed, could not answer. Evdokia was determined. Light in the room from the bedside lamp, shadow-making.

'What was supposed to happen to me? The woman married to the defector?'

He raised his hands as if to calm her.

'What was your plan for my future? What vision did you have in mind?'

'Doosia, I wanted you to have plausible denial. To be able to say you knew nothing and save yourself that way.'

She scoffed. 'Why not say you were happy to send me home in ruins? If not dead, then destroyed.'

'That is not true,' he said. 'Are you denying that in Moscow we would be on the pyre?'

'But whose fault is that?' she said. 'And now it is not us but my family who will burn.'

'The Party won't do that,' he insisted. 'Not with the world demanding news of their plight.' He tried to hold her hand. 'Listen,' he said quietly, 'let's not argue. I know this was a difficult choice for you. Harder for you than for me, as someone without a family.'

'Without family?' she said. 'But me.'

'Well.'

'Did you think I would betray you? Expose you to the ambassador? Was that it?'

'Of course not.'

'Then you were just a coward to go without saying goodbye.'

'Doosia, I am telling you. I wanted to give you plausible denial.'

'What is that? It's some concept you've invented in your head. Don't play me for a fool. I'm not your agent in the field.'

She turned her back on him and looked out the window.

He felt angry. Was it not enough that they were together now? What about sympathy for him? Did she not realise how instrumental he had been in getting her out?

'Look,' he said, 'let us concentrate on the future. It is a remarkable thing that you and I have done.'

'And what have we gained for it?' she asked. 'For this remarkable, irreversible step?'

'Our freedom,' he said. And he could see that she nearly laughed.

After consulting both Howley and Gilmour, he tried to avoid spending time with her alone. The theory was, she needed some space to adjust. He'd been a half-nervous wreck himself.

Because it was her nature to be joyfully polite in new company, the safe-house team organised activities, beginning with dominoes, which they played on a small table in the side yard—Howley, Carter, Evdokia and Elizabeth—with Gilmour taking photographs using a Minox, the device intended to inject a little humour and, Petrov hoped, a degree of perspective into the affair.

The weather deteriorated. Each morning brought less sunlight than the day before, and each afternoon a harsher, more cooling breeze, until on the Friday evening an electrical storm fired white lightning at the bay and rain came down in waves.

During this time the press coverage was immense. Articles explaining in every aspect the international importance of this event. Reporters discovering elusive details about their former lives. How Vladimir Petrov had spent his leisure time hunting and fishing. Which Canberra stores Evdokia Petrova had shopped in. There were articles about the top diplomats at the embassy: Generalov's biography; Lifanov's. It was obvious the reporters had little to go on. They printed strange accounts of telephone conversations with unnamed persons at the embassy, exchanges in muddled English, nonsensical.

He made sure Evdokia saw these reports. It was important that she realise she was being accepted as Australian.

A telegram arrived:

+ PROUD OF YOUR BRAVE ACTION HAVE URGED AUSTRALIAN GOVERNMENT GRANT YOU CITIZENSHIP PROTECTION AND FINANCIAL SECURITY CONFIDENT OTHERS WILL FOLLOW YOUR EXAMPLE + IGOR GOUZENKO

He read it twice to Evdokia. He wanted her to understand what he had always hoped: that in coming across they might join something—a splinter group housed by intelligence agencies across the globe; the gang of defectors, perhaps a modest force in the world but a small and nevertheless real community wedged between two great and global powers.

Evdokia read the message. She said Gouzenko sounded mad; that the telegram read as though he was listing grievances, speaking in a back-handed way to the Canadians. Petrov stared at the note. Maybe, but he didn't think so.

Then pictures of Jack appeared in the *Herald*. The dog Vladimir Petrov had left behind. He found Howley and Gilmour smoking by the back door and demanded again that some rescue attempt be made.

'It's not possible,' said Howley.

'Why?'

'He's Soviet property.'

'He is my property. They hate him at the embassy and they might starve him. If you refuse to fetch him, I will do it myself.'

'Vladimir, please don't.'

'I will. Get me a car.'

Gilmour offered a cigarette. 'If you leave this safe house, that will be it for all our jobs.'

'That's right,' Howley said. 'We've strict instructions to keep you safe.' He paused. 'Now listen, the rumour in Canberra is that the Soviet embassy is about to withdraw. Molotov is furious. At the very least, they're chucking us out of Moscow. So if Molotov doesn't order your colleagues home, we'll be doing it for him. That will be the best time to collect Jack.'

'What if they shoot him?'

'Why would they bother to do that?'

'They will have orders to burn everything. Get rid of everything.'

'I've never heard of anyone scuttling a dog.'

'Hitler.'

'What?'

'It's always a man's dog who wears his mistakes. I should have brought him with me. Let's go and get him. Let's get him because he's important to me.'

Howley shifted on his feet. 'I know, Vladimir. I promise, in good time we will retrieve him.'

That afternoon, he made sure he was more uncooperative than usual in their debriefing. The first thing on the agenda was whether he knew a communist named Ted Hill. He said he didn't. Then he said he'd met him twice, socially, though perhaps that was a man named Hall.

He demanded to know why they were interviewing him and his wife separately. Were they comparing their testimonies, attempting to trip them up?

'Of course not, Vladimir.'

'You're afraid that I'll tell you lies.'

'No. What reason would you have to do that?'

'None at all.'

'That's right.'

Howley was good at the game. His tone hardly wavered, no matter how irksome the mood of their conference became.

But something shifted that evening. Suddenly, he was being asked if he wanted to see Doctor Bialoguski. He put down the dessertspoon he was holding and looked across the table to Evdokia. She had a look that said, please.

'Alright,' he said.

Leo Carter drove him in one car while Howley went ahead in another. It was a twenty-minute trip into Sydney. When they came up on the major intersections, Carter dialled the volume lower and picked up the speaker of the short-range radio clipped to the dashboard in case Howley had something to say.

They took the Bridge and bore left.

Ascending the stairs at Cliveden, Petrov heard music coming from Bialoguski's flat. He thought at first that it was a record player or a wireless. When they knocked at the door and the noise stopped, he realised it had been the doctor playing violin. Petrov had never heard him play before. All this time, the doctor's highest passion, a member of the city's orchestra, and Petrov had never sat down to hear his friend play. Perhaps he was off balance tonight, but this fact, sharp and new, upset him.

'Ah!' said Bialoguski, inviting the group into his flat. 'Here is someone famous.'

They got to drinking straightaway. Bialoguski seemed to know Leo Carter already, or at least no time was taken for an introduction.

The doctor was in a good mood. There was small talk, men's talk. They discussed Sydney's left wing, their pitiful reaction to events. Unimaginative, the way they mimicked the Soviet line. Petrov asked after the boxes in the corner.

'Lady Poynter is returning,' Bialoguski grumbled. 'That, or news of my sacking from the orchestra finally reached London. I'm to vacate by the end of the month.'

The Russian joked that Bialoguski should move to the safe house. If certain communists found out how he'd helped him, the doctor might need the protection.

'That's right,' said Bialoguski. 'That's right.'

Suddenly, and, Petrov thought, quite awkwardly, both the Security men excused themselves, Howley muttering something about checking the cars. They left quickly, their drinks unfinished. Carter caught the doctor's eye and looked instructively at his watch.

Petrov turned to Bialoguski. The doctor looked at him, fetched a whisky bottle, poured them both a glass.

'They've gone because I need a word,' he said.

'Oh?'

'Yes. Let me preface this by saying it is my certain belief that you know what is coming. I wonder, in fact, if it really needs declaring at all.'

'What are you talking about?'

'It's been my desire, of course, to confide in you for a long time. That has not been possible, but you understand how it works.'

'What is this?'

'I must tell you, Vladimir, that I am an agent of the Security organisation. It is my belief that you have known this for some time.'

303

Blank.

'I have been a paid agent for many years,' the doctor continued. 'Since before we met—an important point, I think. Once we became friends, of course, I stopped the rest of my work to concentrate on helping you to remain in Australia. I don't think our friendship should suffer as a result of what I'm telling you. I believe you were aware of who I was; however, the situation dictated that our circumstances remained unspoken. Of course, it was not my job to encourage you. Only to be there if you made your choice. I don't think any of this is news. Nothing that would surprise you. I'm sure you knew or heavily suspected. It would have been no good putting questions or making accusations. What purpose could have been served? So we kept the fact outside ourselves, you and I, a secret that stayed in the background. I believe there were many things your suspicions caused you to hide from me. There should be no need of that now. Please understand also that Security and I were never the same thing. Out of friendship for you, I kept things from them. The women, for example, the escapades with girls—entirely our own affair. Never reported. What would have been the point? Do you understand? That was private and it will remain so, between you and me. The things that brought us together were unfortunate. We should remind ourselves that you were MVD and that officially I was not aware of that also. But now it is all in the open. Yes? And I hope our friendship will grow stronger now that all this secrecy is gone.'

The doctor finished his whisky. 'You are very quiet, Vladimir,' he said.

Bastards.

He drank some whisky and looked past Bialoguski to the kitchen, at nothing. He felt beaten, like a player who, outmatched in the final moment, looks for a rule that has been broken only to find, gallingly, that none has.

He reached forward, performing the only act that seemed to make sense, which was to shake the doctor's hand. To his mind, Bialoguski's blow couldn't have been better delivered, softened by those palatable fibs supposed to allow his friend, Vladimir, to save face. Silently, the Russian finished his whisky and poured another, returning the bottle to the doctor's side of the coffee table but not refilling his glass. 'Of course we are friends,' he said. And that was all.

The Security men returned. As they sat, the doctor told Howley to advise Colonel Spry that he and their prize asset remained friends, true roles out in the open. Howley nodded in a diminished way, lighting a cigarette. They sat quietly until Leo Carter brought up the topic of the federal election, which was locked up, he said, at forty-nine points apiece. They discussed it for a time. Bialoguski joked that perhaps Vladimir ought be issued with a vote. Big laughs. Nervous laughs. They were trying to bring him back, draw him in again, resurrect his ability to trust.

There was a section of road on the return trip that hugged the coastline, bringing the cars to the black edge of the sea. It wasn't a long stretch, climbing slightly uphill for perhaps only a hundred metres. There was a point, however, where the road curved, bracing against the cliff that stood over its dark height. Here, when road conditions were right, travellers could feel the land beneath them dissolving.

He would need to go over everything. The last three years were suddenly a fresh and opaque concern. Too early, he supposed, for evaluations. It was time for considered thought

ANDREW CROOME

and the replaying of events in his mind. Hard to believe. He'd always been a popular man in Moscow; fair with the privileges he'd had; respected as a man and for his work. Friends he'd had then—men who put his interests on equal footing with their own. Pronin, one of his clerks. Unbelievably slender, as if horribly underfed. Fishing partners for years, boating on the River Moskva, venturing to discuss many things, even politics and systems of rule. Pronin was an amateur technologist, a scientist of a type. He admired Petrov's Omega, jesting cash amounts and material inducements to buy it. In Sweden, Petrov bought him one, a newer and more stylish model with a date and day function built in. When he returned to Moscow, Pronin wasn't there to receive it—he had been promoted to head of cypher for the ekranoplan project on the Caspian Sea: huge aircraft prototyped to fly mind-boggling distances over water at an altitude of one metre or less. Petrov sent the watch in the mail—an ambitious idea at best—and it was robbed in transit. Pronin wrote, saying, never mind. They never saw each other again. Strange when friends vanish from your life and you do not give them a second thought.

Leo Carter killed the engine and turned towards him.

'Now that your wife is here,' he said quietly, 'the director thought we should tell you. The girls. No one has any reason to dredge that up. It's a secret between us. Does that suit? Only the case officers saw the details. We're not paying it any mind, and you can be trusting. There'll be none of it that sees the light.'

She was sleeping crossways on the bed, the solid expanse of her back facing upwards, her sides expanding with each breath.

306

The room was only halfway dark, with the curtains open and the twin windows fed by streetlight. He stripped down to his underwear and sat across from her in a bedside chair.

In the far corner was the safe. A black, short-legged structure with an antique appearance, holding a shade under five thousand pounds.

He was thinking that he had never been cut out for this. At one stage he'd thought he was, but obviously he'd never been. These other men—the likes of Kislitsyn, the doctor, the Australians—they were an alien breed in comparison, a peculiar subset of humanity he had thought he could mix with, but—judging by where he now found himself, in this room—he could not. Embarrassing. He had been the world's worst spy: a dupe and a traitor. His only solace was that he hadn't asked for it. They had given it to him, the mantle, insisted that he take it on. Well, they regretted that now. So did he. He wondered what part of this room he should put down to his incompetence rather than Lifanov's and Generalov's greed? What was it a question of? He didn't know.

He looked down at her body and was thankful she was there. For a moment he regretted everything. Every part of what had been done. The room was a sorrow; not of his own making, but of a cohesion of personalities and forces, and who could pick one event or decision as the cause? Strange to be these people in this room. Odd to be doubled in the newspapers and on the radio and to be those people and these at the same time.

No special thing to feel this way about history. He had never been a collector of mementos or keepsakes—something in the impulse struck him as politically unsound. His material connections were a suitcase of clothes, a comb, a toothbrush, some spectacles, the pair of shoes he'd just removed, a key.

Sum total. He saw this as a good thing. Not to be weighted by the past. He had no need of reminders to know the wretchedness at the heart of things.

Desolate views. He looked from the window, the streetlights' electrical glow more stark and less inviting in some spots than in others. There was a jetty or some other fixed object by the water, putting an arc of yellow light onto the sea, picking out whitecaps, barely.

He wanted to vanish now. Escape and use his ransom to buy somewhere to live a life. Go alone. Find an isolated place to reside without ever being found. Such a big country. So many places just like that. Queensland, maybe. Tasmania. Buy a small farm, blocked by sea frontage or a river, some wily route by which to flee should anyone from Special Tasks manage to track him down.

Not possible, of course. He was coming to realise how deeply imprisoned he was by the freedom that he'd bought.

A whole country that knew his face. How long could a man like that hide? He could picture the brute emerging from the everyday haze, a stranger at first like any stranger, a well-dressed insurance seller or a tradesman in overalls, approaching to the sound of cicadas, the same smells in the air, everything regular, nothing amiss—which, he supposed, it wouldn't be—knocking at the door, looking for sales, asking for work, regular, regular. The only plan you could have was to bargain for the pistol and not the pick.

The unfortunate thing about the future is that it cannot be taken back.

He opened the window slightly and Evdokia stirred. He looked down, hoping she would not wake. The bedsheets were white, like hospital clothes, dim in the darkness. He stood and held his breath. He didn't want his wife to become a conscious presence in the room, discomforted by the idea of her seeing him.

Did Gouzenko have a family? Had he taken them with him or left them behind? If they met each other in South America or Africa, two defectors on safe and neutral ground, would friendship be possible? Would they remind each other, awfully, of what their choices had done?

Tamara looked as he imagined Evdokia might have at fifteen. Curls and a movement of body that was athletic and self-assured. He'd taught her in one afternoon how to ride the bicycle her sister brought her from Sweden. They had gone to a square of grass in a park and she had ridden, just clear of his hands, in circles. That was the only time he could think of when they had ever been alone together. Otherwise, he only saw her with Evdokia, the two sisters, Moscow cosmopolitans making the best of their advantages, pretending to be Americans, not quite convincing when they were discussing merit systems in the Komsomol and which play to see of Brecht's.

Was he responsible for that young girl? Weren't there a billion small events that had added up to get them here? Why blame him when any link would do?

He took a pillow from the bed and slept the whole night in the chair.

23

Yes, she was a Soviet intelligence worker, a captain in the MVD. Yes, she had run agents in the field. Yes, she knew something of the espionage situation in Australia. No, she was not aware of the types of document that Volodya had brought out.

Michael Howley's face was mild, a young man's face, pleasant, helpful. They were in the lounge room drinking tea with the translator, Saburov.

Howley asked what she knew about radio equipment. What type of transmitters did the Soviet embassy use?

'Are you able to get news of my family?' she said.

He drank from his teacup and looked at her blankly.

'You must have agents in Moscow,' she said. 'Can't you send a man to check?'

'What is the address?' he asked.

She gave it in English and in Russian. That and the building's telephone number, E-1-31-36. He said the matter would be considered. Whatever help that could be given, it would be done.

Saburov stared at his fingernails.

'We never transmit by radio,' she explained. 'There was an old one, broken. Everything travels by the cable.'

That afternoon she went to the beach. Volodya was anxious about the idea but she did it anyway to spite him. Elizabeth brought several bathing suits for her to try and she decided on a black one with the best fit. There was a good beach in front of the safe house but they didn't risk it. Instead, they drove forty minutes up the coast to a small cove, which was deserted when they arrived. Leo Carter erected an enormous umbrella on the sand. He looked thin and wiry in swimming trunks. The three of them stood in the surf. The water, washy, darkly toned, came up and to their knees.

She felt guilty and ashamed. Unreal. As if she were living a sudden second life, parallel to her own. They ate bits of ham and cheese in the shade. Carter went to sit in the car, leaving her and Elizabeth to chat.

Only they didn't chat. They simply sat there, staring at the sea.

They returned at dusk. Volodya was playing chess with Gilmour at a table in the lounge room. Upstairs, on the bedside table, her carry bag was open. It was one of her few certain possessions and she was sure she had zipped it closed.

She went downstairs. 'What is this?' she demanded.

Volodya and Gilmour looked up, the Security man appearing suddenly afraid.

'Why is my bag open?' she said. 'Who has been in here when I left it closed?'

Volodya moved a chess piece. 'I opened your bag,' he said.

'What for?'

'We were searching for your air ticket.'

'Why?'

'The embassy can gain a refund on the Sydney to Zurich section. The BOAC agent in Canberra needs to see the unused document returned.'

Gilmour was staring. She narrowed on Volodya. 'I thought you had quit the embassy,' she said. 'But still you do their bidding.'

'Don't be snide.'

'Don't tell me what to be. Don't go poking through my things!'

'Hundreds of pounds, the price of that ticket. I am just preventing them from making further accusations.'

'That you are a thief.'

'Yes.'

'The ticket was not there.'

'No.'

'Ironically, you *are* a thief.'

He said nothing.

'Hotel receipts,' she said. 'Not paying the duty on all that liquor.'

Her husband's face screwed up. He asked her how the beach was. He asked in a mocking tone, designed to bring things into focus and to hurt.

'You,' she said. The nearest object was a porcelain ashtray. She threw it across the room. It hit his shoulder high, surprising him more than anything, falling to the floor with a dull thud. Reacting dumbly, his hand came forward and knocked the chess pieces.

Gilmour stood up.

She gave him a painful look and rushed from the room.

***

Grief and the amplifications of night. She stood at the back of the house, facing the hill, a massing blackness. The night was cloudless. The stars were the Canberra stars, the southern stars that Masha thought patternless and rogue. Carefully, she climbed the stairs to the rooftop balcony. Houses below her to the sea. The balcony's railing at her waist. Underneath was the front garden and, with a little effort, the longer drop over the garden wall.

She wondered about her father's cancer. Where it was in his body. How it felt to carry that inside. What about treatment? Would the state provide for his care now?

She guessed that the money she had in Moscow had by now been seized or frozen. Section 1.3 of the USSR Statute of Political Crimes. Funny to have betrayed your childhood, your whole life, the lens by which you viewed the world. She was a Marxist. She believed in the revolution. Capitalism was vulgar, an apocalyptic depravity. How would she make her way here? What was she going to do?

Tell the Australians everything, she supposed. Offer them all she knew about secrets in the Soviet Union, the names, the methods and structures, the missions, the countries, the handlers, the chiefs of sections, the ideals and the cruelties of approach. Tell herself it was a doublecrossing of no choice. Because the Australians had got to her cleverly, it being their job.

Yet how long could that last? A year to remember and recount? Moscow, Stockholm, Japan. The story of her past life. Afterwards, what? Who did she know on this earth but Volodya? And once she'd had the time to reflect on these last few years, would she claim to know even him?

She heard something shift behind her. A face in the darkness; one of the policemen at the foot of the balcony steps. They looked at one another for a moment. His name was Grandelis. They had spoken only once. She thought he might say something but instead he lit a cigarette, a spark of flame and a fiery red circle. Then he turned and vanished with a slow walk, going back to guarding and to listening.

She heard the sound of an accelerating car somewhere in the distance.

Her heart, somehow, was thundering.

She remembered the items she had left for shipping. Would the embassy give her these if she asked? Just as likely, they had already incinerated them, or perhaps sent them to an investigations office somewhere in central Moscow, the subject of a forthcoming paper: 'Items of Suspicion When Detecting Potential Traitors'.

Now we are passing through the curtain, she thought. Maybe you expected your life to unravel, but might you better have prepared for the threads to disappear?

It was a physical feeling. Empty.

She went slinking to the back door and into the kitchen and to the brandy cupboard, poured a midnight glass, the liquid brash and fuming, aftertaste like blood. Grandelis still smoking somewhere, the coarse bitterness of the tobacco a deadening of the air, a starvation. Darkness in the hallway and under Volodya's door.

Standing without reason, holding the glass.

The next morning, she took her time getting up. Nine, and she was just out of bed. Howley and Volodya were already in session in the lounge room. Elizabeth had seemingly been waiting for Evdokia to rise and they ate breakfast together, marmalade on toast.

The woman said, 'They want to know whether you'd like to talk at eleven o'clock.'

'Oh?'

'Yes.'

Elizabeth poured her a juice and told her about the questions that had come by wire overnight. Cryptic lists from the British and the Americans, from the French and the Swedes and other places. Names—there were a number of countries who wanted to know about missing men, missing families of men and missing activists. A lot of people seemed to have vanished recently in Egypt. There were questions of history also, about massacres and war crimes, Katyn Forest, various prison camps.

'I think you will be asked everything,' said Elizabeth. 'The political mysteries of our times.'

Evdokia buttered more toast.

'Of course, the CIA and MI5 have asked to interview you personally,' Elizabeth went on. 'This will be your choice, down the road.'

Evdokia had the feeling there was something she wasn't being told. They were holding something back. A part of the process not yet named, a secret they thought she might resent.

'My husband has Jack,' said Elizabeth.

'*Your* husband?'

'Yes. A policeman in Canberra collected him from your house. He was tied at the back there. He had a bucket of water and seemed alright. They've given him to us to look after. Mr Howley thinks he's too famous, for the moment, to come here.'

Evdokia turned her ear to the lounge room. Volodya's voice seemed happy and cooperative. She was jealous suddenly.

'No news yet of your family,' Elizabeth said.

Outside, the morning sky was grey light, overcast, the noise of bird life in the air. They sat with cups of tea on the balcony and waited. When eleven o'clock came, Howley invited her downstairs. He gave her pencil and paper and asked for drawings of the control structure of the MVD.

'Write in Russian,' he said. 'Saburov can translate it.'

She put herself at the bottom and sketched up and across. The end product was a mess, departments and sections linked in wayward trees. It was supposed to look mechanical, Moscow's secret apparatus, highly structured and well defined.

'We'll draft a diagram,' said Howley. 'You can correct it and we'll add to it over time.'

She described her history in intelligence. Her recruitment and beginnings in the Anglo and Asian sections, her learning of Japanese.

He wanted to know about Rupert Lockwood: Voron. She described the encounter in general terms: the typewritten documents, the pleasantries exchanged. Howley wanted details. What pages or passages did she see him type? What brand of caviar was it that he received? She knew the specifics weren't meant to test her. Howley was already believing everything she said.

'What are these facts for?' she asked. 'You are going to arrest him and make charges?'

Howley looked at her. 'In the end that will be up to the government,' he replied. 'Our job here is simply to get the evidence and the information straight.'

Is this it, she thought. Are they going to ask me to testify in open court?

'It's possible,' Howley admitted when she pressed. 'But the more you can remember, perhaps the less you will be needed.

Whatever facts you provide, we may be able to confirm them in other ways.'

Erase myself, she thought. Give them everything and so avoid appearing in public—the worst of fates, further endangering everyone I know.

They spoke for five hours, not stopping for lunch and finishing only when Howley thought they should. By the session's end, she had given up more details of Russian code systems than she thought she knew. Howley seemed pleased. An hour later, under the pretence that the two events weren't related, he gave her a Grace Bros catalogue.

'We're making arrangements to get you a wardrobe,' he told her. 'The store has agreed to see you after hours any time this week.'

She flicked through the pages. The world seemed suddenly very small.

24

Time now to reinvent the self. He moved out of Cliveden, renting a small one-bedroom flat in Paddington with white walls. He sold his Holden and, using the bounty ASIO had paid on Petrov's defection, bought a Ford Custom Sedan, an American car with ivory duco.

To furnish the flat, he purchased a second-hand armchair. He bought a wooden school desk, a typewriter, a lamp and an ashtray and he set himself up in the middle of the lounge. He got his notebooks, everything he'd recorded as a secret agent, and placed them in a neat pile. He poured a glass of whisky, sat his loaded gun on the desk, stared at the keys in front of him. Time to write the book. My Life Drawing Soviet Defectors Over the Line. It would be a composition of careful construction, not unlike his music, he thought. To begin, he needed a tone, a pitch, a theme inside the words. He crafted a sentence in his mind: a description, as it happened, of his own appearance.

He saw Petrov again. They met at a safe house in the Cahors building under Leo Carter's supervision. The Russian was noticeably fatter. He was sweaty and uncommunicative. They drank beer and didn't say much. The Petrov in Bialoguski's book became more rotund, more incapable.

He gave his first two chapters to Security, typing the drafts using carbon paper. He'd had to agree to it being vetted. It didn't worry him. His plan was to get Security's approval, insert his condemnations of their various petty behaviours afterwards as a surprise assault.

Whenever he left the flat, he carried the revolver. He took it shopping. He took it to the races. At the surgery, he kept it in a desk drawer, the first and second chambers empty so it wouldn't misfire and bullet a patient.

The Royal Commission began: an inquiry into Soviet espionage in Australia, charged with uncovering means and extent and especially the involvement of any Australians. Judges Owen, Philp and Ligertwood were entitled to pursue this inquiry in whichever way they saw fit. Witnesses would be compelled to appear. Lines of investigation would stem from Petrov's documents: the letters written to him by his Moscow command.

There were other documents too. Document H: a slanderous catalogue of the members of the press gallery written by an as yet unnamed citizen for the benefit of Soviet intelligence. Document J: a 'malicious foulness' of a typescript written inside the Soviet embassy by another Australian citizen in an act of 'beastly cowardice' designed to dodge defamation laws. 'Document J appears,' said Mr Windeyer, counsel assisting the commission, 'to be a farrago of facts, falsities and filth.'

On 29 May 1954, Labor, under the leadership of Doctor H.V. Evatt, lost the federal election. The popular vote was won, but not the House. Just five weeks after Evdokia's defection, Robert Menzies returned for a third term. People claimed that it had been the Petrovs' defection, igniting fears of spies and Reds like a magnesium flare, that had cost Labor dearly.

Bialoguski was surprised when John Rodgers, director of Australia–Soviet House, rang him at the surgery and wanted to meet. They had lunch at Ling Nam's, a Chinese restaurant in King Street, and discussed strategies that the Communist Party might use at the commission. Rodgers was certain that, due to his friendship with Petrov, Bialoguski would be called. The doctor pretended to be unsure.

'Petrov was a drinker,' said Rodgers.

'Oh?'

'And a womaniser. A bad one. A shameless, womanising drunk.'

'I believe you.'

'What's most important is the destruction of this bloke's credit. This is the biggest battle for the Party since Menzies tried to ban it. Petrov will name names. But we all know what he was like. If the question of his drunkenness comes up, if his unwelcome attentions to women come up . . . We're just suggesting that you cast doubt by testifying to his habits.'

'Petrov is a traitor,' said Bialoguski. 'Of course I want to help in any way I can.'

The commission hearings in Sydney were swamped by protesters. Some waved placards and a few wore papier-mâché masks. Bialoguski, a hat pulled tightly over his head, watched with subdued amusement as a huge, drunken incarnation of Menzies walked bellowing up the steps of the High Court to be threatened at its doors by a constable with a cudgel.

Vladimir gave his initial evidence over four days. It was revealed that the author of Document H was Fergan O'Sullivan, Doctor Evatt's young press secretary, who, though repentant, was very quickly sacked.

When Evdokia took the stand the press remarked upon how educated and attractive she was. Asked who had written Document J, she stepped from the witness box, paced the front row of the gallery and pointed a finger at Rupert Lockwood, announcing his name.

Bialoguski eagerly awaited his own appearance. It had been revealed now that he was no ordinary, left-leaning doctor but instead a careful and deliberate agent working for the Security service. He practised for his turn, anticipating how the communists would go after him. But before he could appear, events turned strange. Doctor Evatt demanded that Document J be subjected to expert analysis. He was concerned about the way the document was organised, and seemed to be suggesting that certain elements had been inserted.

Bialoguski watched in disbelief as Evatt's theory emerged. It seemed the Labor leader believed that a conspiracy had taken place. At best, Document J had been altered by unnamed forces for the purposes of smearing his staffers and, by extension, Evatt himself. At worst, the whole document was a fabrication, the cruel work of an expert forger, brought into existence for debased political ends. A plot existed, but Evatt was cautious, never fully revealing its shape. Indeed, as the commission progressed, the plot seemed capable of instant transformation, huge twists and turns around the evidence. Empirical facts were in one breath relied upon and in the next breath questioned. The central issue became: was Document J a forgery or was it not? If it was a forgery, who had done the forging and why?

Bialoguski was not amused. Evatt was putting Lockwood, his staffers and himself at the heart of the story. From what Bialoguski could glean, Document J was a pissy little rant, nothing to do with anything. Now it was stealing the show.

He finally entered the witness box. He testified about his double life, the sacrifices and the deceptions. He spoke about his relations with Petrov, the final steps that had led to his defection. Ted Hill, the de-facto solicitor for Australian communists, tried to paint him as a mercenary, a man for hire, paid according to the value of the information he could unearth. Bialoguski denied it. Hill suggested that the doctor was duplicitous. An interesting charge, said Bialoguski, given that that had been his job.

'You have shown interest in the Soviet Union, support for the Soviet Union, have you not?' Hill said.

'Yes.'

'But you were never a member of the Communist Party?'

'No.'

'However, you did belong to the Russian Social Club?'

'Yes.'

'And you belonged to various peace movements?'

'I did.'

'And in each of these bodies to which you belonged, to whose aims you *pretended* to subscribe, you made some close friends, did you not?'

'I made some acquaintances.'

'You made some friends?'

'Not in my mind.'

Hill paused. 'Why did you join Security's service?' he asked. 'Why?'

'Yes.'

'Duty, I suppose.'

'It's a strange occupation, is it not?'

'I don't see how.'

'I take it you dislike communism?'

'I think it is bad for Australia, yes.'

'But why spy? You say it has cost you a lot personally. Why did you involve yourself to such extremes?'

'I wouldn't say extremes.'

'Other people might think so. Devoting your life, as you tell us you have, in this way.'

'Somebody has to. Somebody needs to stand at the cold edge.'

'But why you? That is what I am asking.'

It made Bialoguski uncomfortable that he had no answer. Not, at least, an answer that he was happy with. He would have liked some event in his life to summon, to point at as explanation. The death of his father, perhaps, or of a beloved brother, or a young wife; a motivating tragedy for which communism's bastardry was to blame.

'I don't understand your question, Mr Hill,' he eventually said. 'I would say that it was irrelevant.'

Hill had a last assertion. 'Isn't it true that you, Doctor Bialoguski, conspired with the Petrovs to manufacture Document J?'

Bialoguski groaned. It was exasperating how the commission had been hijacked. It suited the Communist Party, he supposed, to so muddle the evidence with doubts, perceived contradictions and lunacies, thus affording any real proof of espionage the cover of a general circus.

***

He wrote on. He spoke to Clean at the *Sydney Morning Herald*, who said the paper would carry extracts. He met with a representative from William Heinemann. The publisher was interested, offered him a small sum that afternoon to have first option on the final product. Bialoguski explained that a secret second version was in the pipeline—one dealing in detail with Security's foolish ways.

'That's fine,' said the publisher. 'Whatever you want to write.'

One morning, in his flat, he accidentally shot a wall. The gun went off at his desk and the bullet travelled through and into the corridor outside. He retrieved it, returned to the armchair and sat, prepared to concede it was perhaps time to ditch the revolver. Ostensibly it was for safety, but, reluctantly, he knew it was for more. The gun was a way of living. Not in a dying-by-the-sword sense, but in the way it was a secret, a hidden thing, a sort of power over those who could not suspect it.

He had thought he was adapting to his new, open life, the life lived whole, but was it just that he'd found his old habits again in this gun?

It was not something he could readily explain to himself, but in truth he had been feeling, since Petrov's defection, somehow rejected. It was a foolish emotion, not unlike the feeling he'd had when he'd been booted from the orchestra. He knew it was a preposterous sentiment when nothing of the sort had occurred, but there it was: he felt wilfully discarded. Somehow excluded by the world.

Three months later, he'd finished *The Petrov Story*. He particularly liked its concluding chapter, a piece of political analysis in which he called Doctor Evatt an opportunist and accused him of using the commission to divert attention from his own electoral failings.

There was also his final word on the Petrovs. Their future would depend on themselves, he declared. Whether they had the moral courage to know in their hearts that they had done the right thing. Whether they had sincerity of purpose in accepting what their new life would offer.

Sincerity of purpose. He didn't quite know what he meant by it, how precisely it applied to the Petrovs, but he liked the sound.

When extracts of the book appeared in the *Herald*, he expected business at the surgery to pick up. If anything, it dropped off. It was frustrating. All he'd given these people, this nation, and now they could read about it and still he was out of favour.

For a month or two, he turned inward. He rehearsed his violin intently, an element of himself he'd been neglecting.

In December 1955, he found himself in the Spring Street offices of the Orient Line. The more he thought about it, the more it made sense. Get out of Australia. Temporarily. Permanently. What was keeping him here, really? A dying medical practice, a measure of notoriety, a licence to carry a weapon?

He spoke with the director of entertainments.

'I want passage to London as a professional passenger. I can give lectures. I can be charming at dinner. I can even play as a guest in your band, should you like.'

The director looked up from flipping through the pages of Bialoguski's book.

'The Petrov spy,' he said.

'And I want only passage, not payment. It's a good deal for you since the ship will sail anyway.'

Michael Howley wished his former agent luck. He said Bialoguski had played an essential part in securing the defections of the Petrovs and he thanked him for it. He said also that it was perhaps best not to say goodbye to Vladimir and Evdokia. Difficult times at the safe house, he explained.

Instead, Bialoguski wrote a short farewell note to Vladimir, signed but undated, to be handed to the man whenever Security saw fit. He had intended to finish it with a joke, a parting piece of wit between friends, but as he stood with his hand over the paper, waiting for inspiration, he drew a complete blank. Try as he did for several minutes, absolutely nothing came to mind.

1961–1996

25

The New TRUTH
The Independent Newspaper
Melbourne, January 21, 1961

WE FIND PETROVS!
'I WISH I WERE DEAD.'
The secret is out; the Petrovs are found. For the first time their
story of six fear-filled years is told. And TRUTH tells it!

'NOBODY COULD DREAM OF OUR MISERY'
By Bill Wannan and Norma Ferris

THIS WEEK we tracked down Vladimir and Evdokia Petrov, the
Russian diplomats who made world headlines when they defected
and won political asylum in Australia in 1954.

For six years their hiding places have been known only to the
Prime Minister (Mr Menzies) and a few top security guards.

What are they like now, the Petrovs?

How have the years of hiding and subterfuge affected them?

We can tell you.

The Petrovs are lonely, scared people, still dreading an attack from Russian agents.

'No one could dream of our misery . . . I wish I were dead,' said Mrs Petrov . . . Mr Petrov shuffled up looking grey, older than his age and tired . . . 'Quiet, please, somebody is near . . . I don't trust them,' said Mrs Petrov . . . Mr Petrov walked quietly away.

Tears welled in Mrs Petrov's eyes.

'I am frightened,' she said. 'How? How? How did you find us?' she kept asking.

We couldn't tell Mrs Petrov that. We wouldn't tell anyone. But it was along a trail to a holiday resort that we are satisfied no one else will be able to follow.

We found Mrs Petrov an intelligent, ambitious woman, WITH NOWHERE TO GO.

She was trained by one of the greatest political machines on earth to think, act, talk and absorb.

But what is there ahead? Only the humble existence of looking after her husband.

From what we learned of their story from 1954 the Petrovs have had little peace of mind because of what might have happened to their relatives in Russia.

But what is the alternative? Go back to Russia?

Mrs Petrov has lost weight. Her figure is slim and petite. She looks younger, healthier than she appeared during the commission hearings.

Petrov has become greyer. The years have dealt more hardly with his appearance than with his wife's.

'His nerves are very bad,' Mrs Petrov told us. 'He has suffered too much already because of the publicity.'

As she told her story we could see that she had suffered—it was the tragedy of the frail human being caught in the meshes of mankind's political caperings.

When we first approached Mrs Petrov this week, she stood frozen with fear.

'Can you not leave us alone, we have had enough, we cannot bear any more,' she said.

She looked like any other housewife.

Trying To Go On

She was simply dressed in a tasteful cotton frock no one would look at, except perhaps to say, 'What an attractive little woman.'

'Can you imagine what a hell on earth we have been through?' she asked.

'We do not want anything. We are trying to go on but it is incredibly hard.'

With an intolerably sad look in her beautiful china blue eyes, she said: 'No one could imagine what it has been like, no one!'

We assured Mrs Petrov we would never reveal the locality to which we had traced her.

Then Petrov, the man who was once world headlines, joined us.

A stocky grey-haired man in sports clothes and dark glasses, he came in saying, 'What is going on here, what is it?'

He looked pale and nervous.

'I will manage this,' Mrs Petrov said, springing like a tiger cat protecting her young.

When we tried to halt the retreating Petrov, his wife cried out piteously, 'Oh, leave him alone—he has suffered enough.'

There Is No Future

She added: 'Nobody knows us here, but there are some who might not be sympathetic.'

Gloomily, she spoke of an exile's life.

'It is very hard for us,' she said.

'There is no future. There is nothing to live for. I try to live the life of an ordinary housewife. I do the shopping, go to work and look after my husband.'

Were the Petrovs happy in the work they were doing?

Mrs Petrov said that it had taken a long time to find suitable work. Both were now in jobs they liked, but there was always the fear of their identities being discovered. They might have to leave their workplaces if the management knew who they really were.

Had they formed many Australian friendships?

'We have few friends,' Mrs Petrov said. 'It is not easy for us to make friends. For one thing, Australians do not like foreigners or New Australians very much.'

Mrs Petrov continued: 'I feel Australians think only of themselves. New Australians feel they are too often left on their own—in shops, at work, in the streets . . . in fact, everywhere.

'Some people in this country even laugh at migrants.'

'I have many regrets', BUT THIS IS THE ONLY WAY

Mrs Petrov said: 'Some Australians laugh at foreign accents. They do not help these people to become assimilated. They are thoughtless.'

Were the Petrovs lonely?

'Yes,' said Mrs Petrov, 'we lead fairly lonely lives. We have few pleasures or interests.'

'Do you go to see Russian films?' we asked.

'No, never,' said Mrs Petrov, 'but we watch a lot of TV.'

Three times since the Petrovs won political asylum here Mrs Petrov has undergone serious operations.

'I would gladly have died,' she said, 'but I lived.'

'So I must go on. There is nothing else to do.'

Just a Couple in a Car, Maybe Your Neighbours

Maybe you passed this car out driving last weekend. A grey-haired, burly man at the wheel, his wife beside him. Two frightened people trying to forget.

(Car-sick? No fear—I take KWELLS. Kwells prevents all forms of travel sickness. Completely safe for all the family. 3/9 at Chemists.)

Here are some other questions we put to the Petrovs, and the replies given by Mrs Petrov.

Have you contacted your relatives in the Soviet since the Royal Commission, Mrs Petrov?

'No. What is the use? They are dead.'

Have you had any definite word that they are dead?

'No, but I know it. The Russian government would not allow them to live.'

Debt Paid

The pitiful personal dilemma of the Petrovs can be solved only if the Federal Government in particular and the Australian public in general are willing to help.

Consider their case. Up to 1954 Vladimir Petrov was engaged in spying for Russia. He was detected.

From then on events overwhelmed this second-rate spy. Caught in the maelstrom of international power politics, he was faced with this choice:

Go home to his native land and face the punishment; or

Confess all to the country on which he was preying and in return be granted asylum.

The Petrovs chose freedom and stayed in Australia as not very willing and not very welcome guests. The past six years have been, in Mrs Petrov's own words, 'Hell'.

Let those six years be their punishment both for spying on the land they must now regard as their own and for betraying their native Russia.

Let the Federal Government now treat them as ordinary citizens and drop the security mask.

Let the people of this country accept them, not as semi-fugitives living lonely, fearful lives, but as Mr and Mrs Petrov, the couple who once made a mistake and now want to live full, useful lives in the community.

26

1963. She walked home from where she worked, walked through the Melbourne suburb where they lived, walked along the street where they had their house, and saw two men in long coats getting out of a car. The first she didn't recognise. The second was the writer, B2.

'Hello, Evdokia,' the man said, smiling.

She invited them into the house. They took seats at the kitchen table while her terrier barked from the backyard. The younger man's name, she was informed, was Roy. They looked about the room. Just an ordinary kitchen, she wanted to say.

Roy watched her intently as she boiled the kettle, peering at her as if she might constitute a clue to an important question of some kind.

'How are things?' B2 asked. 'Are you having any trouble?'

'Only the journalists,' she explained. They drove Volodya to madness, sitting in cars on the street like the KGB.

It was usually Colonel Spry who visited for these types of conversations. She hadn't seen B2 in at least two years, despite the fact that he had written their book for them; eighteen months spent interviewing, reading and editing in the safe houses.

'Evdokia,' the man said eventually, 'the reason we've come today is to present something to you. I want us to be cautious, however. I think whatever approach we take must be considered. We shouldn't act rashly.'

What was he talking about?

'Received yesterday morning,' he commented, producing a document, placing it between them on the table.

She read:

Dear Sirs,

At the request of woman citizen Tamara Alexeyevna KARTSEVA, we are trying to trace her relatives—sister, PETROVA née KARTSEVA Evdokia Alexeyevna, born 1914 in the village of Lipki, Oblast of Ryazan, and her husband PETROV Vladimir Mikhailovich, who used to live in the city of Canberra, Australia.

The last letter from the persons sought was received at the end of 1953, and there has been no news from them since.

We should be most grateful if you could ascertain, and let us know of, the whereabouts of the persons sought.

Thanking you in anticipation,

Yours faithfully,

A. Titov

Head of Tracing Bureau

Executive Committee of the Alliance of Red Cross and Red Crescent, Moscow

Tamara Alexeyevna Kartseva. The words sat on the page with the other words but they might as well have come alone. She picked up the letter from the table. It was typed in English. It took her several minutes to extract the intended meaning.

'The Tracing Bureau?' she said aloud.

Nine years' silence. Tamara not gone, not dead, but twenty-five years old, existing somewhere, searching for her elder sister.

She agreed with B2 to keep her reply short. She agreed that everything should go through ASIO and afterwards the Red Cross.

Dear Tamara Alexeyevna,

We can hardly believe this letter! Can you confirm that it is indeed you who has made this enquiry in Moscow? Please tell what news there is of Mother and Father—I fear greatly for both of them, such a long time has passed. Have you married? Do you have children? Please write without delay. Please send photographs of everybody. I have none.

E. Kartseva

B2 promised to bring any reply to her the moment it came.

Each night at dusk or just before, she rounded the corner of her street, willing an ASIO car to be there. Two months passed. It was a Thursday and raining when the telephone finally rang. B2 arrived twenty minutes later.

She recognised the handwriting. *Dear Sister.* This was Tamara. There could be no question.

Her sister was sorry for not writing earlier. They still lived at the old address. Their father had died of cancer in February 1959 and their mother was aging poorly but had been 'restored to life' by Evdokia's letter.

Tamara explained she was an engineer—a senior industrial engineer, university educated. She asked where Evdokia and Vladimir were living and wanted to know when they were returning home.

I want to visit you on a holiday, she wrote, *and Mother would like to visit too.*

There were photographs. Evdokia sat on the couch and held them. Her mother looked ancient, smiling from a chair, her hands clasped in front. Her sister looked thirty years old.

She knew there was an oddness to the letter. A gap. Was it possible that, when she and Volodya defected, her family was simply never told? Years of inexplicable silence from your daughter in Australia—was that the punishment Moscow had decided to inflict?

Before I can officially visit you, Tamara wrote, *I must complete a request at the local militia office, and it is necessary for you to complete a questionnaire at the Soviet embassy in Canberra.*

Further letters came. The first was from her mother. It was long and joyful. From what Evdokia could glean it seemed there had been no prison, no arrest. Only long-held, heart-rending fears about what had happened to her daughter. There was a request again for their home address. The letter's pages were numbered and pages seven and nine were missing.

In reply, Evdokia sent photographs of herself with her dog—photographs vetted by B2 to ensure that nothing hinted at their location. She sent warm clothes: two woollen jumpers and a coat.

Tamara's next letter expressed doubt that she could visit. It was the problem of being an able worker—it would be difficult to gain permission. But their mother still intended to come, as long as the Australian authorities gave their blessing. Evdokia wrote, telling Tamara not to give up hope. *Why not apply anyway*, she said, *whether or not you have a chance.*

Tamara's letter said two photographs had been enclosed within the envelope. Had they fallen out in the post?

The next letters were simply news: talk of the Russian winter, snow falling on rooftops and icy streets. No mention of the holiday. Photographs were again said to be included but only one arrived.

Evdokia sent a Moscow flight schedule from a Sydney travel agent. *You should consider booking early*, she wrote, *so there will be ample time to prepare.*

She pictured them vividly, three women walking through the Brighton Beach Gardens, along the esplanade, a slight breeze playing off the waves and along the sand. Her life in this country exhibited; a recompense, countering any resentments her family might hold, demonstrating that what was received was a world less than what was given up.

In her mother's next letter, she questioned whether things weren't best left as they were. Her health had deteriorated and she didn't believe she could manage such a long trip alone.

Evdokia pleaded. The flight was only thirty-eight hours; there was always someone aboard who spoke Russian; the cost of the ticket could be wired straightaway.

B2 was in the habit of placing the stem of a biro across his lips when deep in thought. He caught himself doing it now— tapping a biro against his mouth while sitting here at his desk. In front of him, in the typewriter, was the half-completed draft of a Cabinet submission.

His fingers on the keys. *Mrs Petrov is convinced that the letters from her mother and sister are genuine. The letters have aroused in her a keen desire to be re-united with her family. Mr*

Petrov, while sympathising with his wife, feels that she is not being realistic in her appreciation of the situation and is failing to see the possibility of a KGB plot behind the correspondence.

The typewriter's ribbon needed to be changed. B2 ignored this and wrote several paragraphs cataloguing the good evidence for Petrov's suspicion: the belated nature of the Kartsevas' contact; the Kartsevas' persistent enquiries about the Petrovs' whereabouts and wellbeing; the absence of any adverse note concerning the Petrovs' defection; the apparent censorship of photographs; the suggestion of a visit by Mrs Petrov's sister (then dropped), followed by the suggestion of a visit by Mrs Petrov's mother (now in doubt), followed by the suggestion that Mrs Petrov may have to be content with correspondence contact only—a sequence likely to provoke a strong emotional reaction.

He wrote the heading 'Assassination'. He wrote that the KGB's interest was either this, or to discredit the Petrovs by compelling their return to Russia where they would be made to renounce what they had done. The letters could achieve this by creating a determination in Mrs Petrov to visit her family either in Russia or in a second country from which she could be kidnapped. The KGB might also send a professional operator to Australia posing as Tamara. This operator would threaten Mrs Petrov with her family's persecution, forcing her to return to the USSR.

The biro was in his mouth again. He hadn't even realised he'd picked it up.

In consideration, he wrote, *I have concluded that Mrs Petrov should on no account leave Australia. However, I recommend that the Australian Government furnish Mrs Petrov with permission for her mother and sister to visit her on the condition that the*

*arrangements for such a visit remain in the hands of ASIO, with
any visit to take place at a specially selected house occupied for
the occasion.*

Even as he dragged this page from the typewriter, he knew
that the described visit would never occur. Was the KGB going
to allow any member of a defector's immediate family to set
foot outside the USSR?

Not in a million years.

Correspondence contact only. Little glimpses of a life. Tamara
meeting a man in Kiev while working on a building there, a
university man, a lecturer, well spoken, a voice that could be
listened to. Tamara getting married. Tamara having a son, living
in a room in Moscow, baby pictures sent in the post and seated
carefully on the mantel. Tamara worrying for her husband, his
drinking, his inability to find work. Tamara alone with her son
in the room.

Her mother's handwriting became weaker, her letters
drastically shorter, arriving wrapped inside Tamara's. Evdokia
understood that she was bedridden, even if both she and
Tamara did not say.

She died in the Russian summer, on a date in July. Evdokia
called in sick to the company where she worked and—for
perhaps the third time in her life—went to a church, needing
a quiet place, needing a place to be with her mother, who,
despite everything the revolution had to teach, had never given
up her religion.

Ten days later, America put two men on the moon. Evdokia
watched the moment of the landing but didn't applaud.

Life went on.

They began a series of dinners with defectors. Oysters in a South Melbourne restaurant with Anatoliy Golitsyn. Pasta in Carlton with Igor Gouzenko. Colonel Spry called it Defectors On Tour. Their talk was always of Russia, its weather, the people and places they'd known.

Volodya's drinking intensified. He took fishing trips, which she knew were drinking trips, a man and his dog and his bottle, alone. Coughing fits. Cold sweats and off-coloured urine. She told him in a tone that was caring that he was a chronic drunk. There were periods in hospital; weeks recovering from an illness that wasn't diagnosed. He remained convinced he would be murdered. He inspected the nurses' identification before he took the medicines they were giving.

Evdokia kept carefully within her circle of friends, the women from the company where she worked. The beach, the cinema, the city shows. Everybody addressed her by her new name. Newcomers took years to realise who she actually was.

Tamara's son in his school clothes. Tamara's son in the Pioneers. The boy looked like their brother at that age, thin-jawed and skinny-legged.

Her sister applied to the militia every two years for her holiday. Each time, the answer was Request Denied.

Evdokia suspected it was a life. She had her work and her things to do. She had her dog and she watched TV. At a certain distance, she even made a return to following the bigger events: East and West Germany, America, Britain, the USSR. It was selfish to ask what else there might be.

Spry came occasionally with questions: did you ever hear of such and such a project; do you remember so and so? The director was always lively, arriving with jokes prepared, and the visits rarely failed to cheer her. Sometimes he came for no reason and she supposed they were friends.

Habitually, she walked in the gardens and on the beach, walking the dog at dawn. Neat little waves. Everything flat: the bay, the suburb behind. She stood watching the dog as he sped across the sand. Sometimes it all felt so tremendously unexpected. The sun sparkling on the water, the cold sand underfoot and the dog running. She recalled summer camps with the Pioneer Youth. Tents by the sea. Days of naive thought where the world was a few hectares of coastline, the colour of your scarf, the gloss on your pin. She thought about the promises and potential, the possibilities entertained. The things that were the future then but that would not be. She thought about her work, her friends, the running dog, the bay and her TV. The slight waves broke so close to the sand. She knew that what was left was what had happened. What had happened, and what little remained below the flame.

The streets are a place visited now and then in early hours, buildings towering gravely, streets that are spectral and awash with light. She is here to walk along Great Lubyanka Street. A changing distance: sometimes only a block or two, sometimes close to a mile.

There are the Moscow crowds. Children, adults. They are at once easy and hard to hear, voices like the mutterings of ghosts.

In each recurrence of this world she is a visitor without identity, lacking papers, a passport. She is desperate to blend in, desperate to reach the building at the end of the street, a hotel turned tenement rising six storeys high, a place here but half anywhere, no glass in its windows, and from each gap the sound of conversation, words indecipherable, as if spoken through cloth.

Why is she here? What is she seeking?

If she needs access to this building, its corridors, its stairwells, the body-strewn rooms she knows are inside, it is not granted. It is her fate to stand before it. Outside it, looking up.

It is a dream long suffered. A secret in her sleep, a kind of stitching, she thinks, between lives.

When the historian visits, he sets a microphone on the table and she speaks—an old woman—for the National Library. It is a week-long task. The historian's questions give her the space to betray Volodya, to admit his faults, to commit herself, finally, to the truth. She doesn't. The record is no all-important thing, and what exactly would be the point?

The journalists continue to come, sitting darkly in their cars, spurred by the anniversary of Cold War events.

'Mrs Petrov? Are you Mrs Petrov?'

She calls the police. The matter is brought up by a politician in parliament on her behalf.

Which is why, at 5 a.m. on a day in 1996, she checks the street carefully before going to the taxi. Just an old woman, a nobody headed to Tullamarine without a suitcase.

'Meeting someone?' asks the driver.

'Yes. My sister.'

She waits in the Qantas lounge. Sets eyes on Tamara for the first time in four decades. And the moment is like air. In their embrace is the heat of all things lost that cannot be regained.

They spend the afternoon in the backyard, drinking tea and talking, their voices carrying on the wind. An afternoon long dying. Long veins of grey cloud turning red.

Author's note

This is a work of fiction. While it draws upon historical events and personalities, its characters are speculative versions of their real-world counterparts and many of their traits and actions have been exaggerated or wholly invented. Much of *Document Z* is based on archival sources: either on the records of the 1954 Royal Commission on Espionage, or on the reports, recordings and other files later released by ASIO and now held by the National Archives (some of which can be viewed online at www.naa.gov.au). I am also indebted to the accounts of the affair written by those at its centre, specifically Vladimir and Evdokia Petrov's *Empire of Fear* (London: Andre Deutsch, 1956), Michael Bialoguski's *The Petrov Story* (London: William Heinemann, 1955) and Michael Thwaites' *Truth Will Out* (Sydney: Collins, 1980). I am grateful for Robert Manne's *The Petrov Affair* (Sydney: Pergamon, 1987), the authoritative history to which those seeking to know more about the affair should turn.

Acknowledgements

Document Z began as a PhD thesis and I would like to thank Tony Birch and Ken Gelder for their invaluable guidance and advice over a rewarding four years.

For their knowledge, enthusiasm and expertise transforming *Document Z* from manuscript to book, my thanks to Annette Barlow, Catherine Milne, Alexandra Nahlous, Renee Senogles and all at Allen & Unwin.

For her careful editing, insights and suggestions, I am indebted to Nicola O'Shea.

For their long-standing commitment to Australian writing, thanks to *The Australian* and Vogel's.

Lastly, for all their support, thank you to my family—Roger, Margaret, Helen and Alice—and to Molly Peterson, not least for her unwavering encouragement.

THE AUSTRALIAN
VOGEL LITERARY AWARD

Discovering the best new young writers in Australia

Previous winners:
Belinda Castles
Andrew O'Connor
Julienne van Loon
Nicholas Angel
Ruth Balint
Danielle Wood
Sarah Hay
Catherine Padmore
Stephen Gray
Hsu-Ming Teo
Jennifer Kremmer
Eva Sallis
Bernard Cohen
Richard King
Darren Williams
Helen Demidenko
Fotini Epanomitis
Andrew McGahan
Gillian Mears
Mandy Sayer
Tom Flood
Jim Sakkas
Robin Walton
Kate Grenville
Jenny Summerville
Brian Castro
Nigel Krauth
Chris Matthews
Tim Winton

For more information, visit
www.allenandunwin.com/vogelawards

THE AUSTRALIAN
VOGEL LITERARY AWARD

Discovering the best new young writers in Australia

For 28 years, *The Australian*/Vogel Literary Award—Australia's richest and most prestigious award for an unpublished manuscript by an author up to the age of 35—has been launching the careers of some of Australia's most exciting young writers.

Winners have later won or been short-listed for other major awards such as the Miles Franklin Literary Award, the Commonwealth Writers Prize and the Booker Prize. Often entries that make the shortlist have been published as well.

The winner of *The Australian*/Vogel Award receives publication by Allen & Unwin and a cash prize in addition to normal royalties from sales. To mark the 50th anniversary of the Vogel company in Australia, sponsors Vogel's increased the award prize from $20,000 to $25,000 for 2008 only. Allen & Unwin have matched this with a one-off advance of $25,000—bringing the total award prize money to $50,000 for 2008.

Where it all began ...

The award began its remarkable life in early 1980 when Niels Stevns, originally from Denmark and the owner of Vogel's bread in Australia, approached the literary editor of *The Australian*, Peter Ward, about collaborating on a cultural prize. He wanted to give something back to the nation which had made possible his flourishing business. Following Stevns' call, Peter Ward rang Patrick Gallagher, Allen & Unwin's managing director, which led to the successful collaboration between Vogel, *The Australian* and Allen & Unwin—and to the birth of *The Australian*/Vogel Literary Award.

Find out more at www.allenandunwin.com/vogelawards